THE REFUGEE

Azik Chowdhury

__Definition of refugee__: a person who has been forced to leave their country in order to escape war, persecution, or natural disaster.

A person can be a refugee in their own country. Because it has all the conditions required. War, persecution, and natural disasters. Refugees don't seek a handout, but a fair chance, and that's the right of all humans.

I dedicate this story to my family and friends

3rd Edition

Inshallah – Meaning - God Willing

Chapters

Chapter 1 - Calm

Naguib Ghali sits on the veranda and watches his grandchildren playing. They run around the dusty yard, and three sides of the yard, are lined with flowerbeds. After the death of his wife Rashida, Naguib built the flowerbeds, and planted immortelles. Their small yellow blossoms, seclude this space from the outside world, and it's his sanctuary.

He listens to the children's excited screams and laughter, and they keep watching their grandfathers smiling face. The three grandchildren are his pride and joy, and the youngest and only son, five-year-old Farid, fills him with hope. They share many features, including the same steel grey coloured eyes. While unmarked soft gentle baby skin, frames Farid's eyes. Naguib's face shows the damage of fifty-five years, living under the fierce Middle Eastern Sun.

The two girls, Rafa and Salma, are ten and seven. And at this age, it isn't compulsory for them to wear a headscarf. At home they play with freedom. But Naguib's conservative neighbour, Mrs Kulthum complains.

"Mr Ghali, they're beautiful girls, and they should be covered. You don't want the wrong eyes looking at them. Mr Ghali, don't let the girls get too modern."

Although they've been neighbours for thirty years, Mrs Kulthum always calls Naguib, Mr Ghali. And in public, she always refers to her husband as Mr Kulthum. Naguib finds this strange, and he wonders. How this much formality, allowed them to bring five boys into this world. The older boys are overseas, and only the youngest remains at home.

Rafa screams when Farid runs into the small table. He knocks over the stainless-steel pitcher of water, and matching glasses. Then he stares at his sisters, and they give him a disapproving frown. He bursts into tears. And runs into his grandfather's arms.

"Jadd, I didn't mean to do it. Sorry Jadd!" With his tear-filled apology, Farid clings to Naguib, and rests his head on his grandfather's chest.

"Don't cry Farid, don't cry, it was an accident. Let's fix it, come on. Let's get some more water."

Naguib picks Farid up, and holds him close, and then he tickles him with his bushy moustache. When he starts to giggle, the girls run to Naguib, and they laugh along with their brother.

As they clean and fill the pitcher, Farid holds onto Naguib's shirt.

"Jadd, where's Jadda?"

Jadda or his grandmother, died soon after Farid's birth. Rafa has some recollections but with each day, the memories become more dreamlike. Rafa answers.

"Jadda is an angel, and she's helping other angels. I think she's making covers for their wings, for when it rains." Naguib laughs.

"Rafa, why do you think she's doing that?"

"Well, all I can remember is. When she lived with us, she was always sewing. She made dresses, cushion covers, curtains, and lots of other things." She smiles at Naguib, and he strokes her face.

"Yes, she used to make many things. Farid, that's your answer. Jadda is making clothes for all the angels, and that's why she's not here. She's very busy, because there are so many angels. But one day, many years from now, she will make something for you."

Farid stares at Naguib with sad eyes.

"Jadd, she won't know who I am. When I'm older, I will have a moustache like you, my hair will be white like yours, and I will be as tall as Abbi."

Naguib chuckles, and squeezes Farid.

"Farid, you're a very clever boy, but you don't have to worry. Jadda would know you in a room with a million people."

Rafa wonders about this.

"Jadd, is there such a room. So big, it can have one million people inside it?" With a smile, Naguib answers.

2

"Of course. The Great Mosque in Mecca can hold this many people. I've heard, that more than two million people can go there at the same time."

Rafa's eyes widen at Naguib's words, but she has another question.

"How many people live in our city?" Naguib takes his time.

"Let me think, maybe one hundred thousand, but I don't know the exact number." Rafa loves maths, and she's doing some mental arithmetic.

"Jadd, that's twenty times more than our whole city. That's a lot of people! Are you sure?" Naguib feels blessed with his grandchildren's inquisitive minds.

"Yes, it's a lot of people, but still Jadda would know all of you among millions of faces. Your faces would light up, and she would see the beams of light. That's how we find our loved ones in heaven. Because in heaven, there are trillions of people, and each of us follow the light we can see. For Jadda, you are her light, and she is yours."

As he utters the words, his memories leap back in time, and he recalls the first time he saw his wife. It was during the festival of Eid al-Adha, and it was a blistering hot day. He was thirteen and returning home from the mosque, with his father. As he left the dirt road, he saw a young girl sitting with her sisters, on the wall of Mohammad's farmhouse, it was Rashida. He couldn't take his eyes off her, and he walked into his father.

"Naguib, be careful." This was all Naguib's father said. But he watched his son's gaze, and he agreed with his choice.

Naguib had never forgotten that day. And forty-two years later, the memory is as clear, as if it happened a minute ago. Rashida's dark and depthless eyes, feel eternal.

Rafa and Salma share some of their grandmother's features. But they're more like their own mother Nawal, who has green eyes.

"Come on everybody, Abbi will be home soon. Get washed and ready to eat." Nawal shouts across the yard from the open door. The children scream with excitement, and Naguib's eyes return to the present. With thoughts of his departed wife, he walks into the house.

Chapter 2 - Trouble

Anwar, Naguib's son, works as a mechanic for the army. He's one of the lucky few, whose income is secure, at least for the time being. It was a hard day, full of challenges, and Anwar looks exhausted.

"How is it on the streets?" Naguib asks, but he has a feeling from Anwar's weary expression, that it's going to be bad news.

"Six trucks came back today. There was a lot of damage. Windscreens smashed, parts of them charred by fire, and two of them are beyond repair. We were told, we're getting fifteen armoured vehicles, and they'll be here in the next few weeks." Naguib is shocked.

"Armoured vehicles? Is it that serious?"

"Yes, it is. It's more than a few fed up students. It feels like everyone has an opinion, and they're all shouting at the top of their voice. And it's an angry voice, which is attached to a flying rock."

"Please be careful. We need you back here in one piece." Since she doesn't want to scare the children, Nawal whispers. Naguib nods and asks.

"Are you being careful son?"

"Yes Abbi. We leave everything that connects us to the army base before we leave work. But people are starting to recognise those coming out of the base. The base commander offered to drive us home, but we told him, that would only draw attention to us, and people would know where we live. He agreed to drop us at the edge of town, so we could walk the rest of the way. It's only three kilometres. I used to walk further than that to school."

Anwar thinks about his school days.

"Abbi, do you think those peaceful days will ever return?"

"I wish I knew the answer. But I don't think they will. Not exactly the way they were. Because things always change. But one day, there'll be peace. Because people can't fight forever. I think people see how we live compared to the west, and for us, life hasn't changed in years. People here, want the same chances, the west offers."

After answering, Naguib gazes at Anwar. He notices, Anwar has the same expression on his face as Rashida, whenever she was scared. Anwar looks at Naguib and speaks.

"I suppose having the same leader for thirty years, is bound to cause problems. People are fed up with the same things, all the broken promises, and all the poverty, but what can we do?"

Naguib isn't sure how to answer, and he utters a single word.

"Leave."

Anwar stops eating and stares at his father.

"Leave? You mean leave our home, our city, our country?"

"Yes, that's exactly what I mean. If you live in a village where the water dries up, you leave, and you find another home. Son, for us, in this country, hope is drying up, and so we have to leave."

To Naguib this makes sense. He knew of many who left, and many more, who were desperate to leave. Anwar now thinks. *'How do I get everyone out? There's six of us. How much will it cost?'*

Anwar has always been careful with money, but six passports, cost of travel, and starting a new life, in a new country. He wonders if he has enough money for that.

"Abbi it will be expensive." Anwar looks at his father, and Naguib answers.

"Some prices are worth paying. If money buys hope, it's worth spending. Very few things in life can buy hope."

Anwar stares at Naguib and asks.

"Abbi, do you want to do this?"

Without emotion, Naguib answers.

"As a father and a grandfather, I have to do things which help my family. It's your job to do the same for Nawal and the children. I read about a town. It's only a two-day journey from here. At this place, entire families died, and most of the homes were destroyed. We have to get out before that happens to us."

He then hands Anwar the newspaper, and he points out the article about their neighbouring town.

"I haven't seen today's paper, but let's talk when the children go to bed."

Father and son sit on the veranda. They sip the sweet black tea. After draining his cup, Anwar asks.

"Abbi, were you serious about leaving?"

Naguib puts his cup down.

"Yes, I was. When I see these horrors, and what's happening in our country. I know in my heart, there's no hope. It's not like two farmers arguing, or a camel owner's dispute. This is far more dangerous. It's a vicious attack. And it's got a tight grip on everyone's throat. People don't know who or what to trust. Neighbours squabble over the pettiest things. Women are scared to go to the shops, and they're scared to let their children play outside. It makes you feel like a prisoner in your own home, like animals in a zoo."

Anwar pours them both a fresh cup.

"I remember reading about the Indian people. Mahatma Gandhi fought for more than twenty years, to gain independence for India. He succeeded, but India still ended up, a divided country."

Naguib left school at eleven, and he didn't get beyond an elementary level of education.

"I don't know anything about this. But twenty years, is a long time to fight. Imagine what twenty years of fighting would do to Salma, Rafa, and Farid. What kind of people would they become? Would they even survive twenty years?"

As Anwar thinks about this, Naguib lays a gentle hand on his son's arm.

"My son, I believe that all we want as parents, is for our children to live with hope. And every generation, is better than

7

the last, not worse. You talk about India, and I only know that it's a country. You tell me about a man from India, that I've never heard of. So, you're an improvement on me. One day your children could visit India, and see where this man lived, and they'll be an improvement on you. But you must give them that chance."

Anwar responds with genuine amazement.

"Abbi, I'm not an improvement on you. Please never think that. All that is good in me, came from you and Ummi."

Naguib smiles.

"Then listen to me my boy. You must do this. Your future, and all that you and your children can achieve in life, depends on leaving. This country will crush poor people like us, and if we stay, the system will enslave us. Our hopes for the future, will mean nothing. But enough talk, it's getting late."

Anwar thinks about this, and he makes up his mind.

"I'll ask around, and I'll see what we have to do. My old friend Abdel is a senior official at the passport office. He has good friends at different embassies. I'm sure he has connections at the U.S. embassy."

Naguib's expression changes and he looks stern.

"Do you mean Abdel, Hassam Elneny's son?"

Anwar's eyes flicker with doubt.

"Yes, Uncle Hassam's son. Abbi, is that a problem?"

Naguib's face remains stern.

"Yes Anwar, it's a problem. Hassam has his fingers in many pies, and many of them, are illegal. Hassam is a dangerous man, and the less he knows, the better. The best thing is to involve only those you must. Involve no one else. Jealous people are dangerous people. Don't let people become jealous. Say only what you need to say, no more. Don't speak to anyone at work. Just listen and do what you must. Is that clear?"

Anwar answers.

"Yes Abbi. Inshallah things will work out." Naguib repeats the word.

"Inshallah."

He smiles, strokes Anwar's arm, blesses him with a prayer, and heads into the house.

Once Nawal sees Naguib re-enter the house, she joins her husband. She sits down, and then she points to the sky.

"There's a crescent moon tonight. Perhaps it's a good omen." Anwar faces Nawal and smiles.

"Perhaps it is, my beautiful woman." Nawal gives a shy smile. Anwar used to call her my beautiful girl, but after Rafa's birth, he changed it to my beautiful woman.

Anwar stares at his wife, and then he speaks.

"Can I ask you a question?"

Nawal nods.

"You can ask me anything you like, my beautiful man."

He holds Nawal's hand, but within a second, his smile disappears.

"How would you feel about leaving our country?"

Anwar is careful not to say city. He wants to make sure, Nawal understands the full impact of his question. Nawal's eyes dilate with fear, and she rubs her hands together.

"Are the troubles so bad, and do you think we're in danger?" Without looking away he answers.

"Yes, the rioting and fighting is getting worse. You'll see when you read today's paper, and every day there's more violence."

As he stares at her, his eyes soften. Nawal looks at him.

"You and the children mean everything to me. I know you love me, and you've never given me any reason to doubt you. Both my parents are gone, and my brother and two sisters live in America. You have much more to lose by leaving, than I do. Are you sure?"

Anwar's eyes light up, and he thinks. *'My brother and sisters in law, are in America. Even if they cannot help, they can give some valuable advice.'*

"I'm absolutely sure. Nawal, the people in my life, are the same as you. Other than you, the children and Abbi, I don't have anyone else. My older brother Nassef has a good life in Dubai, he'll not return here. And Ummi, she's gone. My life's work is to provide for my family. Not just with money, but to make sure, I give them a future…"

Anwar's words fade into a sigh, and Nawal knows how much her husband loves her.

"I'll write to my sister Shadia in America. She'll know how to help us. She's studying law. Will you post the letter for me?"

Anwar puts a finger to his lips, and again Nawal's eyes dilate with fear. She looks left and right, then she stares at the tall wall surrounding the veranda. And all the time, her heartbeat speeds up. She stares at her husband, and he holds her gaze. When Anwar hears Naguib snoring, and silence from the children, he stands up. Nawal also stands, but she's frightened, and she presses herself against him.

"Anwar, you're scaring me. What is it?"

Anwar puts his arms around Nawal, and he holds her. He feels her heart thumping against his chest, and he whispers in her ear.

"I wanted to make sure everyone's asleep. So I can tell you, I love you."

Nawal faces her husband. She holds his strong jaws in her hands, draws him in, and presses her lips against his. As they kiss, Anwar pulls her closer.

Chapter 3 - Questions

After Friday prayers, Anwar heads into town to visit his friend Abdel.

Abdel Elneny lives in the busiest part of town, since his father Hassam, owns a thriving electronics repair shop. And the family live above the business premises.

Hassam also dabbles in the black market. He provides sought after electronic goods, at hugely inflated prices. There's no warranty, other than Hassam's personal assurance.

"If anything goes wrong. Bring it back to me, and I'll fix it for a very low fee."

Although he says this with a friendly smile, there's also an element of menace. And the real message is.

"Don't say a word to anyone, or I'll cut your balls off!"

To Anwar this is Uncle Hassam, the gentle giant with a big heart. Despite his reputation, Anwar knows that Hassam does a lot to help the elderly. He fixes their electrical problems, without charging them a penny, and provides free radios for those with fading eyesight. But Anwar also knows what can happen if someone crosses or betrays him, or if they owe him money.

As he walks through the store lined streets, his senses come to life. The delicious smell of koshari invades his nostrils and makes him feel ravenous. To distract himself, he looks across the road to a shop selling kitchenware. Then the unmistakable sweet syrupy smell of the kanafeh, wafts into his face, and his stomach groans. To escape the mouth-watering aromas, he walks briskly.

When he turns the corner, the smell of food disappears and then he sees it. "Elneny's Electrical Supplies." It's still the same, but he notices that with age, the weather, and general neglect by the government. The store, and the old town looks ugly. Perhaps it was always ugly, but he hadn't noticed it before.

He wonders. *'Can I only see the horrors because, I've decided to leave? Can I not see beyond the ruin? I loved this place. It's narrow streets and alleyways, were full of adventures. We played hide and seek. We played cops and robbers. Can I not the see the fun we once had?'* He looks again, and this time his fond childhood memories return. Despite the exposed and broken bricks, the dangerous tangle of wires leading to the telegraph poles, and the flaking washed out paint. Now he remembers the countless childhood games he played with Abdel. And slowly, the ugliness disappears.

Nearing the store, he sees Hassam step out of the door with a cup of tea in one hand, and a cigar in the other. Anwar wonders about the cigar, since it's too expensive for most people, and he thinks. *'Uncle must have got this from one of his contacts. I wonder what type of contact?'*

Hassam spots Anwar, and shouts.

"Anwar! Is that you?"

"Yes Uncle Hassam! As-salaam-alaikum. It's me, and it's good to see you."

Despite all the rumours about Hassam's business activities, Anwar will never disrespect his uncle. Since Hassam, has only shown him love and affection.

"Wa-alaikum-salaam my boy! My goodness! How you've grown! How long has it been?"

Anwar is embarrassed by the question. Because it's been at least five years. He remembers Naguib's request. "Stay away from Hassam. His criminal activities could put your job with the government, in danger. Don't risk losing a well-paid job. Not in this country!" He obeyed his father, but he still feels embarrassed. And his voice is full of regret.

"It's been about five years Uncle. Sorry, but time just gets away from us."

Despite feeling hurt by the exclusion at Rashida's funeral. And not being invited to celebrate Farid's birth, Hassam smiles.

"Yes, time goes very quickly. But never mind that, have some tea with me." Anwar and Hassam hug. Feeling his uncle's warmth, Anwar thoughts are full of regret. *'I wish I hadn't listened to Abbi. I wish I had stayed in touch.'*

"It's really good to see you Uncle. I've missed you."

Hassam accepts this as an apology.

"Don't worry. You're here now, and that's all that matters. But look at you. I forgot how tall you are. When I think of you, I always see the ten-year-old running around with Abdel. You must be over six feet tall."

"I'm not sure how tall I am. How's Aunty, Abdel, and the girls?"

Anwar smiles, he needs to make sure there's no bad blood between them. And he's trying his best to repair some of the damage. He knows, if he is to get any help from Abdel, he has to do this.

Hassam answers.

"They're all doing well. The girls are in England, a place called Sheffield, and they're happy. In their last letter, they said the winters in England lasts for ten months. Aunty is sad because she can't see her grandchildren. But Abdel still lives with us, and she's happy with that. Although, I wish Abdel would find a nice girl."

Hassam strokes Anwar's back affectionately, and smiles.

"I'll shut the shop now. I'm not usually open, but I was expecting a delivery today. I guess the driver must be having some trouble on the road. Armed police are everywhere, and they can cause chaos by stopping one truck. Let's go upstairs and have something to eat and drink." Once they enter the shop, Hassam pulls down the shutters and locks the door.

At the dinner table, there's an uncomfortable silence. Abdel looks across at his oldest friend. He wonders why they haven't seen each other in over five years. The distance between their homes is less than five kilometres. Then, he wonders. *'Why didn't we just bump into each other? Did he go out of his way to avoid me?'*

Hassam feels the tension, and when his wife Samir furrows her eyebrows, and leans her head, he raises his voice.

"Abdel don't be rude. Life gets in the way sometimes, and Anwar has a wife and three children. From what I hear, he works long hours. So, what if you haven't seen each other for a while. With all the troubles, you should be grateful that you can see each other today, because tomorrow you may not get that chance."

"But Abbi…"

Abdel starts, but Hassam talks over him.

"Whatever problems you have, sort them out. But don't let an old friendship die. Nothing is worth that. Now take your drinks, go and sit on the roof, and fix things." Samir squeezes Hassam's shoulder, to show her thanks. Abdel answers in an apologetic tone.

"Yes Abbi. Come on Anwar, let's go."

On the roof, Anwar and Abdel sit on the old wicker chairs. Anwar feels tense, but he knows he has to make the peace.

"Abdel I am sorry. Really, I am. And there're no excuses, so I won't insult you by trying to make one up. Please accept my sincerest apologies."

Abdel sighs.

"Anwar, you don't have to apologise to me. As friends, we've argued and fought, but we've always made up. This isn't about me. It's about how hurt Abbi and Ummi were, when they couldn't say goodbye to Aunty, and hello to Farid."

Anwar needs to tell his friend the truth.

"Abdel I must tell you something. Around the time, Farid was born, and Ummi was sick. I had my interview with the army, for the mechanics job. They do background checks, and one of the questions they asked me, was about my connection with Uncle Hassam. I told them. You and I went to the same school, and we were in the same class. And because of our friendship, I spent a lot of time at the Elneny home. They were happy with that answer, but when I told Abbi. He told me to cut ties, not permanently, but until my probationary period was over. During this period, Farid was born, and soon after Ummi died. And I hadn't invited you, or your family to either of these things. I felt so bad. I couldn't bring myself to visit. I know I've hurt Uncle and Aunty, and I hope they can forgive me."

Abdel listens and it makes sense, but he's concerned for his father.

"What did they ask about Abbi?" Anwar answers.

"They asked me. If I had anything to do with Uncle's business. I said, he's my uncle, and I've never done anything for him, not even, run an errand or go to the shops. After that, they didn't ask me any more questions. For some reason, Uncle Hassam is on their radar, but I don't know why."

This wasn't true. Anwar knew it was to do with guns. Everyone knew that Hassam could get guns, and the army were more interested in his suppliers. An army facing rioters with rocks and verbal abuse, is under no real threat. It's a very easy fight. But facing people with guns, that's far more dangerous. The army and the government wanted to avoid this.

Abdel accepts Anwar's explanation.

"Yes, Abbi has some very strange friends, and I hope he's being careful. Do you have any other confessions my old friend?"

Anwar comes clean.

"Yes, I do. I need your help, and I'm sorry that it took something I needed to step through your door, but I just want to make sure there are no lies between us."

Abdel gives a sincere smile.

"Thank you for telling me the truth. I have so many new friends because of my job at the passport office. I'm guessing it's to do with passports and visas?"

Anwar nods.

"Yes, it is. And it's for the whole family."

Abdel leans forward and holds his hands together, as if he's praying. And then he speaks.

"To get a passport, all I need, is a birth certificate, or something official. But it must state, the date of birth. It can be a midwife's report, as long as it can be traced back to an official organisation. Like a hospital, or a registered doctor. I also need two photographs of each person. If you go to this photographer, he'll look after you."

Abdel writes down the address and carries on.

"Just tell him Hassam sent you. He'll send his invoice to Abbi, and he'll make sure he doesn't delay. It also means, there's no record of you having seen him. It takes a few months for the passports, but I can speed this up a little. Let's deal with the visas once we have the passports. I'll get the application form to you. And as soon as you get it back to me, I'll start the process."

Anwar's answer is immediate.

"I'll get that back to you withing 24 hours. Shukraan Abdel. You're a good friend, and you are my oldest friend. If Allah blesses me with another son, I will call him Abdel."

The two friends stand, embrace, and kiss each other on the cheeks. Although this is customary, it's much more than a gesture. It's their way of reigniting their friendship.

Once they sit down, Anwar remembers his conversation with Hassam, and asks.

"My friend, why have you never married? You're getting beyond the age of marriage, and I think Uncle and Aunty are a little worried."

Abdel grins, and then chuckles.

"Did Abbi mention something to you?"

Anwar laughs.

"Yes, but in a good way. I guess he just wants to see you settled. Or maybe he wants an Elneny junior." They both laugh, and then Abdel sighs.

"There are many reasons. Abbi and Ummi are one reason. They're on their own, and I worry about them, especially Ummi. She's at her best when the house is full of people. Even now, she finds it impossible to cook a meal for three people. Don't be surprised if Ummi asks you to eat with us. Can you smell the cooking?"

The two friends laugh, and Abdel carries on.

"But this is the real reason. On my first week with the passport office, I went to a function at the American embassy. During this function, I met a woman called Rebecca. She's

American. To me, she's the most beautiful woman I've ever seen. She has blonde hair and blue eyes, and I've been in love with her for the last five years. She has bewitched me to the point, where I cannot see the beauty of our own women."

Anwar breaks into a smile.

"I see! Now it makes sense. But does she feel the same way about you?"

Abdel looks away, and then he fixes his eyes on Anwar.

"I don't think so. She's a married woman, and I know the rules about that. If nothing else, I'm a Muslim man who respects a woman."

"What will you do?" Anwar asks. And with a sigh, Abdel answers.

"I don't know, but I guess I'll wait for her. That's what my heart is telling me."

Anwar raises both eyebrows.

"Brother that could take years, even a lifetime. My Nawal has green eyes, and so does her older sister, Shadia. Shadia isn't married, and she lives in America. She's an American lady now. Do you want me to see if we can arrange something?"

Abdel touches Anwar's arm.

"When you've looked into eyes, that are the colours of the ocean, nothing else will do."

Anwar reaches for Abdel's hand.

"But sometimes, the colour of the ocean is green as well. Maybe, a compromise is needed. Also, what else do you have in common with this American woman? Culture? No. Religion? No, Food? No. You have nothing in common. Even if a match was made, it would be difficult. Am I making sense?"

Abdel has never confided any of this to anyone. But he's glad, he can speak to his oldest friend. And his answer is more optimistic, than realistic.

"I believe, that when two people love each other, love finds a way to overcome these things. The things you mention are manmade obstacles, and nothing to do with the purity of the heart. The biggest problem is. Only one person is in love, and so I have to be patient."

17

Anwar isn't sure Abdel is making the right choice. In watching his children, he recognises how quickly time passes, and he wonders. *'Is Abdel wasting his life by waiting. After all, he's already waited five years.'* And he's not willing to give up on his friend.

"No Abdel, there's a bigger problem. This woman is married. You'd have to wait for her to divorce. You don't know if she will ever do that. Abdel, let me talk to Nawal about her sister. You never know, you may be able to give your heart to someone else. Let me do this for you?"

Abdel isn't sure.

"You're making a lot of sense, but the heart can't help what the heart wants. In any case, after so many years in America, Shadia may not want a boy from the old country."

Anwar is now sparring with Abdel, and he must win. Otherwise, he can see years of loneliness for his friend.

"At this time what your heart wants it can't have. If you were thirsty for orange juice, wouldn't you settle for water to quench your thirst? I don't know if Shadia will like you, I can't tell you that. What I can tell you is. If you wait another five, ten or twenty years, they'll be the loneliest years of your life. My friend that's not living a full and happy life. It's putting yourself in prison when you can be free. And what about your happiness? Are you willing to let that go?"

Abdel stares at Anwar, their eyes lock, and gently Abdel's lips form into a smile.

"We'll have to talk to Abbi and Ummi. Since you're here, let's do it today. I've already wasted a lot of time. Thank you brother. I needed someone to straighten out my thinking, and I'm glad it was you."

Anwar feels elated. As much as he needs Abdel's help, he's happy that he can help his friend. As they shake hands, Anwar speaks.

"Inshallah, all will be well."

The boys sit at the dinner table with Hassam, while Samir dishes out the food.

Once they're about to eat, Abdel speaks.

"Abbi, Ummi, Anwar has an announcement."

Anwar is nervous, and when Hassam asks.

"What is it my boy?" It takes away some of the tension.

"Uncle, Aunty, I'd like to make a marriage proposal. This isn't a task that falls on someone like me, but under the circumstances, it might be the only way."

Hassam shifts on his seat, and it distracts Anwar for a few seconds. But then he continues.

"My wife Nawal has a sister, she's two years older than her, and her name is Shadia. She lives in America and is unmarried. She's a law student. Please don't worry, she's a traditional girl. I think she and Abdel would be a good match, and with your blessing, I would like to start the conversation."

Hassam and Samir stare at Abdel, and Samir asks.

"Abdel do you want this? Abdel looks at his mother.

"Yes Ummi." Immediately his head drops, and he is again the little boy, who cannot face his mother, when he's in trouble. Samir walks over and she cups his face.

"Then let's leave it with Anwar. Let's see what he can do. Inshallah, everything will work out and you'll be happy. Now smile. Because my heart is spilling over with joy."

Hassam claps his hands in a thunderous round of applause. He jumps from his chair, wraps his huge arms around Samir and Abdel, and showers them with kisses. Once the joy subsides, Hassam turns his attention to Anwar.

"Thank you Anwar. The most unlikely messengers answer prayers. But thinking about it, you are the most likely person, to bring this message. I always considered you as family, but if this happens, we will be family. If you need anything from me, ask. There's no charge, no debt, but only the joy of giving. Please let Naguib know this. I know he doesn't always approve of me. But let him know what I've said."

Anwar feels the heat rising in his cheeks. He understands that Hassam knows, how Naguib feels about him. And when he looks into his uncle's eyes. He realises that Hassam is willing to forgive, and he will never hold a grudge.

Samir now starts to fuss.

19

"Come on, no need for all this seriousness! Let's eat and drink. This is a celebration. I've made koshari and afterwards we have kanafeh!"

The two friends laugh, and Samir stares at them and asks.

"What's so funny? Anwar I've made lots, so you'll be able to take some home for your family. Hassam where are those picnic boxes?"

The boys roar with laughter, and Hassam joins in without knowing why he's laughing.

Chapter 4 - Proof

"**Nawal,** do you have all the birth certificates, and other legal documents for the family?"

Anwar asks during the evening meal.

"Of course, everything is in the suitcase, on top of our wardrobe. Why?"

"I need them for the passports."

While Anwar feels safe talking in his own home, Naguib thinks his son is being far too reckless. The proof comes within a few seconds, and Rafa asks.

"Abbi, why do we need a passport, are we going somewhere?"

Anwar realises his mistake, and he's about to speak, when Naguib breaks the tense silence. In a gentle voice, he answers.

"No Rafa, we're not going anywhere. But it's good to have a passport, because it lets you prove that we are all family."

This is the best spontaneous answer Naguib can find. In trying to support his father, and make amends for his earlier slip up, Anwar speaks.

"Jadd is right, and no, we're not going anywhere."

The two younger children are busy with a petty squabble, and they've missed this conversation. The adults eye one another with concern. They know, Rafa is an intelligent girl. Nawal can see the cogs turning in her daughter's head, and she decides to talk to her later. They finish the rest of their meal in silence.

Once Nawal sees the children asleep, she wakes Rafa. Rafa rubs her eyes, yawns, and asks.

"Ummi, what is it? Is it morning already?"

"No darling, it's not morning, but I need to talk to you." Nawal holds out her arms, and Rafa raises her body, and puts her arms around Nawal's neck. Nawal carries Rafa to the front room. Sitting on the chairs are Naguib and Anwar, and Rafa panics.

"Jadd, Abbi, Ummi what's wrong? What have I done?"

The adults drop to their knees and surround Rafa, and Nawal's voice is almost a whisper.

"Sweetheart, you haven't done anything wrong." All the adults reassure Rafa, but she's anxious.

"Then, do I have to leave school?"

Naguib tries to soothe Rafa.

"Do you want to leave school?" She stares at Naguib with a frown.

"No Jadd! I love school. I love reading. I want to be a doctor and make sure you don't go to heaven like Jadda. I'm going to stay with you, Abbi, Ummi, Salma, and Farid. But only when Farid is not annoying me. And following me around."

All the adults smile and Nawal speaks.

"You can keep going to school, and you can be a doctor. But we must speak to you about passports. We need you to keep a big secret. You mustn't talk to anyone about passports. Not your best friend, not your teacher, no one. Do you understand sweetheart?"

Rafa rests her small gentle fingers, against Nawal's upturned palms.

"Why Ummi?"

"Because if people think we have passports, they'll ask questions, and these questions could get us into trouble."

Rafa is now wide-awake.

"So, are we going away?"

The adults look at one another and Naguib answers.

"We may have to. Because of all the fighting in our country. Sweetheart this is last week's paper, let me read you the story about our neighbouring town, and how people have been hurt. And how some are in heaven with Jadda."

Rafa listens, but she doesn't understand the full horrors of the situation. Naguib sees the questions forming in Rafa's mind, and he thinks. *'Why should a ten-year-old understand these things.'*

Nawal also sees confusion on Rafa's face. And she needs to make things simple enough for a child.

"I need you to swear on the Qur'an. I need you to promise, not to say a word about this."

Anwar's eyes are wild, and he objects.

"You can't ask a child to do that." Naguib understands Nawal.

"Anwar, under the circumstances, it's the right thing. Don't worry."

Nawal takes Rafa's hand and places it on the Qur'an.

"Now repeat what I say my darling girl." Rafa repeats her mother's words.

"I swear by almighty Allah, that I will not speak a word about passports to anyone."

Rafa's large innocent eyes stare at all the adults. She sees the tears in their eyes, but she doesn't understand why.

They all share one simple thought. *'Why would you put a child through such an ordeal.'*

After Rafa goes back to sleep, Anwar brings out the beaten-up old leather suitcase. He stares at all the documents and asks.

"There's a lot here. Where do we start?

Nawal smiles, and shuffles closer.

"Don't worry. I have all the birth certificates in one envelope." She finds the envelope, and inside are all the papers.

Anwar sifts through them, and he puts them in order.

"Here are Farid, Salma and Rafa's birth certificates. Nawal this is yours and this one is mine. Where are the others?" Nawal stares.

"What others?

"Abbi's birth certificate. Where is it?" Anwar looks at Nawal, and then turns his attention to Naguib. Naguib's eyes narrow and he answers.

"I know where it is." With relief, Anwar sighs.

"Abbi where is it?"

Naguib scratches his stubbly chin.

"I'm afraid it's lost. It was at my family home, and during the last troubles, my Abbi destroyed all documents, and many photographs. He took this precaution in case soldiers caught us.

He wanted to make sure the soldiers couldn't connect us. He also wanted to make sure, they didn't know where we came from. I'm sorry. I know it's not what either of you want to hear. Anwar, my name is on your birth certificate, can we do something with that?"

Anwar is worried, but he stays calm.

"I need to speak to Abdel and see what we can do, leave it with me Abbi. Inshallah, we can do something."

Naguib watches Anwar as he speaks. He recognises the expression. Rashida had the same expression when she was unsure. Naguib repeats the word.

"Inshallah."

In bed Nawal turns to her husband.

"Anwar, will you be able to do anything for Abbi?"

He faces her.

"I'll do everything I can, and the rest will be in Allah's hands."

Nawal kisses her husband, and he returns the kiss. While she closes her eyes, his are wide open and anxious.

"Abdel, Abbi's birth certificate is missing. I think we'll have a hard time getting any official documents. My Jadd destroyed anything with the family history during the last troubles, and that was fifty years ago. Is there nowhere centrally we can prove Abbi's birth?" Anwar asks Abdel when they're alone.

And Abdel considers the question.

"I'm surprised Uncle even had a birth certificate. Many people from that time don't have very much at all. I need to think about it, but in the meantime let's get these ones sent. I have all the forms, so let's fill them in, and get things started."

As they fill in one of the forms, and paper clip the photograph, Anwar asks."

"Have you ever dealt with anyone who couldn't prove their birth?"

Abdel stops what he's doing and answers.

"Yes, many times."

Anwar stares and asks.

"What did you do?"

Abdel looks straight into Anwar's eyes.

"Legally, there was nothing I could do, but through some of Abbi's contacts, they got forged documents. Please understand, this is not what Abbi does, and he plays no part in it. One more thing, you cannot rely on the quality of these documents. I remember one man who had a fake passport, and the forger spelled the name of our country wrong. Can you imagine that? I looked at it and said, is this a joke? Also, it can be very expensive."

"How expensive?" Abdel looks at Anwar.

"For middle ranking civil servant like you, it's one year's salary." Anwar doesn't take his eyes off Abdel.

"I can afford that." Anwar knows this will use most of his savings. But at this point, he's desperate to find an answer. The thought of leaving his father behind terrifies him.

Chapter 5 - Passports

A month after the passport applications, Abdel phones Anwar at work. Anwar doesn't have a phone at home, but then very few do. Since the phone company is government controlled, and too expensive for most. When Anwar answers, Abdel speaks, and his tone is business-like.

"Mr Ghali, the parts for your ceiling fan have arrived. Do you want us to deliver them, or will you pick them up?"

This is the secret message the two friends agreed. Anwar knows the passports are ready, and answers.

"I'll collect the parts. I'll be at the shop between four and five." This is another coded message. Whatever two numbers Anwar said, added up to the actual time he would see Abdel. In this case, it was nine o'clock.

While Anwar is excited, he's also apprehensive about Naguib's passport. He realises, the only way he can get a passport for his father, is through illegal means. While Hassam offers to pay, Anwar won't accept it.

"No Uncle, you cannot do that, it's too much money." Hassam still wants to help.

"Fair enough, if you won't accept the money, at least let me set you up with an honest crook. At this time, Khaled Sharif, has working for him, the best forger in the country. You don't need his real name, but they call him. "The Grand Muzuir." Now, if he does the work, which I hope he will. Then nobody will know, the difference between an official document, and a fake one. I heard a rumour that he created many death certificates, and with these, he got millions from life insurance policies. This forced the insurance companies not to give new policies to anyone from our country. Imagine that!"

Anwar feels reassured, but then he gets scared when Hassam warns.

"When you negotiate the price with Khaled, never lose eye contact. He does everything with his eyes. He'll disarm you with his eyes, until you are left standing naked, and pissing yourself with fear. Again, I say, never lose eye contact. Remember the going rate for a document such as this, is usually ten thousand. But you must start at two thousand. Khaled will laugh, and he'll start at twenty thousand. Don't get distracted by the laughter. Then he'll go to eighteen thousand. Keep saying two thousand, until he drops to fifteen thousand. When he does that, you move to four thousand. He'll then give you some line like. The more you pay, the better the quality. Say nothing, just repeat your price. When you reach the price, you want to pay, give a simple answer. Agreed. Extend your hand to seal the deal. Keep your eyes on him, and never look back when walking out of his office. Walk, as if you're taking a stroll in the park. Can you do this?"

Anwar nods.

"Yes Uncle, I can do it." Hassam gives further instructions.

"Only say what you have to. Yes and no are sufficient. This isn't a social call. You don't need to discuss anything else. Stick to a simple yes or no as much as you can, and don't say anything about your family. Khaled isn't a nice man. He's a dangerous man. Promise nothing, do your business and walk away."

Anwar thinks about everything Hassam says. And a part of him panics. But he understands, and he's determined.

At home, Nawal stares at these alien documents with photos of her, Anwar, and the children.

"God, this makes me look like I have an enormous nose. I'm glad no one else will see these photos."

She asked for copies. Since she only has few photos of her children and her husband. But for her, these images are significant. As they document the beginning of a new life. She promises herself. *'One day, I'll have photos where we're all smiling.'* Then she smiles.

"Passport photos are so miserable." Anwar has a serious look on his face.

"I'm meeting with Khaled Sharif tomorrow, to get Abbi's passport."

Within seconds, Nawal's smile disappears, and she fidgets.

"Is there no other way?"

"No, this is the only option left." Anwar feels like he's walking into the jaws of death, and he's paying for the pain.

Khaled Sharif's office is an old warehouse, and it's on the outskirts of town. It's set back five hundred metres from the main tarmacked road. To an onlooker, it resembles a deserted structure, and the only thing that gives away the existence of human life, are the tyre tracks leading up to the building.

Hassam and Anwar sit in the car on the main road, and Hassam points to the entrance.

"Ask for Khaled and let them know I sent you. I'll be back in thirty minutes to pick you up. If I'm not here because you finished early, start walking into town, and I'll pick you up on the road. Don't hang around. Thirty minutes is plenty of time. And as I've already said, this isn't a social call. Have you got half the money in an envelope?"

"Yes Uncle." Anwar reaches into his pocket and with his trembling hand, he hands the money to Hassam.

"Try to stop your hand shaking." Hassam now gives Anwar his final instructions.

"The way to do this. Is visualise Khaled taking a big shit, and he finds himself with nothing to clean his arse. Reduce him to a vulnerable state."

Anwar starts to chuckle, and in a calm voice, Hassam asks.

"Show me your hands." The shaking has stopped.

"That's better. Now keep that thought in your head, it will give you the courage to neutralise Khaled's stare."

Anwar walks to the front of the building, and he knocks on the only door he can see. When the door opens, he cannot see anything beyond the monster standing in front of him. It's a human eclipse. This man is over two metres tall, he has a huge head, and no visible neck. But when he speaks, his voice is almost feminine.

"Are you lost Sir?" Anwar is amazed at the contrast between the gentleness of the voice, and the giant proportions of the man.

"No, I'm not lost. I've come to see Khaled Sharif. Hassam Elneny sent me."

"Come in and please be seated. May I have your name, and would you like a glass of water? It's a very hot day."

"My name is Anwar Ghali, and yes, I would like a drink. Shukraan."

The Giant brings a tall glass of ice-cold water, and then in silence walks out of the office. Anwar is petrified and gulps down the water. Within ten minutes, the giant returns.

"Please follow me Mr Ghali. Mr Sharif will see you now."

With an uneasy feeling, Anwar follows the man. The building is an industrial unit, but with one difference. It's empty. The space is at least one thousand square metres, or around a quarter of an acre. Anwar wonders. *'Why is it empty?'*

At the end of the building, there's an office. This has windows, and it gives the room, a hundred- and eighty-degree views of the warehouse. The two men head for this office.

Anwar steps in, and inside there's a large desk. Khaled is sitting behind the desk, and from this position, he appears to be an average sized man. As soon as Anwar sees Khaled, his heart starts to pound. For a second, he looks at Khaled, and Anwar thinks. *'His face looks thin. He's so bony. The bones around his jaw and eye sockets are sharp. They look ready to tear the skin around his face.'* Then Anwar looks at Khaled's hands resting on the desk, and they look shrivelled and old.

But as soon as Anwar walks in, the stare starts. Khaled watches Anwar's every move. Anwar remembers Hassam's final instruction, and he imagines Khaled sitting on the toilet in a state of panic. Anwar's lips quiver and he stops himself from smiling. He shows no emotions.

"So, how do you know my old friend Hassam?" Khaled asks.

Anwar thinks about this and wonders. *'How do I answer this with a yes or no?'* But he answers.

"Growing up, I was in school with his son, and we became good friends." Khaled's eyes are like a hawk watching its prey. He looks for dilation of the pupils, and he listens for an inflection in the voice. He's looking for signs of fear. And he's looking to exert his authority. He says nothing, and realises that either Anwar is telling the truth, or he isn't scared. Without any emotions, Khaled asks.

"What can I do for you Mr Ghali?"

"I need a passport for my father?" Anwar answers.

"Have you spoken to Abdel, Hassam's son? He can get you a legal one. Have you tried him?" Khaled's almost caring questions confuse Anwar, and his brain works hard to find the shortest possible answer.

"Abdel is unable to help, because Abbi has no proof of birth." Without taking his eyes off Anwar, Khaled answers.

"I see. That's a common problem with people of your father's age." He pauses and then gives a cold response, as if the previous conversation was meaningless.

"It will cost you twenty thousand."

Both men's eyes lock. Neither of them shows any fear, and then, Anwar makes his offer.

"Two thousand."

Khaled laughs.

"Well Mr Ghali, it's been nice meeting you, and good luck with getting a passport." Anwar gets up and heads for the door. When his hand is on the doorhandle, he hears Khaled.

"Fifteen thousand." Anwar turns around and stares at Khaled.

"Five thousand."

The men look at one another, and neither of them flinch. Khaled smiles.

"I like you Mr Ghali. I also like Hassam, and I know your father is a good man. You have shown a lot of courage, and I

30

respect courage. But let's be reasonable. The middle number between my fifteen thousand, and your five, is ten thousand. If we can agree on this, you'll get the best passport. In fact, it will be a real passport. We buy these from people we know. Some people have terrible drug problems, and they'll give up just about anything for another smoke, or injection. Are we agreed?"

Anwar feels the menace in Khaled's words. He needs to get away from this evil man, and in silence he extends his arm. Without getting out of his seat, Khaled raises his hand and shakes on the deal. Anwar pulls the money out of his pocket and places it on the desk.

"Here's five thousand. I'll give you the rest when I've received the passport. I want Abdel to inspect it before the final payment."

Khaled gives Anwar a piercing look.

"I'm not used to people making demands, but as I said, I respect bravery. As you wish. I need three weeks." Anwar nods, turns around and walks out of the office. He walks to the road, and he sees Hassam waiting.

"Well, how did it go?" Anwar looks ahead.

"Five minutes was all it took, but it was just as you described Uncle. Shukraan." Hassam puts his foot on the accelerator.

"Don't thank me, you did the hard work. Anyway, let's see the passport first, before we thank anyone. This isn't something you buy from a shop. There's no guarantee that you'll get what you paid for, and you can't ask for your money back." Anwar looks straight ahead, and to relieve the tension he jokes.

"No, Khaled didn't give me a receipt, or a cooling off period."

Hassam roars with laughter.

"My goodness that's hilarious! A receipt, a cooling off period! Can you imagine such a thing! Oh my God Anwar, you better drive, before I piss my pants laughing."

Once they switch seats, Hassam asks.

"What did you make of Khaled?" Anwar puts the car in gear and then answers.

"The stare was incredible. I think he could melt ice with that stare. Physically, I could only see from the chest up. He looked thin. Skinny face and skinny hands. I kept thinking. If I have to fight him, it wouldn't be that tough."

Hassam is amazed.

"Are you sure you saw Khaled. He was never skinny, athletic but not skinny."

Anwar answers.

"I'm sure it was him. Who else could it be?" Hassam thinks about this.

"I guess so, but I think you might want to get your eyes tested. Remember one thing. You never want to fight a man like Khaled. If you fight him. Then make sure he's dead. Because if he survives, he'll kill you, and then he'll kill your family. Also, he's the dirtiest fighter I've ever known. He would have no problems biting your balls off."

While driving, Anwar stares at the landscape in front of him. He wants to imprint every feature in his mind. He watches the swirls of dust coat everything it touches, and when he looks in the rear-view mirror, he sees a spiralling cloud of sand. The scene is desolate, but underneath the sand, dust, and blazing sun. There's life, and a society. And there are thousands of memories. And the thought of parting with all those memories, breaks his heart.

Chapter 6 - Visa

Abdel is at his desk when the phone rings.

"Hi Abdel, its Rebecca." Abdel's heart races and he summons all his mental strength, and he remains calm.

"Hello Rebecca, how are you?" Rebecca sounds breathless, but she's business like.

"Abdel, this is a very brief call. I'm just letting you know, the Ghali documents are complete, and with me. I'm calling from a public phone. Shall we meet as discussed?"

Abdel answers.

"Yes, that'll be fine. I'll see you on Thursday. Thank you."

When Rebecca doesn't respond, and the phone clicks to end the conversation. Abdel realises, that in asking Rebecca to fast track the visas, he's put her at risk.

On Thursday, when Abdel arrives at the café, Rebecca is already there. She has chosen a seat near the window, but there's also a column, and it offers some privacy. She doesn't want to signpost to other customers, that this is a clandestine meeting. And her seating choice, is to avoid suspicion.

She orders tea and biscuits. Abdel watches her from the café doorway, and his gaze lingers longer than a business acquaintance should. A man barges past him, and yells.

"Why don't you stand in the doorway like a stubborn mule?" Abdel smiles and thinks. *'I see the Arab art of sarcasm is still alive.'* He walks to Rebecca's table.

"Rebecca, how are you?"

She smiles, and points to the chair opposite her.

"I'm well, and are you taking care?" Abdel returns the smile.

"As much as anyone can in this heat. But I'm used to it."

Once Abdel is seated, Rebecca hands him a box of tea.

"This is the best tea on the market, and it's very special. I hope you enjoy it."

When Abdel stares at her with a quizzical look, she holds his gaze, and he understands. All the passports are in this box.

"Thank you, this is very kind of you. But what's the occasion?" Rebecca's eyes soften.

"Let's call it a going away present." Abdel's heart starts to race.

"Where are you going?"

Rebecca stares at the box, and he knows the answer is inside. He's devastated and he reaches for her hand. He stares at her and mouths. "I love you."

Her head drops, and he notices tears fall from her eyes. They land on the white tablecloth. It stains the cloth, but in the arid air, it dries up within a second. Rebecca stands up, dabs her eyes, and she holds out her hand.

"I'll be leaving early tomorrow, so I'll
say goodbye. But if you ever find yourself in D.C. look me up. I hope this country treats you well."

Abdel stands up and takes her hand with both of his. Again, the moment is longer than it should be. Rebecca takes a last glance, and a frail smile traces her lips. Then she turns around, and like a fading whisper, she's gone.

When Abdel gets home, he goes to his bedroom. He opens the box of tea, and underneath the loose leaves, there's a brown envelope. With care, he removes the envelope. When he sits on his metal framed bed, it creaks, and he waits for silence. He hears Samir.

"Abdel is that you?" He shouts.

"Yes Ummi, I'll be down soon, I'm just having a nap. The heat has really got to me today." He waits for her acknowledgement, and then he hears her singing while she cooks.

Inside the envelope, are the passports. He inspects all of them, and he sees the entry visas for the U.S. They're all in order. Then there's a neatly folded letter, and he unfolds it and reads.

"Dear Abdel,

It's with sadness that I have to say goodbye to you. Due to the escalating troubles in this beautiful country, central government, is minimising the number of staff who'll remain. A memo came out to say. That for security reasons, those with active or reserve duty experience, would staff the embassy. And I don't fall into either of those categories.

I've never forgotten how you saved my life. How you got me to safety when the street fighting started. Without you, I'd be dead. I can never repay that, and that's why I promised to help you. And in my absence, Bob Ciszek will help. You can trust him.

From our first meeting, I knew how you felt about me. Since there's one thing a woman can always figure out, and that's the love that comes from a look.

I also have feelings for you, but I took a vow when I married. Until death us do part. I took that vow in the house of God, and I can't break that vow.

I hope you find someone who will make you happy. I'm sure you'll make her happy. And if you look at her, the way you've looked at me, she'll give her heart freely.

If you're ever in the U.S., please get in touch. I'll be in D.C. and in case I move, I've put my mom's address on the back of this letter. She'll always know where I am.

Inshallah, there'll be peace in this beautiful country. I pray, the people won't suffer.

Take care of yourself my beautiful Arab man. You and your country will be in my prayers.

Rebecca

Abdel stares at the letter, and after folding it, he places it in his wallet. He now feels free to marry Shadia.

A strange feeling comes over him. It's a sense of fulfilment. He understands that Rebecca felt his love, and in her own way, she loved him.

Chapter 7 - Celebration

Anwar stares at the visas, but he cannot celebrate, since Naguib's is missing. He has the fake passport, and Abdel approved the forgery.

"My God, this is fantastic, first class! I can't find a single mistake. No one would suspect, this is a fake."

Abdel asks.

"So, can you organise the visa?" Abdel's eyes drop.

"It may take a bit longer than usual. You see, Rebecca was my main contact at the embassy, and she has returned to the U.S. But I have a meeting with Bob Ciszek at the embassy next week, and he's a good man. Let me see what I can do, and what my new contacts are like."

This wasn't the answer Anwar wanted, and he asks.

"Do you think there might be a problem?"

Abdel doesn't know.

"It's hard to say. While I've dealt with many people at the embassy, there's only one now, and that's Bob. He's the only one who can influence anything. Also, I know that the U.S. embassy is receiving more applications than it can handle. I can't promise anything right now. Inshallah, all will be well." Anwar says the word, and throughout the day, he keeps repeating it.

Abdel walks through the doors of the U.S. embassy. He's apprehensive about this meeting. And his instincts tell him, there's a good chance of bad news.

At the front desk Bob Ciszek, a lifelong civil servant, greets him.

"Abdel my old friend, how are you?"

"I am well Bob. You've still not mastered the traditional Arabic greeting." Bob Laughs.

"I have, but with my broad New York accent, I always feel self-conscious. I'm sorry, but please don't be offended."

Abdel smiles, and pats Bob on the back.

"Bob, I know that. There's no need to apologise, I was teasing you. So, what's the latest according to U.S. intelligence?"

Bob ponders the question.

"I'm not sure how an analyst locked away in a room at Langley, understands what's happening on the streets of this country. As for U.S. intelligence? I wonder if such a thing exists." Bob raises one eyebrow, gives a wry smile, and carries on.

"How can anyone make a judgement based on a report that has been filtered, re-filtered, and changed, so that a decision can be made? Anyway, let's go to my office so that we can talk in private."

Bob's office is in the shaded part of the building. Despite the outside temperature being over forty-Celsius, his office is refreshingly cool.

Abdel looks around, and he sees the obligatory photo of the current president, hanging on the wall.

"Bob, I wonder how the president of America would feel about my country, and my people, if he had a meal with me and my family. You know. An informal meal, where families are talking about their day, and having fun."

Bob sighs.

"Maybe that's the way to find peace. Not by talking to another guy with an ego bigger than his country. But talking to the people who have to deal with the aftermath of that ego."

Abdel nods.

"I wish it was that simple. Okay Bob, what's the latest?"

Bob pulls out a folder from his desk drawer.

"Abdel, you need to read this. It's to do with a man called Khaled Sharif. Do you know him?"

Abdel takes the folder and starts to open it. It allows him to look away and hide the truth. He did know Khaled. With a nonchalant air, and without taking his eyes off the file, he answers.

"No, I don't know this man." Bob carries on.

"Well, he's a pretty big fish in this country. Now this is off the records, but it concerns someone you know." Bob stares.

38

Abdel feels tense, but he doesn't let it show, and he pretends to be surprised.

"Someone I know, who?" Bob answers.

"I'll get to that, but first, and again this is off the records. Khaled has done a deal with the U.S. government, and part of that deal is to give up his contacts, as far as trading counterfeit documents. The police have arrested someone called. "The Grand Muzuir." Now, this guy, may go down as one of the world's best forgers. From his premises, the police recovered this list, and it details all the illegal passports in the last six months. I'm giving you a copy. Before Rebecca left, she asked me to protect you. I think she had real feelings for you. If you have connections with any of the passports on this list. Disconnect yourself and destroy the documents. Am I making myself clear?

Abdel stays calm.

"Yes Bob, thank you. But you said, it involved someone I know. Who are you talking about?"

Bob's eyes lock onto Abdel's.

"Again, this is strictly off the records, and you're not gonna like this, but your dad's name keeps coming up. There's no other way to say this, but your dad's gonna do some prison time. Unless he can get out. The only thing I can do is to help you, and this is for you."

Bob hands Abdel his passport. Rebecca had asked him for it, and he'd given it to her. And now he remembered her words.

"Abdel, it could come in very useful to have a U.S. visa...." He never asked her for this. When he opens the passport, he sees the U.S. stamp and a green card.

"Bob, I never asked for this! Why did Rebecca do it?"

"Like I said, she had real feelings for you. And she wanted to protect you, but she can't protect your dad. According to local police, he's definitely in the mix. Can your mom and dad leave the city? Do they have family somewhere else?" Bob doesn't take his eyes off Abdel.

Abdel takes a deep breath, and answers.

"I don't know. I know we have family in the south, but they're Bedouins. I think you call them gypsies."

Bob nods.

"Tell your dad, to get him and your mom out of the city. Khaled Sharif has cleared out everything that could incriminate him. The local brass, and other interested parties want to pin something on someone. And it looks like your dad's head is on the chopping block. I'd say your dads got three to four weeks."

Abdel looks out of the window. Then he turns his eyes.

"Bob, what am I supposed to do with this passport?" Bob smiles.

"Rebecca told me that she'd helped a family called the Ghali's at your request. No one else knows about this but me. She shared their documents, and I've managed to get you all on a ship headed for New York. These are all your tickets." Bob hands Abdel an envelope, and then he touches Abdel's arm.

"It isn't first class, but it will get you to safety. My friend, go to the U.S. Don't stay here. It will get far worse in this country before it gets better."

Abdel's head is in a spin.

"Bob, I don't know how to thank you. My only thoughts are for Abbi and Ummi. Right now, I can't think of anything else. Forgive me for not showing the correct gratitude."

Bob swallows hard.

"I understand, and I can see how sincere you are, and that's more than enough. Abdel my parent's entire family were lost in the Second World War. I'm doing this because you're a friend, and you are a remarkable person who deserves to live. A man by the name of Gideon Frieder said. Whoever saves one life saves the world entire. You did this. You saved Rebecca's life. I just wish I could do more, but I can't."

Abdel stares at Bob.

"May Allah bless you and your family my brother." The two men shake hands and Abdel walks out of the U.S. embassy.

Once he's clear of the guards, he runs as fast as he can.

Chapter 8 - Run

Abdel runs through the streets while people stare, and many, jump out of the way. He looks like a thief, but there are no police behind him. An old friend shouts, "Abdel! Abdel! What's wrong?"

Abdel doesn't even hear the question, and he carries on running. By the time he reaches home, he has run over three kilometres in the blistering heat. The sweat from his body has soaked his clothes, and more sweat runs from his head and onto his face. When Samir sees Abdel, she holds back a scream, but yells.

"Hassam, come here now!"

After barking a few orders to the young man who works in his shop, Hassam runs up the narrow flight of stairs.

"What's wrong, what's happened?" Then he sees the exhausted and grubby state of his son. He panics, and horrific thoughts of violence flash before his eyes.

"Abdel what's happened?" Abdel doesn't know where to start, and gasps.

"Water, please, some water." Samir gets the jug of ice-cold water from the fridge. Abdel doesn't wait for her to pour it into a glass. Snatching the jug, he empties half the contents down his throat. Then he pours the remainder over his sun-baked head, and lets the ice-cold water run down his face and body.

"Abbi, Ummi, I love you." Samir starts to cry, and Hassam moves closer to Abdel, and holds him in a strong grip. Yet his words are gentle.

"What is it my boy, has someone hurt you?" Abdel starts to cry.

"Tell me the bastard's name, and he'll regret the day he was born!" Abdel holds Hassam's strong arms, as if he's trying to stop him, from committing such a crime.

"No Abbi, no one has hurt me." Hassam's tone softens.

"Then speak my boy. There's nothing you can't say to us. You are our lives, and we'd never judge you."

Abdel now reaches for both his parents' hands. In that moment, he remembers that when he was a child, Hassam and Samir would hold his hands, and lift him up as he giggled. Abdel leads his parents to the sofa. And after catching his breath, and gathering his thoughts, he tells them as much as Bob revealed. And then he pleads.

"Abbi you have to get out of the city. Get as much money, gold, silver, and anything you can trade. You must go south and stay with Uncle Ismail. You must stay there until the troubles are over." Hassam looks at Samir.

"We'll do that, but not before making sure, you have everything you need for America. You must go to America. I order you to do it. You're my only son, and you carry the family name. You must live."

Abdel hesitates.

"Abbi, if you wait for me to leave, you'll run out of time."

Holding Abdel's hand, Hassam smiles.

"I have to make sure you get on that ship with the Ghali's. I have enough contacts to get out of the city. Don't concern yourself with that."

Hassam is lying. Khaled's deal with the American's has scattered his contacts. Many are already in prison, and those that aren't. Are now on the run. He knows he'll get very little help. And he knows, it's only a matter of time, before he faces the courts, or worse, ends up in jail. The thought of jail fills him with dread. He met a few who made it out of prison, and they were never whole again. The torture stole their humanity. And the lucky ones, were the ones who died there. Under his breath, Hassam hisses his hatred for Khaled. "You'll pay for this. I promise you'll pay for this." He turns to Abdel and again his tone softens.

"Abdel, go and wash. Put on some clean clothes. Let's eat and enjoy every minute we have left."

In between sobs, Samir prepares the food, and when Abdel leaves the room, Hassam walks over to her.

"Things will be fine, you'll see. I'll take care of everything." Samir turns to Hassam.

"Can you? I've never asked about your business, and even now, I don't need to know. Because you've always looked after us. But this is more trouble than you've ever faced before. This isn't a mad business partner, this is the government, and they want blood. Hassam I can't live without you."

Samir holds her husband as if her life depends on it, and for the first time in their marriage, Hassam sheds a tear. He knows this is the biggest fight of his life, and it's a fight he must win.

Once his parents are asleep, Abdel writes down the number from Naguib's passport, 8010028728. He folds the piece of paper, holds the number like a ruler, and runs it down the page. There are four pages, and each page has three columns. When he completes a page without finding a match, he sighs with relief. Page 2 checked. He looks to the heavens, and mouths, thanks be to Allah, *'alhamd lilah.'*

He checks page 3, column 1, no match. Column two, no match. And then he gets to column 3. His eyes zoom in on the numbers, and he gasps. "A match!" He checks, and then he double-checks. He washes his face, in case his eyesight is failing him, and he checks again. It's a definite match. Naguib's passport is on the wanted list. He stares at the paper and thinks. *There's no way Uncle can get a visa. My God, I have to tell him.'*

A knock at the door startles Naguib. He looks at his watch, and it's 2.15 a.m. He looks through the chink in the door, and in the dim light, he thinks he recognises the face.

"Abdel, is that you?" Abdel answers.

"Yes, Uncle Naguib it's me. As-salaam-alaikum." Naguib responds, but he's confused.

"Wa-alaikum-salaam. Is everything alright?"

"I wish I could say everything is alright, but it's not. Uncle if you don't mind, Abbi is with me." Abdel then beckons to Hassam, and he walks out of the shadows.

The two older men stare at one another, and Hassam sticks out his hand. Naguib grabs Hassam's hand and then draws him into an embrace. He pulls away and looks into Hassam's eyes.

"It's good to see you my old friend." Hassam's face creases into a sad smile.

"And you brother. It's been too long."

When they enter the house, Anwar and Nawal greet them. Without answering the greeting, Abdel asks.

"Is there somewhere we can talk without being disturbed?" Anwar shows them into the main room, where the family eat their meals. He closes the windows, shuts the doors, and turns on the ceiling fan. With five adults in the room, and the windows and doors shut, the humidity levels soar.

From inside Abdel's shirt, he pulls out a small leather document holder. Then he pulls out the list.

"Uncle Naguib's passport is now on a list, of wanted fake documents. If we try to do anything with this, it will be suicide. This passport is worthless, and it cannot be used."

Anwar's eyes bulge.

"You mean Abbi cannot get a visa?" Abdel stares at Anwar.

"Yes, but worse than that. As long as this list exists, you can never use this passport. And if the authorities find it, Uncle will go to jail. My advice is, burn all of it tonight. And never speak of it again."

Anwar is frustrated and angry.

"Ten thousand I spent on that. How did this happen? Did Khaled double cross us?"

Hassam answers.

"Anwar I'll give you the money. Khaled sold us out, and that's how he's managed to stay in business for so long. He would sell out his mother to save his skin. Bastard!" Although Anwar's face twists with anger, he remains polite.

"Uncle, I'm not worried about the money, please don't think that…"

Naguib touches Anwar's arm, and then he looks at Hassam.

"I guess this is the same Khaled Sharif from the old days?"

"Yes brother, the same." Hassam spits out his contempt, and Anwar stares at the ground. Naguib stares at Hassam, and they both know, their ability to leave their country is unimportant.

Naguib fixes his eyes on Anwar and Abdel, and when they look back at him, he speaks.

"Children listen to me. Hassam and I have grown up in this country. We're no longer young men, and perhaps the best years of our life are behind us. We've always tried to do our best for our children. The next step of doing the right thing, is to tell you. You must go to America. You must live with hope, and you must give your children the best chance possible, just as Hassam and I are doing right now."

"But Abbi…" Naguib stops Anwar.

"No buts, you're going to America. And I'm staying here. I want to make sure, you still have a home, if you get the chance to visit. Is that clear?"

When Abdel and Anwar's heads drop, Nawal speaks.

"We'll send for you, and we'll all be together again." The entire room speaks in one voice.

"Inshallah."

Abdel asks.

"Uncle, is there somewhere we can burn the passport and the list?" Naguib nods.

They all walk out onto the veranda. They place the passport and list in a metal bucket. They set fire to the papers, and as Anwar watches the flames take hold, he sees his hopes disappear in a black cloud of smoke.

That evening when Abdel gets home, he lingers in the doorway. He cannot believe how quickly things can change. When Samir and Hassam have gone to bed, Abdel traces his fingers along the walls. He stands where Samir prepares food. He holds the pestle and mortar that Samir uses to crush herbs. He picks up the pestle. He can feel the shape of Samir's fingers. Since they've left their imprints, after thirty years of using this utensil. He picks up Hassam's sandals. He runs his fingers along the grooves made by his toes and feet, and he starts to cry.

In his room, Abdel flicks through his books from university. He picks up a copy of The Crime of Sylvestre Bonnard by Anatole France. He doesn't know why he'd kept this book. As he flicks through the pages, he sees a quote. It strikes a chord, but it also gives him comfort.

"All changes, even the most longed for, have their melancholy; for what we leave behind us is a part of ourselves; we must die to one life before we can enter another."

Chapter 9 - Departing

It's the day that Naguib, Hassam and Samir will say goodbye to their children. Their emotions are raw, and not knowing when they'll see each other again, causes heartache without relief.

Hassam has borrowed an opened backed truck. While he, Naguib, and Samir sit in the cabin, everyone else sits on the cargo bed. As Anwar, Nawal, and Abdel look at the people, the streets, and the beige landscape. They all wonder if they'll ever see their country again.

Anwar thinks about all the days, he spent playing in this desolate place. He realises, that despite the heat, and the vastness of the desert that surrounds them, it doesn't erode the love they feel. If anything, it makes the love even stronger, because it can withstand the hostile and torturous climate.

At the harbour, Naguib and Hassam are busy with the suitcases. It allows them to hide their sadness from their children, but both men teeter on the edge of despair.

Samir cannot hold back her tears. And the only relief comes from the children's questions. Salma clutches Samir's hand, and then the children surround her.

"Don't cry Aunty. We'll come and visit you soon, and then you can come and visit us." Samir looks at Salma's beseeching eyes, and she gives her a tearful smile.

"Yes darling, and that will be a wonderful day." Nawal sits with Samir and the children, and when she speaks, her voice shakes with sadness.

"That's what you have to tell yourself Aunty. That at the end of this goodbye, there'll also be a hello." Although Nawal says this to comfort and reassure Samir, she wants to believe her own words.

Samir has the children close to her, and despite not having blood ties. From this day, there's a connection, and it creates an unbreakable bond.

As they wait, they hear an announcement over the crackly speakers, first in Arabic and then in English.

"Will all passengers please go to the departure area. Please make sure you have your passports, visas, and tickets. Anyone without these travel documents will not be allowed to board the ship…"

As the echoes of the announcement fade, they all stand up. The children still cling to Samir, and Samir hangs on to them. She needs their support more than they need hers.

All the adults listen as the children say goodbye to Naguib. They adore their grandfather, and while Farid sits on Naguib's lap, Rafa and Salma have their arms around him. Farid nuzzles into Naguib and asks.

"Jadd, will you come and live with us?" Rafa has a feeling it's unlikely, she seems to understand. Salma screams with excitement.

"Yes Jadd, come and live with us like now, and we can play together." Farid clenches his little fists, and cheers. It's breaking the adult's hearts. Naguib looks at all of them, and answers in a gentle voice.

"I will visit you in your dreams. Remember, when we're good, and Allah sees this, he makes our dreams come true. But you must be good, for that to happen."

Farid is fascinated.

"If you visit me in my dreams I'll never go to sleep. Because I'll wait for you, so that we can talk, and I can tell you about my new school."

Naguib squeezes Farid.

"You can write to me. So, it's important, that you learn to write. And when I get your letters, I'll write back." Rafa listens and then in a tearful voice, she speaks.

"Jadd, if you visit me in my dreams, I'll never wake up. I'll sleep and dream every day and night." Samir puts her hand

48

over her mouth to stop herself from sobbing, but all the same, her body shakes with pent up tears.

Nawal and the children say their goodbyes. Anwar and Abdel linger a while longer. Abdel hangs his head, not with fear or shame, but with an overwhelming sense of loss. Hassam feels the same, but he holds back his sorrow.

"This is a new adventure for you, and it will challenge you. But remember where you came from." Abdel chokes back his tears.

"I'll never forget anything. You are my heart, and I hope my heart doesn't break without you."

Samir moves closer to her son.

"As with everything we lose, for a while we hurt, but after a time we learn to cope. Our heartbeat adapts to our new surroundings, and we get through. You'll get through, I know it, and every day you'll be in my prayers."

Abdel's head sinks even further, and Hassam supports him.

"Be strong my boy." Abdel puts his arms around Samir and Hassam's neck, and they hold onto their son. As they watch Abdel walk away from them, Hassam, and Samir's face sags. And in that moment, they look a hundred years older.

Anwar keeps his eyes locked on Naguib.

"I'll send for you Abbi."

Naguib doesn't look away, and then he asks.

"Do you remember what I said to you about leaving?"

"Yes Abbi, I remember."

Naguib summons all his strength and speaks.

"Let me remind you. Your future and all that you and your children can achieve in life, depends on leaving. So don't leave with a heavy heart, just understand that this is the right thing to do. Stay strong for your family, and always put them above everything else. I'm happy to have done what I can. You are everything I could have wished for in a son."

Father and son embrace, and whisper in each other's ears.

"I love you."

Without another word, Anwar turns and walks away without looking back. Naguib also turns away and walks towards Hassam and Samir. He sees their bodies withering with pain. Their eyes remain glued to the ship. They hope they'll see Abdel one more time. When Naguib reaches them, he puts his arms around them, and sweeps them away from this torture.

On the ship, Abdel gazes back at the shore, but Anwar only looks to the horizon. Anwar cannot look back, he knows, it will weaken him. While the two men are different in how they deal with this parting, they both feel the same love for their family and their country. They're both proud Arab men.

Chapter 10 - Alone

Hassam drops Naguib at home, but for the entire journey, none of them say a word. They're all silenced by sadness, and they reflect on the separation from their loved ones.

Outside Naguib's house, Hassam speaks.

"Naguib, come and stay with us. You're alone now. But you don't have to be."

Naguib rests his hand on Hassam's arm.

"Thank you my friend. I'll come and visit later. But right now, I want to straighten the house. Also, I need to figure out, what I do next." Hassam nods, and Samir gives a weak smile, but there's no joy in her eyes.

As Naguib locks the door, he steels himself, and then he turns around. The overwhelming emptiness brings him to his knees, and his tears flow.

An hour later, Naguib wakes up. He realises, that he passed out. He knows it's due to the exhaustion, caused by many sleepless nights, and heart-breaking days. It's the dead of night, and with no one else in the house, he hears every sound. He slows his breathing and listens. A part of him is hoping to hear his grandchildren sleeping. He used to smile when he could hear Farid giggling in his sleep. He wonders. *'What was going on in Farid's innocent mind? I wish I had asked him what he was dreaming of. Why didn't I ask him?'*

It dawns on him, that he'll never know the answer to this question. And he may never really know his grandchildren. From this day on, there'll be no shared experiences. Whatever they're about to face, they'll face without him.

He looks around the front room, and he sees the newspaper that Anwar was reading the day before. He picks it up, and he sees some scribbled notes. He runs his fingers across the indents. He folds the paper, and places it in the centre of the room.

He goes to Anwar and Nawal's bedroom. The bed is made, but when he opens the wardrobe, he sees some clothes still hanging there. As the door swings open, some of the hanger's rattle and it breaks the silence. He gathers the clothes and puts them in the centre of the front room.

Naguib then walks into the small room where the three children shared a bed. His heart aches when he sees some of the toys they left behind. With tears streaming down his face, he piles them in a line on the bed. He finds a toy police car, a doll with a missing arm, bits of paper with drawings of flowers, and little notes. He looks under the bed, and there's a small pair of sandals, and a ball. Farid left his ball behind and Naguib thinks. *'He loves that ball. He will miss it.'*

He gathers all the tokens and remains of his family. He puts them in a neat pile. Then he brings out the small, battered suitcase and fills it. And finally, he places the newspaper on top. It's a way of remembering the day, although he doesn't need any reminders. He knows, he'll never forget the day, he said goodbye to his family.

As the sun rises, he opens the windows. He stares at the suitcase. He decides to put it away. He knows, it will be hard enough to remove the feelings of loss, but he doesn't want a constant reminder.

He makes himself tea, and then sits on the veranda. Looking across the yard, he shuts his eyes, and he remembers the sound of his grandchildren's laughter. During his daydream, there's a knock at the door. The sun has only risen, and he wonders. *'Who could it be?'*

When he opens the door, he's surprised to see his neighbour, Mrs Kulthum. She has a tray in her hand, and as soon as the door opens, she speaks.

"As-salaam-alaikum Mr Ghali."

"Wa-alaikum-salaam Mrs Kulthum. How are you, and what brings you here?" Mrs Kulthum hands Naguib the tray.

"I made food. But I made too much, so I thought, I'd share it with you."

Naguib smiles.

"Shukraan Mrs Kulthum, this is very kind of you." It's all he can say. Since his neighbour's kindness overwhelms him. Mrs Kulthum stares at Naguib's watery eyes.

"Mr Ghali, you don't have to sit on your own, please come and spend time with us."

Naguib blinks hard to stop the tears.

"I just need a little bit of time. From not having a space to think in, I now find I have too much space, and too many thoughts. I suppose that's Allah's blessing and curse. He gave humans time to feel, to think, and to reflect." With a gentle hand, Mrs Kulthum touches Naguib's arm.

"Whenever you're ready Naguib. Please call me Yousra." With those words, Yousra Kulthum breaks the barriers of formality, which have existed for decades.

"Thank you Yousra."

Naguib's words are sincere, and as he re-enters the house he feels blessed. He understands that the new rhythm of his life will involve his neighbours, as well as others like him. He knew of many who said goodbye to their loved ones, and now he understands the sadness he sees in them. He understands where that sadness comes from.

Through his pain, he learns another lesson. You can repair a broken family. But the time they lose, is gone forever, and nothing can bring it back.

Chapter 11 - Police

Hassam sits outside his shop, while Samir packs what they need for their journey. Business is almost at a standstill, and with more than half his suppliers locked away, he doesn't have the essential supplies he needs, to make things work. The slow trade doesn't bother him, because he knows he has to walk away from everything he's built.

As Hassam sips his tea, a question races across his mind. *'Would Abdel be proud of me if he knew, how I've earned money?'* He thinks he knows the answer. *'Abdel wouldn't be proud of his father.'* As he mulls over the answer, he decides to write off every debt, his creditors owe him. He walks up the narrow stairs and calls to Samir.

"I have some business to deal with, and I'll be gone for the rest of the day. How are you doing with the packing?" She sits with him.

"What business? Please Hassam. No more business. We have enough. All my wedding jewellery and the cash, we have more than enough. You don't need to do anything else. Let's just leave while we can." Hassam reaches into his back pocket and pulls out his notebook.

"In this book, are the names and addresses of all the people who owe me money."

Samir stops him.

"We don't need the money…"

Hassam holds her hand.

"I'm not going after the cash. I'm visiting these people to say they owe me nothing. I want to do this. This will let me cleanse myself of some guilt. I want to be the person I once was. I don't want to look over my shoulder. I just want to look ahead."

Samir understands.

"Go, you have my blessings. But I beg you, please be careful, and get back before nightfall. I have lost too much, and I can't lose you. We'll grow old together, or not at all."

As Hassam walks onto the street, a police car pulls up. He stands still and calm, but he's aware that he's unarmed. As he stares at the car, the chief of police for the city gets out. His driver gets out as well, unclips his holster, and he stands with his hand on the butt of his gun. The chief shouts.

"Put the gun away Shoukry and sit in the car! This is a civil matter." The young police officer obeys, and the chief walks toward Hassam. He waits until Shoukry is out of earshot, and then he faces Hassam.

"As-salaam-alaikum, how are you and Samir?"

Hassam looks at Chief Youssef Sobhi and smiles.

"Not as well as you my old friend. I see the police force has made you put some meat on your bones."

Youssef smiles.

"Do you remember the first time; I walked through the neighbourhood in my police uniform. People were laughing and saying. That boy hasn't got an arse, look at him, he looks like a beanpole."

With their backs to Shoukry, the two men laugh at a joke that is over thirty years old. Still smiling, Youssef asks.

"Is there somewhere private we can talk? I don't want Shoukry to hear this conversation. Bloody force has got us spying on each other."

Hassam answers.

"If you don't mind Samir hearing the conversation, we can go upstairs." Youssef nods.

The two men sit at the table while Samir makes tea. Youssef doesn't waste any time.

"I have a warrant for your arrest Hassam. I can delay taking official action for three days, no more. Can you get out of the city?"

Samir puts the tea down, and answers before Hassam gets a chance.

"Yes Youssef, we can. What day will you come back?"

Youssef answers.

"Tomorrow is Friday, and most things will be shut for Jumu'ah prayers. I suggest you leave after sunset on Friday. Make sure you go to prayers at the mosque. This way, you won't draw attention to yourself. I'll not arrive at your door until Sunday morning. I can find an excuse or create a fake emergency. So that I don't have to come on Saturday, but by Sunday, I'll have no choice. If you're still here on Sunday, I cannot help you."

Youssef looks at them, and Hassam speaks.

"I'll make sure everything is done as you ask. What about Shoukry?"

Youssef answers.

"Today is Shoukry's last day with the city police, and his shift ends in three hours. I'm keeping him with me until he finishes. That's why I brought him. I got him a promotion at another station, hundreds of kilometres from here. He thinks I'm here because you cheated a customer, who wants to take you to court. He doesn't know my real reasons for this visit. And even if he work's it out, I'm hoping you'll be gone by then."

Hassam stares at Youssef.

"I don't know how to thank you, because I know you're putting yourself in danger."

Youssef stares back at Hassam and grabs his hand.

"Hassam, you're my family. You looked after my mother and me, when my father died, so you're my older brother. You protected the skinny boy that everyone teased, and your kindness stopped me from having a life of hell. I promised myself, that if I could ever repay you, I would. Please accept this payment from a grateful man."

The two men stand up and embrace. Hassam pulls back, and he looks into Youssef's eyes.

"Youssef, you owe me nothing. It is I, who owes you everything."

They walk to the front of the shop. They agreed on a parting message. Chief Sobhi shouts with a sarcastic tone.

"I'll see you very soon Mr Elneny! I suggest you either pay up, or you get a lawyer." Shoukry laughs when he hears Youssef's words, and grinning he responds.

"That's a good joke boss, a lawyer." Hassam gives Youssef a hard stare. Then he turns his gaze on Shoukry, and glares at him with real hatred.

Hassam borrows a motorbike from a neighbour, and visits over twenty people who owe him money. The last person he visits is a young man, named Mido Ibrahim. When Mido spots him, he bolts. Hassam speeds after him, and after a frenetic chase through the busy streets, he catches Mido down a dead end.

With wild terrified eyes, Mido pleads.

"Mr Elneny, I'll have the money in one week. I promise! You know I borrowed it to pay for my mother's medicine."

Fearing for his life, Mido breaks down in tears. Hassam can see how much people fear him, and it fills him with shame. He calms Mido, and in a reassuring voice, he asks.

"Mido, please come here." The gentleness surprises Mido, and with caution he walks towards Hassam.

"I know why you borrowed the money, and I'm not here to collect. I've come here to say, you owe me nothing, and your debt is repaid."

The terror now turns to wonder, and Mido asks.

"Mr Elneny, it's a lot of money, the medicine was very expensive. I need to know why you're doing this. As grateful as I am, I need to know." Hassam gets off his bike.

"Let's go to a café and speak as men." At the café, the two men sit facing one another, and as Mido picks up his cup, his hand trembles. Hassam looks into Mido's eyes.

"Please don't be afraid. I won't touch you. But can I ask you a question?"

Mido nods and Hassam asks.

"Do you think a bad man can ever be good? Can he ever face Allah, and know that he's tried to mend the past?"

Mido ponders the question. He didn't have an extensive education. But as a boy he had Qur'an classes, and he searches those memories for an answer.

"I remember reading this line from the Qur'an. *Even if your sins were to reach the clouds in the sky, I would forgive you.* Mr Elneny, Allah is merciful, and he's not cruel or vengeful. You must never lose hope in the mercy of Allah."

Hassam puts a gentle finger against the edge of Mido's hand.

"You amaze me with your knowledge. You're bound to do great things one day, and I'm happy to know you as a friend."

Hassam reaches into his pocket and pulls out the equivalent of a month's wages.

"Take this. I hope it will help you and your mother." Mido stares at the money, and then he looks at Hassam.

"Mr Elneny, you are my friend, and you have my blessings."

When Hassam gets home, Samir has prepared a meal, and as they eat, she speaks.

"All our children are safe. I can't remember the last time we were alone like this. And starting a new adventure."

Hassam nods.

"Yes, it's just like when we first started out. We have a bit more than we did, but back then, all we needed was your headscarf to keep us warm at night." Samir blushes and reaches for Hassam's hand.

Chapter 12 - Friday

When Hassam returns from the mosque, he doesn't recognise the house. Everything is spotless, and Samir has put everything away. He looks at her and asks.

"Why have you cleaned the house?"

She smiles.

"It was the only way I could find all the valuable things. Remember what Abdel said. Get things you can trade. There are four suitcases. One with clothes, one with things we can trade. And the two small ones, have cash and jewellery."

Hassam is amazed.

"What sort of things are we trading?"

Again, Samir smiles.

"I looked in the shop, and there were ten small radios. Handheld things, and still in their boxes. There were batteries, lightbulbs, fuses, these types of things. Small things which fit into a suitcase, but essential for trading if we needed to."

Hassam wraps his arms around her.

"What a woman you are."

But Samir has other plans.

"We're both going to dye our hair, and you're going to shave. The police will be looking for two older people. This disguise may give us a few more kilometres."

Hassam dreads the idea of dying his hair, but he knows it makes sense.

"I've traded in my truck for a sedan car, not a new one, but an old model with a good engine. That truck would be as easy to find, as a camel with two heads." They both laugh. It's the first time, there's been laughter in this room since Abdel left.

Samir's hair is long, it reaches the small of her back, and it takes a long time to dye. While the dye is taking hold, Hassam takes his razor, lathers his face and shaves. When he comes out of the bathroom, she grins.

"You look sixteen years old! Is it even legal for me to go to bed with you?" Hassam gives Samir a playful smack across her bottom, and he starts to laugh. His laughter is a roar, and for a moment, it lifts them from their despair. Samir smiles.

"I'm going to wash this stuff out of my hair. God, it smells like a three-day old fart! Let me finish, and then it's your turn."

Hassam screws up his nose.

"Why would you want to make me smell like a three-day old fart?" Samir grins and heads into the bathroom.

Hassam checks every room to make sure they haven't left any clues. He removes all family photos from the picture frames, and then hangs the empty frames back on the wall. It's an attempt to hide the discolouration between the surrounding walls. But in his heart, he hopes, they'll return to this place. He doesn't want others to think, he's abandoned his home.

In the bedroom, he pulls out a leather holdall from under the bed. He opens it, and inside there are four guns and about a hundred rounds per gun. He pulls out his favourite, a Sn P-51251. It has a 9 mm bore, and 8 shots. He strokes the handle and whispers. "My friend, I hope I don't have to use you. I hope you'll remain silent."

He looks in the bag, and he pulls out a CZ .32. And then there are two MAC MLE's. The MACs are effective and since they're semi-automatic, they're easy to use. Point and pull the trigger. He wants to make sure, Samir knows how to use one, if she needs to. He decides to give her lessons, once they're on the desert road.

"Hassam, where are you? Come on, I need to colour your hair." Hearing Samir's voice he shuts the bag, walks down the stairs, and puts the holdall in the trunk of his car.

When he enters the front room, his heart starts to thump. Standing in front of him is Samir, and she has shiny jet-black hair, a sight he hasn't seen in over twenty years. She smiles at his gaping mouth.

"What is it?" He moves closer.

"My God, you're so beautiful. You just took my breath away."

Samir hugs him, and answers.

"Come on, it's your turn." Once they're ready, they stand next to one another, and they stare at their reflection. It's the first time they've looked at a mirror together. Their thoughts linger on the faces looking back at them. They had an image of themselves, but it isn't the image staring back. They can see, their best physical years are behind them, but there's still a lot of life left.

Hassam turns to Samir and asks.

"Ready?"

"Yes." And with her answer, they leave their home of the last thirty-five years.

It is a home. Because a home, is where souls live. It's where laughter, happiness, and love, caress the walls. And the floor, makes those walking on it, feel safe. Despite his criminal life, he made sure, his home was a sanctuary. And where, he and his family thrived.

Sitting in the car, he grits his teeth and squeezes the steering wheel. Samir looks straight ahead, and without looking back at the house, she speaks.

"Let's go."

The car moves away, and within a minute, they turn the corner. Samir closes her eyes. She cannot look at the neighbourhood or the city. For her, it's just too painful. Hassam takes a quick sideways glance at her, and he speaks.

"I want to see Naguib. It will be a short detour." Samir nods. She's exhausted, and as Hassam drives, she leans against the window, and falls asleep.

When they arrive at Naguib's house, he brings the car to a stop, and he wakes Samir. When Naguib opens the door, the dyed hair surprises him, and he looks twice. Once inside he questions the new look.

"Are you trying to recapture your youth?"

Hassam answers.

"No my old friend. We're leaving the city, and it's a disguise. But we wanted to say goodbye to you, and we wanted to say a few last words."

Naguib makes tea, and once they're all seated, he asks.

"Where will you go?" Hassam knows he can trust Naguib.

"We'll go South, to stay with my brother Ismail. It's peaceful down there, and no one knows us."

Naguib asks.

"Is Ismail in the same place?

When Hassam nods, Naguib carries on.

"This will be a big change. There are just cattle and goat herders down there, and sand as far as the eye can see. Even the revolutionaries don't go that way."

Hassam knows that after the buzz of the city, this is going to be a big change.

"Naguib, if I don't leave the city, I will go to jail. And that means, leaving Samir. It also means, I may never see her again. Very few come out of that jail alive. I cannot leave her by herself. Khaled is to blame for all of this. He's shit on all of us."

Naguib stares at Hassam.

"Yes, Khaled has ruined a lot of lives."

Hassam nods and stares at Naguib.

"Yes, he has. But he's done a lot more."

Naguib is intrigued and asks.

"What do you mean by that?"

Hassam looks down at his hands. He keeps squeezing his fingers, and after his initial hesitation, he speaks.

"Understand something. I heard this a long time ago, and with time, the memory remembers what it wants to. Also, I knew. If I said something to you, all hell would break loose."

Naguib has fire in his eyes.

"Tell me."

Hassam takes a deep breath.

"These are the rumours, but as with all rumours, sometimes there's an element of truth. Some of the old boys told me, that one day when Rashida was at Khaled's shop, she overheard him talking about a murder he committed. A murder that involved a member of Rashida's family, a hot-headed cousin, I think his name was Fouad. I believe Fouad was a bit of a gangster. People said, when Khaled walked away from that conversation, Rashida confronted him. Her last words to him were. 'You'll pay for this.' And then, she walked out of the shop. People told me, Khaled took immediate action, and ordered his men to follow her."

Hassam stops, and Naguib's stare is fierce.

"What happened?"

Hassam clears his throat.

"Khaled told his men to run her over. To make it look like an accident. Naguib, please remember, these are rumours, and the only one who knows the truth, is Khaled. I don't have any hard facts."

Naguib stares and asks.

"Why didn't you say something before today?"

Hassam answers.

"Because I don't know the truth. And I knew if you went after Khaled, he would kill you, and your family. I didn't want that. Since your family is safe now, I felt it was the right time to tell you."

Naguib's eyes stay locked, and he asks.

"Do you have a gun?"

"Yes." Hassam goes to the car and brings back the holdall. He hands Naguib a gun.

"This is a MAC. It's very simple to use, and here are the extra rounds. Do you want me to show you how to use it?" Naguib stares at the gun.

"No, I've used one before."

Hassam knows what his old friend intends to do. He knows it will be useless to try to stop him, but then he feels guilty.

"Naguib, what I've done in telling you this. Is a very bad thing. I've put murder in your mind. Please, think twice, before you go after Khaled."

Naguib looks at Hassam.

63

"Don't worry about what you said, and I'll be careful. I know Khaled, and I know how devious he is."

Hassam perches on the end of the sofa.

"Naguib, we have to go."

As Hassam and Samir stand up to leave, Naguib speaks.

"I'm sorry for being such a bad host, but after what you've told me, my head is elsewhere. Forgive me." Hassam reaches for Naguib's hand.

"There's nothing to forgive. Please be careful. Khaled is like a cat, he has nine lives, and as far as I know, he has three to spare." Naguib grits his teeth.

"I will do what I need to. I need you to do me one last favour." Hassam answers with caution.

"What is it?" Naguib asks.

"Is there anyone I can trust, to tell me what Khaled is doing? Where he goes, and who he visits?" Hassam thinks of all his contacts, but most of them have a connection with Khaled, and then he remembers Mido.

"There's one boy. His name is Mido Ibrahim. Please don't put him in danger. He's struggling to provide food, shelter, and medicine for his sick mother. If you go to see him, give him this money. If he's willing to help, please tell him not to make direct eye contact with Khaled. He needs to be a casual passer-by, and not draw attention to himself."

Naguib nods.

"I promise to take care of Mido. I just need to know one thing. Is there a time in the day when Khaled is alone? Once he gives me that information, I'll not ask anything more of Mido. How will I recognise him?"

"He's about six feet tall, and he's very skinny. Please make sure you give him a good meal. The striking thing about him is his honey-coloured eyes. Once you see those eyes, you'll know it's him. Naguib, he's a good boy, and he's not a crook. I beg you, please look after him."

He writes down the address of the restaurant, where Mido works. When he and Samir get up to leave, the two men embrace. And when they pull away, Naguib's voice is full of sadness.

"My friend, be careful on your drive. I look forward to the day when I'll see you both again. Inshallah." Hassam and Samir repeat the word.

As Naguib stands in the doorway, he watches the brake lights of the car flicker. Within thirty seconds, the car turns the corner and as the dust settles, he shuts the door. His thoughts turn to this goodbye, and he wonders. *'How many more goodbyes do I have to suffer?'*

As Hassam drives along the desert road, he sees the fading lights of the city in his rear-view mirror. He glances at Samir, and she's asleep, and her breathing is gentle and even. He looks up at the sky, and the stars are magnificent. Without the light pollution of the city, he sees the wonders of the universe. His eyes follow a shooting star as it flies out of sight, and he makes a wish.

In the silence and with only his thoughts, he thinks about the life he's leaving behind. He remembers when he, Naguib, and Khaled had, what he thought, was an unbreakable brotherhood. And he remembers, how it fell apart.

Hassam smiles as he thinks of their lives forty years ago. Back then, they were known as the Robin Hood Gang. People gave them the name, because of the way they distributed some of their profits, to those most in need. They dabbled in the black market, and they could get most things the people of a growing city wanted, and always at a premium.

Naguib had always been careful with money, and before he reached his twentieth birthday, he bought his house. Hassam and Khaled preferred to live the life of young playboys, and money for them, was easy come easy go.

Their partnership ended when Khaled made a new connection. It was with a group of men from the U.S. Military. He'd struck a deal to buy guns from them, and in exchange, they would buy hashish and other drugs. Naguib had gone mad with Khaled.

"Why are we getting involved in guns and drugs? Once we do that, everyone will be after us! We make enough money. Let's not get greedy. Once we get involved with stuff like that, the police will never leave us alone." But Khaled could only see the money.

"We can make a hundred times more than we're making now. We can pay off the police, and as long as they get a good share, everyone will turn a blind eye."

The argument went on like this for over three days, and in the end, Naguib decided to walk away.

"I want nothing to do with this. I'm getting out before I end up in jail. I have a young wife now, and I am already finding it difficult to explain my days to her. Sorry, but you two are on your own."

When they were alone Hassam pleaded with him.

"Naguib please stay. I'll manage Khaled. You're the brains, and you know when to be cautious, and when to take a chance. Please stay, for me." Naguib answered in a gentle voice.

"And as the cautious one, I'm telling you to get out. Don't go any deeper. Once you go into the deep end, your feet will never touch the ground, and you'll forever be treading water. Khaled is greedy for money, and soon he'll be greedy for power. Work with him if you must. But keep him at arm's length. You can make a good living from electronics, cars, bikes, motorcycles. This will give you more than enough money, and it will not make people jealous. Remember, Khaled wants to own this city, but that will never happen." In the end, Hassam asked.

"What will you do?" Naguib smiled.

"I'll get a job. I'm not a bad carpenter, and I can train with my uncle in his workshop. He makes a great living making furniture for people. My house is paid for, and I have money in the bank. When I'm a master carpenter, I'll earn good money, and it will be honest money."

Hassam smiled.

"You were always the smart one, but I can't live that life. I can't read and write properly, and I'm too old to learn." Naguib put his arm around Hassam's shoulder.

"You're never too old to learn, and you're never too old to do the right thing. Khaled is the devil. He whispers honey coated promises. But remember, wherever there's honey, there are bees, and bees can sting a man to death."

Hassam had heeded Naguib's word, and he never got involved in drugs. He traded most things, and sometimes for a trusted person, he could get a gun. This helped Hassam to keep the police off his back, and make sure they left him alone.

Khaled did become the underworld king of the city, but he paid a huge price. He lost most of his real friends. They saw him filled with so much greed, they didn't trust him.

Hassam now remembers, how sad Naguib was by the changes in Khaled's character. He knew, Naguib hoped for Khaled to make a clean break. But as the wealth and power increased, it looked less likely.

Hassam knew, it wasn't money alone, that Khaled craved. It was also, seeing fear in people, and Khaled mistook that fear for respect.

As he drives on the desert road, Hassam sighs. And while it's a sigh of regret, it's also a sigh that carries hope.

Chapter 13 - Revenge

Naguib sits on the veranda and thinks about what he's going to do. He thinks about the act of revenge, and he remembers reading a passage from the Qur'an, when he was younger. He walks back into the house, opens his copy, and finds the passage.

"If you want to retaliate, retaliate to the same degree as the injury done to you. But if you are patient, it is better to be so."

When he reads these words, he doesn't understand the full meaning, and he decides to visit the mosque. The next day he visits Imam Ali.

Naguib and Imam Ali step out of the mosque, and into an office adjoining the library. Imam Ali starts the conversation.

"It's been many years since we last spoke. The last time was when you built the table we're sitting at. Whenever I sit here with the council, I think of you. So, what brings you here today Naguib?"

"Shukraan Imam Ali, I am happy that the table is still serving you well."

Then he falls silent, and Imam Ali smiles.

"I'm sure you haven't come to check on the sturdiness of your carpentry skills. I'm guessing, something is on your mind. So, what is it?" Naguib feels a little foolish, but he needs a clear and simple explanation.

"I was reading the holy book, and I saw a passage on revenge. I wanted to know what it means."

Imam Ali asks.

"Do you remember the passage?"

Naguib answers.

"No, but I can find it." Imam Ali walks to the library, and he comes back with his copy of the Qur'an.

"Show me." Naguib finds the passage and hands the book back. After reading, Imam Ali stares at Naguib.

"Why are you reading these words? And what is really troubling you?"

Naguib's eye's flicker with hesitation, but when he gets a reassuring smile from Imam Ali. He tells him of the rumours about Khaled's involvement, in Rashida's death. The smile vanishes.

"Do you have any proof?" Naguib shakes his head, and then his voice rises in anger.

"Imam, what good is proof? Khaled is too clever, and he's probably killed the man who ran over my wife." The Imam shows no emotions, but he tries to soothe Naguib.

"Look, if we have proof, we can use the proper legal system." Naguib struggles to stay calm, and he takes a deep breath.

"Imam Ali, with all due respect, Khaled has powerful connections. Even if I had proof, it might be useless. Khaled has also done a deal with the American's, and he's a protected man." Imam Ali listens, and he remains calm.

"Naguib, do you know what I did before I became an Imam?"

Naguib shakes his head.

"Well, I was a teacher. I taught teenagers, and my subject was mathematics. So you see, my training has always been logic." Naguib is confused, and Imam Ali sees the confusion.

"You're wondering, why I'm telling you all of this. Right?"

Naguib forces a smile and Imam Ali answers.

"Well, I'm telling you this because. Lessons are learned through understanding why we're doing something. When I taught algebra, I had to teach my students, that algebra is the study of mathematical symbols. And it's about learning the rules for manipulating these symbols. Without knowing how the symbols work, they couldn't get any further in mathematics. Everything in life is about learning, what we should and shouldn't do. So, I want to talk to you man to man, and not as an

Imam. First, I need you to answer one question, but be honest. Are you looking for revenge?"

Naguib stares at Imam Ali.

"Yes."

It's a cold answer. Imam Ali strokes his beard, and then he looks into Naguib's eyes.

"Man to man, this is what I think. While, my faith shapes my opinions, what you should understand is, these are also my beliefs. Even if I didn't believe in God, I would believe in this. I'm sure the passage you showed me, is saying. Even if someone harms you, you can respond with patience and forgiveness. This has more value, and it shows that you're human. Naguib, try to understand, that religion has nothing to do with this. It's simply about doing the right thing. When we seek revenge, it's because, we want to hurt someone, but understand something. If every person was to seek revenge, imagine how awful this world would be."

Naguib understands, but he's also looking for something, which makes his actions right.

"Imam Ali, I accept what you're saying. Please tell me what it says in the Qur'an about revenge."

The Imam sits up.

"According to scriptures, there are two levels of revenge. The first is, equal revenge, and the second is, you forgive the other person's bad actions. Although, in balancing an injustice, you can take revenge, there are strict conditions. The revenge sought, must be of equal proportion. It cannot exceed the others' bad actions. That is the religious answer, but again, I'll talk to you man to man. In the real world of humans, revenge isn't such a simple choice. Because it's such a difficult act. If a person loves life, he won't take this action. This option is hypothetical, or an option, which exists as a concept. A good person such as you Naguib, won't take revenge. This ensures that society, doesn't become murderous, and so there are two real choices. The first is to forgive, and the second, is to use the judicial system of the land. Don't take the law into your own hands. Otherwise, the law can take your life."

Naguib takes a deep breath and asks.

"Imam, do you understand the pain I suffer, when I know the man who killed my wife is free. He goes unpunished, and by all accounts, untouched?"

Imam Ali locks his eyes on Naguib.

"I do know. I had a wife once and she was killed. Believe me, when I say, I understand those feelings."

Naguib is embarrassed.

"I'm sorry, I didn't know. But how did you rid your mind, of the need for revenge?"

Imam Ali's gaze softens.

"Don't worry, it happened a long time ago, and I am at peace. Although we've just discussed what the Qur'an says, I found an explanation, which was easier to understand. And it came from a non-Muslim. These are the words of the Roman Emperor Marcus Aurelius, and he lived nearly two thousand years ago. *The best revenge is to be unlike him who performed the injury.* In other words, don't be like your enemies, but be better than they are. As humans we can choose to forgive, and this isn't a heaven-sent choice, it's a human choice. I know of all the bad things you talk about, and I know that right now, you're alone. And when we're alone, that's when we suffer the most. Because we forget the love of our family, and so we strike out against ourselves. Revenge does not fix a problem. It's only capable of leaving a sour taste in our heart, mind, and soul. And the taste will stay with you, until the day you die."

Naguib's head is in a spin. He's now more conflicted than before. He half expected the Imam to give his blessing, but this wasn't the case. The only thing Imam Ali's words do, is to prick his conscience.

Before leaving, Imam Ali and Naguib embrace. Breaking away from the embrace, Imam Ali looks at Naguib with sadness.

"Come and see me whenever you want to talk. Sometimes, just sharing a problem makes it easier. It can lift the confusion. I didn't learn that from religion. But from some of my students, who struggled with the most basic maths."

71

That evening as Naguib sits on the veranda, he thinks about the conversation. His mind can only focus on one element. That revenge must be of equal proportion. He chooses to forget the rest of the message. While he waters his flowers, he thinks.

"I must kill Khaled, and it has to be quick. One bullet to the head, and one to the heart. He will be dead in less than thirty seconds. This is less than the months of pain Rashida suffered. This is what I must do."

Chapter 14 - Mido

Naguib walks through the hustle and bustle of the grand bazaar. He hates this part of town. It's noisy and during the midday heat, it smells of raw sewage. And the smell lingers till sunset. Despite his home only being three kilometres away, the suburbs are in total contrast to the city centre.

He walks to the restaurant where Mido Ibrahim works, and the manager tells him.

"Sir, I'm very sorry, but Mido, is making a delivery, and we expect him back in about 30 minutes. Would you like to take a seat?" Naguib sits down.

"Could you get me a cup of tea, a tall glass of water. And if you have it, a slice of basbousa?"

The basbousa, is his favourite. It's a semolina yoghurt cake flavoured with brown butter and honey, and doused with rose, lemon, and cardamom syrup. The waiter nods.

"Of course Sir. This is a speciality of our café, and the best in town."

Once his food and drinks arrive, Naguib sips his tea, and watches the scene. He sees armed police patrolling the area. A few years ago, this was a rare sight, but now it's as commonplace as the street vendors. Some police carry machine guns, and he cannot understand why they need them. He's sad to see this peaceful city turning into a police state.

Across the road from the café, he sees a shoe-shiner, with his polished box, and a small mat for customers. The man sits between two shop fronts, and Naguib wonders. *'Why is he here? He won't get many customers here. He's better off in the business district.'* He looks at the man, and he realises, he's too old and frail, to carry the heavy box far. Naguib keeps staring, and he sees the man leaning to one side, and occasionally dusting the box. The shoe-shiners face is a mass of wrinkles, and his beard and moustache are pure white. Naguib looks at his own feet, and he wonders. *'Should I ask him to clean my shoes? All he needs is enough money for a meal.'*

As this thought crosses his mind, two police officers approach the shoe-shiner. And the older one, who has a grand greying moustache, asks.

"Jadd, can you polish our boots please?" The shoe-shiner gives a gummy smile.

"Yes, of course sir. Two for the price of one today, it's a special offer." The older policemen smiles, and answers politely.

"No Jadd, no need for that, here's the money for both." The younger officer is about to object, but the older one glares at him.

As the officers walk away, Naguib acknowledges the kindness of the older man, and the police officer greets him.

"As-salaam-alaikum." Naguib smiles and responds with sincerity.

"Wa-alaikum-salaam." The younger officer clenches his jaws in an act of defiance, and his face looks scarred by the arrogance of youth. Naguib thinks. *'One day, you'll get old, and I hope, you learn compassion before then.'*

Then he picks up a newspaper left behind by the last customer, and he reads the latest decree by the president.

"We will stop these revolutionaries from destroying our homes. We will have peace in our country…"

He smiles at the hypocrisy of these words. And with sarcasm he thinks. *'Mr President, you're to blame for the state of our country. You're responsible for the killings and mayhem. How do you intend to fix it?'* He knows that to say such a thing in public, will land him in jail, or worse, they'd execute him.

In the sports section, he reads how his country beat Ethiopia at football. And while it isn't a major international team, it gives people a glimmer of hope. As he turns another page, a gentle voice breaks his concentration.

"As-salaam-alaikum sir, my boss told me, that you're looking for me. I am Mido." Naguib stands up and shakes Mido's hand.

"Wa-alaikum-salaam Mido. My name is Naguib Ghali, and I'm a friend of Hassam Elneny." He sees fear flicker across Mido's eyes.

"Has Mr Elneny changed his mind about my debt?" Naguib is intrigued.

"I don't know anything about a debt. What arrangements did you have with Hassam?" Mido tells Naguib why he borrowed the money.

"But the last time I saw Mr Elneny, he said he'd written off the debt, and that I didn't owe him anything." Naguib smiles. He's happy, and he knows, Hassam is trying to change his life.

"No, I'm not here for that. Whatever you and Hassam agreed is fine with me. I have a different kind of request, and I need your help. Do you have time to talk?"

"Right now, I can't talk. As you can see, I'm working, and I won't be finished until late. I have a day off tomorrow, but I'm busy in the morning. I'll be available after midday. If you want, we can meet here at two o'clock?" Naguib doesn't want to discuss the matter in public.

"Can I visit you at your home tomorrow?" Mido feels scared, and he answers with caution.

"You can, but can you tell me a little bit more?" Again, Naguib sees the fear.

"Mido, I promise you, I'm not here to harm you, and it's better for us, to talk in private. Please take this money. I hope you'll understand from this gesture, my intentions aren't bad." He then hands Mido half the money Hassam gave him.

"Very well, shall we say two o'clock?" Naguib agrees.

"Please let me have your address." Mido writes his address on the edge of the newspaper. Tearing the piece of paper, Naguib puts it in his wallet.

At home, Naguib fights his conscience. He can see that Hassam was right. Mido is a good and honest boy. His eyes are clear and alert, and his hands are gentle, like his voice. They're the hands of a musician or a poet, but not a criminal. He understands Hassam's protectiveness, and he thinks. *'I'll ask him, and if he says no, then I'll find another way.'*

The next day he walks to the address Mido gave him. It's in a part of town, which looks abandoned. There're only a few inhabitants left, and looking at their faces, he gets and uneasy feeling. They stare at him as if he's a foreigner, and it makes him feel unwelcome.

Everywhere there are broken walls, and some of the walls are peppered with bullet marks, like a badly pock marked face. Windows are smashed, and many doors hang loosely by their hinges. Some houses are unrecognisable. They look beyond repair. While other's stand, they look too fragile to be a home. The rubble is everywhere, and amongst this, the children carry on playing. The children look like ghosts. Their faces, hair, and clothes have a grey powder coating. Looking around, he thinks. *'This is where Mido lives. My God, it's a place where hope has moved out.'*

Naguib spots Mido and calls out his name. Mido meets him halfway down the street.

"Mr Ghali, please follow me and come to my house. We don't get many visitors. It's just my mother and I who live here. Naguib asks.

"Where's your father?" With a sad smile Mido answers.

"Dead, but that's another story." Naguib stares at the ground. He's embarrassed by the bluntness of his question.

"I'm sorry."

"It's not your fault, no need to apologise. In this part of town, and probably all over our country, there are many broken families. And some families which are gone forever..." Mido's words trail off, and for both of them, the tragic reality of their world is clear.

Naguib follows Mido, to what he thinks, is a derelict house. The side where the kitchen once stood, is in ruins, and the windows have strips of wood crudely nailed to them. It's a poor effort to board them up. Somehow, the roof is hanging on, and it's the only thing, which gives this building the shape of a house.

"This is where I live Mr Ghali. There's only one good thing, it costs nothing." With a grim expression on his face, Naguib asks.

"What about electricity and water?"

"Water we get in buckets. As for electricity? Well, there's none. We have candles or lanterns, and inside, I have a radio with batteries. The radio gives my mother something to listen to, rather than sit in silence all day." The more Mido speaks, the less Naguib wants him to do this job.

Inside the house, it's clean. A curtain separates the space where Mido's mother sleeps, but everything else is in one room. The collapsed wall left a hole, and Mido has done his best to cover it with old sheets, and a piece of tarpaulin he scavenged in the debris. Mido grabs the only chair they have, and hands it to Naguib, while he sits on a stool. He then starts to brew tea on a homemade cooker. Mido made the cooker from old bricks neatly piled in the shape of a box, with an opening at the front for fuel. An iron drain cover sits on top, and this is the hot plate. He lights the fire, and then he places a kettle on the hot plate.

"It won't be long Mr Ghali, in the meantime please have a glass of water." Naguib's heart is breaking at the wretchedness of what he sees.

"Water is fine. Shukraan Mido." Naguib drinks a mouthful of the cloudy water. He doesn't want to be disrespectful. But then, he gets straight to the point.

"Mido, do you know a man by the name of Khaled Sharif?" Mido clenches his jaws.

"Yes Mr Ghali, I do." Naguib stares at Mido.

"Have I upset you?" Mido relaxes.

"No Mr Ghali, you haven't upset me. But Khaled Sharif, killed my father. I cannot prove it, but in my heart, I know it was him." Naguib is worried.

"So, does Khaled know what you look like?" Mido takes a mouthful of water, and after swallowing it, he answers.

"I don't think he does. My father died when I was ten, and I've changed a lot. I'm sure he doesn't know who I am, or what I look like. Nowadays, it's just me and my mother, and we keep a very low profile." Naguib feels relieved.

"That's fine. What I want you to do. Is keep an eye on Khaled? I want you to find out, where he spends his days. It will be at his shop, or his home. And if he isn't at one of these places, he'll be at his premises out of town. I don't want you to make any contact with him, I must insist on this. I only need to find a time when he's alone. Can you do this?"

"I can do what you ask, although there's a lot of risk involved. I must ask why you need this information." Naguib finishes his water.

"Because I am going to kill Khaled." Naguib fixes Mido with a cold hard stare.

"Mr Ghali I'll do it, but if anything happens to me, I need you to promise me one thing."

"Anything." Naguib waits, and then Mido stares at him with tear filled eyes.

"Look after my mother." Without losing eye contact, the two men shake on the deal. Handing the rest of the money to Mido, Naguib speaks.

"If there's anything you need, please get in touch with me. My address is on this piece of paper. Keep it safe."

Mido takes the money and the paper, and he answers.

"Thank you Mr Ghali. I think the tea is ready. Will you join my mother and me for a drink? If you're hungry, I have some nuts and fruit. Let me introduce you to my mother, her name is Madiha."

When Naguib looks across the room, he feels his heart quiver with pain. Smiling back at him, is a frail old woman. These two people hardly have anything, and yet they share the little they have with him.

"It will be my honour, to eat and drink with you. Mido what was your father's name? With a smile, Mido answers.

"My father was Saad Ibrahim." Naguib's eyes bulge with amazement.

"Saad Ibrahim! The politician?" Mido nods.

"Yes, the same. He wanted to clean up the city, and I guess, Khaled was one of the parasites he wanted to bring to justice."

Naguib's head is in a spin. He cannot believe that the son and widow, of the only honest politician for the last forty years, live in abject poverty. But it makes him realise, where the gentleness, charisma, and charm Mido possesses comes from. He is his father's son.

Chapter 15 - Spying

Three weeks pass since his meeting with Mido. And Naguib wonders. *'Has Mido fled town? Can you blame him?'*

The sun has set and Naguib is watering his flowers. He always does this at night, because during the day, the water evaporates as soon as he pours it into the flowerbeds. He watches, as the soil drinks the water, like a thirsty man coming in from the desert. When he's finished, he sits on the veranda, but within seconds, he hears a knock at the door.

He looks through the chink, and he gasps. "It's Mido!" He opens the door and almost drags Mido into the house.

"Mido, my God it's you! I was starting to give up hope. I thought, you left town. Mind you, I wouldn't blame you if you had. Anyway, how are you?"

"Mr Ghali, I'm sorry it's taken so long. With my work and trying to look after my mother. I only had two days a week, where I could carry out any surveillance. And even then, I needed at least three weeks, to see if there's any pattern in Khaled's days." Naguib nods.

"And no one spotted you?" Mido shakes his head.

"I don't think so. In any case, no one really knows me. I often run errands for the restaurant, so it's not unusual for me to walk about town." Naguib is happy.

"Let me make tea, and then you can tell me what you've learned."

As Naguib makes tea, Mido sits on the sofa and looks around. To him, this is luxurious. Despite, having spent his early years living a good life, he cannot remember those days. And after Saad's death, all he and his mother have, was the small derelict house. Mido asks.

"Mr Ghali, do you live here on your own?" Naguib has a pained expression, but he answers with good humour.

"Yes, for the last three months, I've been on my own. I used to share the house with my son, his wife and their three children. But now, they're in America."

Mido asks.

"Mr Ghali, why didn't you go with your family?" Naguib sighs.

"I tried, but I had a problem with my passport." And the response is sympathetic.

"I'm sorry you're on your own, it must get lonely." Mido's voice is calm and soothing, and Naguib smiles.

"So, what have you learned about or mutual enemy Khaled Sharif?" Mido finishes his tea.

"As I said, I observed him for three weeks and there's a pattern. From what I saw, he spends every morning, until eleven in the shop. People come and go, but I have no idea what they discuss. However, I kept seeing the same two visitors, and every day they came at the same time. These men are huge, they look like bodyguards. I'm not sure, but whatever they are, they look violent. They stay for twenty minutes and then leave. After that, Khaled goes home and spends time with his wife and children. He has two children, a boy who is maybe seven or eight, and a girl who is five or six. His wife is very young, maybe half his age. Then, between three and four, he comes back to the shop, and he stays there until sunset. Then the two big men return, and Khaled goes with them in a car. I'm guessing, it's at this point, he visits his premises out of town. I had no way of following them."

Naguib listens, and then he asks.

"Is there a time in the day when he's alone?"

"Yes, once they get back around ten, he walks home, across town and through the park. His house overlooks the park. Mr Ghali, your window of opportunity is very small. You have about ten minutes, while he walks across the park. There's only one place, where you can hide. It's a hedge. I know this because I've hidden in it. From that vantage point, you have maybe three minutes, in which you can approach Khaled." Naguib nods.

"I don't need three minutes. One minute is enough." Mido is concerned.

"Mr Ghali, if you use a gun, the police will catch you. This is where all the rich people live, and police patrol the neighbourhood. If they hear a gunshot, they'll be on you before you can run. Please don't take this the wrong way, but you're not a young man. I doubt you could outrun a healthy police officer." Naguib strokes his chin.

"I'm not worried about them catching me, but I understand your concern. I do have a gun, but I'll use a knife. It's messy and has to be done at close quarters." Mido asks.

"Mr Ghali, have you ever taken a life?" Naguib stays impassive and Mido carries on.

"I've heard, it's not easy to take a life. People say. That a person who takes a life, carries so much guilt, the only atonement they can offer, is their own life. I'm saying this as a friend. I'm saying this, because with so much death and destruction around us, it seems meaningless to take another life. Even the life of someone like Khaled Sharif."

Naguib's eyes glaze over, and he blinks hard to stop the tears.

"Hassam thought very highly of you, and I can see why. You have the same goodness as your father. One of the reasons I turned away from crime, was because I listened to the speeches made by your father. And I can see, you have the same caring heart." Mido sighs.

"I don't know if I have my father's brains. My education was cut short after his death. All I have are my instincts, and they're all I need to make sure my mother doesn't suffer. I don't know where my future is. I don't know if we have a future in this country."

The two men sit in silence. After pouring two more drinks, Naguib asks.

"Mido, what can I do for you? Just say, and it will be done?" Mido hesitates, but then he opens up.

"It's something which may put a huge burden on you." Naguib leans forward.

"Tell me, and I can decide if it's a burden."

Mido struggles. His voice falters with heartfelt emotions. But after a minute, he finds the courage to ask.

"Mr Ghali, my mother is very sick. According to the doctor, she has three months, maybe a little bit more. The winter is coming, and the nights are cold. I can cope with it, but she won't survive. Those three months could easily become less. I need to find a better place for her, but I don't have that kind of money…"

Mido's words trail off, and Naguib knows what he has to do.

"She will live here. I have plenty of room, and you're also welcome." Mido's eyes fill up, and he asks.

"You would do that Mr Ghali?"

"Yes Mido." Naguib feels the weight of Mido's love for his mother. Mido places his hands over his face and starts to cry. There's no sound. And as the tears run down his chin and fall to the floor, Naguib moves closer. He puts his arm around Mido's shoulder and whispers.

"Don't cry Mido. You and I will do what your mother needs. We'll make her comfortable, and she'll get good treatment."

Mido's head falls against Naguib's shoulder. In an attempt to stop his own tears, Naguib clenches his jaws, and he thinks. *'Here's a boy who hasn't known a father figure since the age of ten. But in this torn and tortured land, he's one of many. When will it stop?'*

The following day Madiha comes to Naguib's home. He gives her Anwar and Nawal's room. Naguib has cleared the room and he's put a small table next to her bed. And on it, he's placed fresh flowers.

Despite asking, Mido won't stay.

"Mr Ghali, what you've done is enough, and I'm happy. Because I know, my mother's last days, will be in comfort. That's all I need."

"Mido, I have plenty of room, why won't you stay?" Naguib questions him, but Mido insists.

"Because sir, I have to look after my father's house. I have to remember him as well." Naguib doesn't question Mido any further.

"Then take the spare keys. Come and visit your mother whenever you want." Mido takes the keys.

"Shukraan Mr Ghali, but I have one more favour. Would you mind if I call you Uncle?" Naguib smiles.

"I wish you would. All this Mr Ghali business, makes me feel like a policeman." They both laugh.

That evening Naguib visits Mrs Kulthum.

"Naguib, what a lovely surprise, please come in." He hesitates.

"Mrs Kulthum…" She stops him.

"It's Yousra. Remember?" Naguib smiles.

"Yes of course. Yousra, I need a favour." Mr Kulthum comes to the door. Although Naguib has seen Mr Hussein Kulthum, many times over the years, it was always from a distance. They didn't really know each other well, and they had only spoken on a few occasions. Standing only a meter away from Hussein, leaves Naguib speechless. Hussein is a short squat man, and hairy all over, except his head, which is as bald as a new-born baby. He smiles, and Naguib notices the nicotine-stained teeth. Hussein asks.

"Naguib, how are you my old friend, and what do you need?" At first Naguib hesitates, but when Hussein smiles, he answers.

"Hussein, Yousra, it's a rather delicate matter. Will you come to my house?" Hussein barks some orders to their son, after which he and Yousra follow Naguib. Yousra doesn't waste any time.

"Naguib, what is it?" Again, Naguib hesitates, and then he whispers.

84

"Right now, I have a guest at my house. It's a woman, and she's the wife of Saad Ibrahim. Her name is Madiha." Hussein is astonished.

"Saad Ibrahim, the politician? Are you joking?" Naguib relaxes.

"No Hussein, it's not a joke, but it's a long story. Here's the short version. She's dying. She has three, maybe four months. She was living with her son Mido, in the worst conditions you can imagine. He helped me, and I'm doing this as repayment." Yousra looks around and raises her voice.

"Where is she? Have you hidden her?" Then they hear Madiha.

"No my dear, he hasn't hidden me, I'm in this room." When they enter the bedroom, they see her. As soon as Hussein lays his eyes on her, he claps his hands.

"Oh my God, it really is you? You're still beautiful. You know all the guys had a thing for you. We used to see your photos in the papers when you married Saad." Madiha giggles and Yousra scolds.

"Don't listen to him Madiha, he's an old charmer." She nudges Hussein and he starts to laugh. In the front room, Naguib looks embarrassed, and again he whispers. But this time, it's even quieter.

"Yousra, Madiha needs help to bathe and other things. I cannot do that. She's a woman, and I must respect her modesty. I know it's asking a lot, but could you help me. Please."

Yousra sees the vulnerability, but she doesn't hesitate.

"Yes Naguib, I'll help, and I'll cook for both of you." Naguib feels relieved, and smiles.

"Shukraan Yousra, may Allah bless you." Naguib turns to Hussein.

"Hussein, you old crook, how did you end up with such a good woman?" Hussein gives a hearty laugh.

"I told her I was a millionaire, but little did she know, I didn't have two pennies to rub together."

The three neighbours laugh, and as their laughter subsides, they hear Madiha softly snoring. She is warm, cared for, and safe.

Chapter 16 - Madiha

Having Madiha in his home, makes a huge difference to Naguib's life. But still, he cannot rid himself of his hatred for Khaled. This is the negative effect of having her stay. Watching someone dying, reminds him of Rashida's last days.

He enjoys listening to conversations between Madiha and Yousra. Their lives couldn't be more different. And yet, their humour connects them like two old friends. As Yousra combes Madiha's hair, she asks.

"What was your life like in the old days? You know, the servants, the chauffeurs, the gorgeous clothes, and the jet set parties?" Madiha's eyes sparkle for a second and then fade.

"It's not as glamorous as you think. I know you saw us on the covers of Vogue and Tatler. Those photos embarrassed me so much. Because I knew how much the people were suffering. Let me shatter the image everyone has about glamour. To get one cover shot, the photographer may take two hundred photos. Do you know, it takes a whole day to take that many photos? I'd often walk off because I needed to fart."

Yousra is in hysterics, and Madiha carries on.

"Don't be fooled by the glamour. It's a perfect moment conjured up by the artistry of a good photographer, but it isn't real. It's an illusion. Whether a person is rich or poor, at times, we have the same issues. Self-doubt, fear of the unknown, happiness, and sadness. We all share the same emotions, but under different conditions, and in different clothes. The parties were awful. The men would try to outdo each other, with their clever talk, backstabbing, and sucking up to the president. The women would talk about jewellery, the houses, the shopping, and other mundane things. Very shallow, but I must confess, at times it was fun." Yousra wants to know more.

"What about children? Who looked after the children?" Madiha sighs.

"Often it was the nanny, but for me there was a reason for this. I was nearly forty-six when Mido was born, so I wasn't a young woman. Saad and I always saw Mido as our miracle child. So you see, the nanny was there to help me, while I recovered. The nanny situation reached boiling point, when we had to fire her. We suspected her of stealing. Mido was only four years old. You can't imagine how much he cried. Because for the first four years of his life, she was always there, and I wasn't. I realised, I was a shit mother, and from that day, I never left Mido's side. Wherever I went, he came with me. Whatever I did, he was involved. I stopped going to parties, but at that time, Saad was taking an opposing position to the president, and the party invitations stopped arriving. Nobody wanted to show support for Saad. At least not in public. In public, those people we thought were friends, didn't want anything to do with us. Despite the political turmoil, it was a time when Saad and I were at our closest, because all we had was each other and Mido."

Yousra is silent, and her tears well up. To lighten the mood, she asks.

"Come on, let me put some lipstick on you." Madiha agrees. Then she looks in a handheld mirror.

"My goodness, this is very red. We used to say that when a woman wanted another baby, she would wear this colour to entice her husband." She follows this with a mischievous chuckle. Yousra laughs and Madiha squeezes her hand.

"Thank you Yousra."

Yousra asks.

"For what?"

And Madiha answers.

"For making me feel like a woman. It's been many years since I had that feeling." The two women embrace.

Naguib sits in silence. He is humbled by Madiha's words, and by her ability to laugh, despite all the tragedies in her life.

Chapter 17 - Letter

Naguib is returning from the Doctors surgery, with Madiha's medicine. And he sees the postman outside his front door. He shouts.

"Nour, I'm here, wait." As Naguib gets closer, Nour smiles at him, with the seven teeth that are still in his mouth.

"As-salaam-alaikum Naguib, how are you my old friend?" Naguib returns the greeting.

"Wa-alaikum-salaam Nour. I'm well, and you?" Nour's face turns sour.

"Could be better. I'm still working, but nothing is certain. We're all surprised that we still have a job. The situation is so bad, sometimes the post doesn't get to us for months. And we can't guarantee, that the replies will get to their destination either. The only things that seem to get through, are the bills!"

The two men laugh and Naguib asks.

"You have something for me today?" The gapped tooth smile returns.

"Yes, indeed I do, and the stamp is an American one! It must be from your son!" Naguib's heart starts to race.

"Come into the house, let's not stand out here talking." Inside the house, Nour hands Naguib the letter, and the two men go out onto the veranda. Nour asks.

"Where in America does Anwar live?" Naguib knew where the ship was going, but he didn't know if that was Anwar's final destination.

"I think it was New York. That's where the ship was headed. But we'll know more once I open the letter." Nour smiles and asks.

"Oh, they call it the Big Orange, isn't that so?" Naguib grins.

"No my friend, I think it's the Big Apple." Nour laughs.

"Big apple, big oranges, or big banana's it doesn't matter, he's safer there. But listen, I must go now, but can I come back later to hear what he has to say?" Naguib agrees and after letting Nour out, he checks on Madiha, and she's reading.

"Naguib, is everything alright, I heard voices?"

"Yes Madiha, it was Nour the postman. He brought me a letter from my son in America." Madiha sees hesitation and pain in Naguib's face, and she asks.

"What is it, have you not read it yet? Naguib, please don't be offended, but can you read?" For the first time, Naguib shows fear.

"I can read Madiha, but I'm scared to read the letter. I'm scared, it will break my heart. Will you read it please?"

Madiha agrees. Inside the envelope, there are photos along with the letter. Naguib gazes at the family pictures and the tears stream from his eyes. Madiha touches his hand, and she tries to comfort him. With his hands shaking, he hands the letter to her, and she starts to read.

"Dear Abbi,

I hope you're well, and you're eating properly. We all miss you very much, and the children go to sleep and dream about you. They tell Nawal and me that you come to them in their sleep.

Rafa and Salma are at school and they're enjoying it. They can speak enough English to make friends. Farid goes to a nursery, but he doesn't like it, and he cannot make himself understood. He said to me, I'm going to run away, and I'm going to live with Jadd. His sisters are trying to teach him, and the school is giving him extra English lessons. He will be fine once he makes some friends.

I have a job as a janitor at a local school, the work is good, but sometimes people around me talk very fast. Nawal is trying to learn English from the girls. She's suffering with homesickness. Maybe it's just to gossip with the other women,

90

but all the same, she's struggling, and we're all trying to help her.

Abdel stayed with us for the first two-weeks, but with his contacts at the U.S. embassy, he got himself a good job, and he moved to Virginia. He and Shadia have met, and they like one another. We're hoping something good will happen, please let Uncle Hassam and Aunty Samir know the good news.

It's very different here. And the first thing, is the weather. Last week we had over a metre of snow, and the temperature did not go above minus ten degrees. For us, it's cold enough to freeze your blood.

This is a strange country. I work with a black man and his name is Marcus. I think, a long time ago his family were from Africa. He reminds me of the Sudanese people, who sometimes visited our city. Marcus is a good man, but he warned me about how Americans view foreigners. Most Americans are very nice, but many don't like refugees, and Muslims. They seem distrustful of us. I read the papers and sometimes we get news of home. I worry, but at least the American newspapers seem to understand our countries problems. I hope something good can come from so many people reading about our home.

Farid sat with me when I was writing this letter, and he asked if I could put him in a parcel and post him to you. It was funny, but I wished I could do the same.

I hope you enjoy the photos and if you can, I would love to get a photo back from you, and of course a letter. The photo of you might put my mind at rest. I will end this letter now, and I will write again soon.

Please pray for me as I will pray for you. Inshallah I will see you soon.

Your loving son

Anwar

Madiha holds onto the letter, while Naguib carries on staring at the photos. He listens to every word she utters. After a minute's silence, Madiha touches Naguib's arm.

"Naguib, it's a good letter. And it sounds like, Anwar will thrive in a country where there's opportunity." Looking down at the floor, Naguib answers.

"My brain understands, but my heart doesn't. And sometimes I get tearful, I'm sorry." Madiha sighs.

"Naguib, there's no need to apologise. As a nation, we weep, and families mourn their losses. Whether those losses are, permanent or temporary."

Naguib understands her words, but today, he doesn't want to think about it. He decides to ask a question, which has played on his mind, since he first met Mido and Madiha.

"Madiha, I need to ask you something." She smiles.

"Anything you like Naguib." Pushing back his own feelings of sorrow, he stares at Madiha.

"You and Saad had such a great life, how did you come to live like a beggar?" Madiha thinks about this for ages, and then she answers.

"When Saad saw the criminal way the president, and his henchmen held onto power, he knew something had to be done. But it isn't easy. It's like walking a tightrope. And below, there are daggers pointing at you. And below that, there are ferocious animals waiting to devour you. And even below that, there are vultures, and they'll make sure. That even the memory of you, does not exist." Madiha takes a sip of water, and then she carries on.

"For years, the secret police have bugged most of the minister's homes and offices, and those who are influential when it comes to public opinion. Saad was one of those. We used to speak freely at home, not knowing that someone was listening to us. There was a day the president's office summoned Saad, and the president asked. Whether he could count on Saad's support. But Saad hesitated. He told the president. That he didn't agree with everything that was happening. That was his biggest mistake." Madiha takes another sip, and then she continues.

"Saad had shares in an oil company, and he owned a small hotel, which his father left him. The president decreed that the oil industry would be nationalised. Saad got less than five percent of the share value. And it was enough, to buy the small house Mido and I were living in. The same house, you visited. This house was our first home when Saad and I married, but in those days, we rented it. That's why, Mido won't leave that house. Then, there was a compulsory purchase order for the hotel. We were told, the land would be used for a new airport. Again, Saad received about ten percent of the hotel's value. The hotel was bulldozed, but they never built an airport. Whatever money we had. We spent a long time ago."

Madiha stops and stares at Naguib. For the first time, he sees a flash of anger in her eyes. But within seconds, the anger disappears, and the kindness returns.

"Naguib, the worst thing is, if the president decides to break a person, it becomes an unofficial decree. And no one, will deal with that person. Not if they value their lives."

Naguib feels his anger rising.

"What about blood relations?"

Madiha sighs.

"Saad and I, are only children, and our parents died a long time ago. I have one uncle, but he's in Europe. He left during the last military coup, and I have no idea where he lives. Saad had two aunties, and they could have helped, but the secret police threatened them. The police said. If they helped us, their sons would be forced to join the army, and they would fight the deadliest battles. Saad decided not to involve them, and I agreed with him."

Naguib is confused.

"But by then Saad was powerless to do anything. How could he be a threat to the president?"

Madiha answers.

"You would think this is the case. But it wasn't, and this is where Saad made his second mistake. This mistake led to his downfall. Saad was approached by a politician who wanted to gain power. And his name is Zulfiker Sakka."

Naguib's eyes bulge with amazement.

"Zulfiker Sakka! The foreign minister? The second wealthiest person in our country?"

Madiha gives a mocking smile.

"Yes, the very same man. He suggested a coup and promised support from the army. Saad went along with the plan. Zulfiker revealed the plan to the president, and Saad and the soldiers involved were arrested. Zulfiker suggested to the president, that he should not kill Saad, but show mercy. It was a public relations exercise, and because of it, our country got a lot of assistance with modernising the oil industry. After that, Zulfiker was the president's favourite, and he could do no wrong. They stripped Saad off all power. They even denied him his pension. But Zulfiker knew, Saad could implicate him, and so he had Saad killed. This part is rumour, but it also makes a lot of sense."

Naguib remembers his conversation with Mido, and he asks.

"Mido said, he suspected Khaled Sharif. Do you think the same thing?"

Madiha answers.

"Yes Naguib, I believe this. Since Zulfiker and Khaled Sharif have known each other a long time. People say, Khaled offered to have Saad killed, and he could make it look like an accident. In exchange, Khaled wanted amnesty from prosecution, and for the police to turn a blind eye. From all accounts, Zulfiker agreed to these terms. Even now, Khaled walks without fear, because Zulfiker has made him untouchable. Zulfiker and Khaled are very similar, and in a guarded way, they trust one another, but they're both ruthless."

Naguib knows, Khaled likes to make murder look like an accident. A car crash, or slipping aconite into someone's food or drink, to induce a heart attack. But always something, to hide the truth. Naguib asks.

"Do you have other reasons for thinking it was Khaled?"

For a while Madiha thinks about this, but then she stares at Naguib.

"Yes, I do. At the time, Saad had a driver, and his name was Hazem. When Saad lost his job, he also lost the government car, and Hazem became Zulfiker's driver. Hazem witnessed some of the meetings between Zulfiker and Khaled, and he overheard some of the conversations as well. Hazem warned us because he liked Saad as a person, but Saad didn't take any notice. He thought it was paranoia, and he said to me. 'They've taken everything. There's nothing else to take.' He was wrong. And that was his final mistake, and it was fatal."

Naguib grits his teeth in anger, but he says nothing. Madiha notices the rage, and she squeezes Naguib's arm.

"Naguib don't let your anger rule your heart. I've seen this before, and the damage it does is devastating." Naguib looks at Madiha.

"I don't feel anger towards Khaled. I feel nothing for him. To me, he's less than a dog. Whatever I do, I'll do it with my eyes wide open, and my mind clear of emotions."

Naguib squeezes Madiha's hand to acknowledge her words. He picks up the letter and photos, and he walks out onto the veranda. His breathing is calm, and he knows what he needs to do next. He stares at his flowers, and to stop himself thinking about murder, he waters them.

Chapter 18 - Plotting

"**Mido**, how did you get into this hedge? There's not enough room in here for a child?" Mido laughs.

"It wasn't easy Uncle, but this is your cover." Naguib scratches his head, and while he's shorter than Mido, he's much wider. His body has thickened with age, and he isn't flexible enough to fit into such a small space.

"Mido, we have to think of something else. Even if I could get into that space, I wouldn't be able to get out in time. Can you imagine the scene? Khaled standing there, and watching me trying to get out of that hedge? I'll look like a clown! Unless I want to kill Khaled with laughter, we'll have to find another way."

Mido smiles at the macabre humour, but he realises, Naguib is right. And they'd only have one chance at this ambush.

"Uncle, do you have a black galabeya, and a black turban?" Naguib doesn't know where this is going, and why he needs a new shirt.

"No, but I can easily get them. Why do I need new clothes?" Mido answers.

"Because there's a blind side to this hedge, which means, if you stood on that side, dressed all in black, you wouldn't be seen?" Naguib likes this, and smiles.

"Perfect, that's what we'll do. The thought of hiding in this hedge is horrible, and I know I'd miss my chance."

Once they stop talking, the murderous intentions that brought them to this place, sinks in. In silence, they walk back to the house.

As Naguib sits on his bed cleaning his gun, he knows he has to buy a decent dagger. It must be functional, like a butcher's knife. It must be capable of slicing through flesh with ease. He's trying to think of the last time, he was involved in any kind of violence. As a young man, he was a capable and determined

96

fighter, but that was over thirty years ago. From thirty years of non-violence to this act, worries him. But he pushes his doubts to the back of his mind.

In the next room, Mido is talking to Madiha, and they're sharing the precious time they have left. Naguib thinks. *'It's strange. In one room, there's love and a longing for life. And I'm planning to take a life, and all I feel is hate. And both these emotions, live under the same roof.'*

Mido has been worried about Naguib's intention from the start, and before leaving, he speaks.

"Uncle, I hope you know what you're doing. You don't have to do this for me and my family. No good can come from another death. But you already know my feelings on this, and I know Ummi shares those feelings." Naguib understands.

"I know Mido. I've listened to you and Madiha, since you know what I intend to do. But here's my view. If Khaled were a virus, then we would do our best to wipe him out. Think about it. Despite not having a blood connection, the Khaled virus has affected our lives, and we don't know how many other lives he's infected. His drug connections could have killed many more. Have you ever seen a drug addict? They're like a walking corpse."

Mido listens and when there's a pause, he answers.

"Uncle, Khaled is one of the wheels in the criminal world. Even with him gone, the other wheels will continue to turn. You also need to think about his wife and children. They have names, and they're human. His wife is Zeina, his son is Gamal, and his daughter is Hanan. He gave his children these names because he loves them. Underneath this so-called virus, is a man. Just one last thing. Uncle, please don't make two more children live without a father."

Naguib hugs Mido, and he says nothing else. As he sits on the veranda, his mind is in torment. He wonders if his hatred is blinding him, and he remembers Madiha's warning.

As he stares at the flowers, he thinks about Rashida and her suffering, and the hatred floods through his veins again.

He decides not to take Mido with him, since he doesn't want to put him in danger. He'll complete this task on his own. He knows it's full of risks. Since there'll be no one on lookout.

The following day he visits the shops and purchases a black galabeya, a black turban, a butcher's knife, and a leather sheath.

It's the dead of night, and while Madiha sleeps, he tries on his new clothes, straps the knife around his waist, and grips the gun in his hand. He stares at his reflection with ruthless determination, and his eyes stare back without blinking. He's ready for this murderous mission.

Chapter 19 - Kill

While eating with Madiha, Naguib is quieter than usual, and she notices.

"Naguib, is something troubling you?" He swallows his food.

"I was just wondering. How you can tell if you're doing the right thing?" She thinks about the question, and when she sees him staring, she answers.

"There's a quote by Rumi which might help you. *These pains you feel are messengers, listen to them.* Do you understand what this means?" He looks at Madiha with inquisitive eyes.

"I think so. Are the pains Rumi writes about, referring to doubt?" Madiha nods.

"Yes. I believe they are. When we do the right things, we're not doubtful. We do not question our actions, and it's as natural as breathing. When we make the wrong choices, our moral compass goes haywire, because it's confused. The confusion makes our brain go in different directions. It's like walking on an uneven surface, and when we do that, we have to keep adjusting our footing."

Naguib asks.

"But what if you know in your heart. That what you're about to do, is right. In that situation, why do we feel so much conflict?" Madiha touches his hand.

"The heart can lie. Hatred can fill the heart with lies. For example, when we become jealous for no reason, the heart is lying. And it causes us to treat someone we love, in a bad way. Whenever there's doubt, it's reasonable to say, the action is not right. Even if your heart tells you a hundred times, that it's right, your moral compass will try to put you on a different path. It's a way, for humans to stay in balance."

Naguib thanks her, and when he spoons Madiha her medicine, she gags and coughs. Her body shakes until she takes a mouthful of water. It reminds him of the time, he spent nursing Rashida, and he grits his teeth with anger and sadness.

Naguib changes into the black clothes. He straps the knife around his waist, and he puts the gun in the side pocket. He wraps a long black shawl over his shoulders, and this hides the knife and the bulge of the gun.

He steps out of the house, and he locks the door behind him. It's late, and there are only a handful of people on the streets. As he walks towards the park, some of the stores close their shutters for the night. He stays on the darkest part of the road, and the black clothes are doing their job. Other than the occasional sound of his footsteps, he is unseen.

While he walks, he has one wish. *'Why couldn't I be like a sniper? Killing people from a distance, and not knowing anything about those I kill. I wish I didn't know Khaled.'*

Before getting to the hedge, Naguib relieves himself, and stands with the gun in his hand. The minutes drag on, and he feels his hand tremble, and his mouth getting drier by the second. He picks up a small smooth pebble, cleans it as best he can, and pops it into his mouth. As he sucks on the pebble, saliva starts to return, but he wishes he brought a drink with him.

He leans against the hedge, and it almost gives way. He stumbles, but straightens himself, and thinks. *'God I'm making enough noise to wake the whole city.'* In the silence, every noise echoes, and rebounds, as if he's playing the drums. He takes a deep breath, and exhales, and slowly, he feels his heartbeat settle.

There's a noise! He peers from the hedge. It's two police officers on patrol. He crouches behind the hedge. He watches them pass by while they talk.

"I didn't get my overtime this month. I'll have to speak to the paymaster." The second police officer is angry and complains.

"They're making more mistakes every day. You wait and see. It won't be long before they forget to pay us. If it wasn't for my extra income, I don't think I could cope."

Naguib understands that extra income means, bribes the police take, to turn a blind eye.

Another ten minutes pass, and in that time, more lights in the surrounding houses go out. Then he hears more footsteps. He looks again, and it looks like Khaled. But he feels unsure. There's something different, and he thinks. *'He looks a lot thinner. Is this Khaled?'*

Then he takes a longer look, and he recognises the walk. It is Khaled. Naguib grips the gun, and despite being a cool evening, he feels sweat all over his body. With a quick movement, he wipes his hands and the butt of the gun on his shawl.

Once Khaled passes the hedge, Naguib steps out.

"Stop!"

Khaled freezes, and then he turns around. His movements are slow and confident. He cannot make out the face, but he sees the gun. Khaled asks.

"Do you know who I am?" Naguib steps out of the shadows and answers.

"I know exactly who you are. You could say, I know you better than most people. Because I crawled out of the same gutter as you." Khaled thinks he recognises the voice.

"Naguib?"

"Yes, it's me." All the tension leaves Naguib's body, and he steps forward.

"And I'm here to put an end to your evil." Khaled doesn't flinch.

"Naguib, you're not the first person to try and kill me. But for old time's sake, I'd ask you to listen to me." Naguib thinks. *'Even a dying man gets a last request.'*

"Fine, go ahead and talk." Khaled stares at Naguib, and when he speaks, his tone is calm.

"Not here. Please come to my house. It's five minutes away. There are no guns in my house, there are no weapons, my wife and children live there. Let's talk there." Naguib asks.

"And you don't have a gun on you?" Khaled raises his shirt, and then he does a full three-hundred-and-sixty-degree turn.

"If I'm caught with a gun, there are too many questions. That's why, I never carry a weapon."

Naguib understands, but he doesn't trust Khaled. In the old days, he saw Khaled slash another man's face with a pen. He knows what Khaled can do.

"Walk ahead of me. One false move and I'll shoot." Naguib keeps his distance and follows. And all the time, he points the gun at Khaled.

Inside the house, Khaled asks.

"Naguib please put the gun away. Whatever you think of me, please respect the sanctity of my home. This is where my wife and children live." Naguib feels a surge of anger, and he thinks. *'You ask me to show you respect? Did you respect my life?*

Gripping the gun harder, Naguib enters the house. It's quiet, and Khaled shouts.

"Zeina, I'm home. I have some business." Zeina comes out of the bedroom.

"Do you and your friend want tea?" Khaled shakes his head.

"No, you go back to sleep. I'll make tea if we want it." Naguib peers through the gap between the door and the doorframe, and he thinks. *'Yes, she's much younger than him.'*

Khaled gets a pitcher of water, two glasses, and leads Naguib to his study. Naguib looks around, and the emptiness of the room surprises him. There's a simple desk facing the window, and it overlooks the park. There are two chairs, and a bookshelf with a dozen books, and a photo of Khaled's children.

When they sit down, Naguib keeps his hand in his pocket, and a tight grip on the gun. Khaled pours two glasses of water, and then asks.

"So why have you come to see me?"

Chapter 20 - Confession

"I have come to kill you." Naguib says the words, as if he's ticking off a list of things to do.

Khaled answer shows no fear.

"I always knew, I might die at the hands of someone close. So, I guess, it might as well be you." This is going to be harder than Naguib imagined. He knows, a cold-hearted killer, would've pulled the trigger by now. He stares at Khaled and asks.

"Why did you kill my wife?"

Before he pulls the trigger, he needs an answer to this question. Khaled's eyes flicker, but he remains calm.

"Is that what you think? Is that what you believe?" More doubt creeps into Naguib's mind, and he answers.

"Yes, that is what I believe." Khaled looks at Naguib with genuine sadness.

"It's a lie. I had nothing to do with Rashida's death." Naguib asks.

"Is it true, that Rashida overheard you talking about Fouad's death?"

"Yes, it's true. But I was talking to a contact, who knew how Fouad died, and who killed him. There's no point telling you the killer's name. Because he died a long time ago. I know this because I killed him. On that day, I didn't know Rashida was in the shop. She overheard some of the conversation, and she confronted me. She asked me. Who killed Fouad? She was shouting, and a crowd gathered around the shop. I tried to stop her from screaming, but she kept saying. Tell me before I go to the police. I tried to calm her, and I told her I would take care of it. I asked her to trust me. By then, someone in the crowd who worked for this other man, spoke to him. This other man killed

Rashida. I knew this, as soon as I heard about her accident, and eventual death. And that's when I killed this man."

Naguib doesn't move or take his eyes of Khaled. His head is thumping, and he keeps hearing the word. Liar. He forces himself to listen, and then he asks.

"Who was this other man?" Khaled answers.

"I suppose it doesn't matter now. It was Abdul Nabawy. He was this city's chief of police, and he was the most crooked man I've ever met. And coming from me, that's a big accolade." Naguib frowns.

"Where's your proof?" Khaled closes his eyes for a second, and once he opens them, he answers.

"Naguib, why would I keep proof of something, which means, the death sentence for me? Would you keep a souvenir of that day?" Naguib feels his resolve weakening, but he's determined to get more answers.

"I don't believe you. You've survived this long. Because you've mastered the art of avoiding blame. You killed Rashida." Naguib now wants this to be true, and he squeezes the gun. Khaled takes a sip of water.

"Naguib, I'm many things, and I've done things for which I deserve to die. But I didn't kill Rashida. Do you remember when you told Hassam and me, that you were getting married? Do you remember, how happy we were? You were a brother to me, and that made Rashida my sister. Why would I kill my sister?" Naguib presses on.

"Hassam and I spoke before he and Samir left the city…" Khaled stops him.

"I had to let Hassam believe what he needed to, and I knew he wouldn't say anything to you. One thing about Hassam, he knew when to keep his mouth shut. But I suppose, he felt you needed to know. I had to let the rumours die out. I couldn't tell anyone the truth about who killed Rashida, and I was under orders from Zulfiker Sakka, not to make trouble. But once Abdul Nabawy fell out with Zulfiker, it cleared the way for me to kill him. But even Zulfiker, doesn't know, I killed Nabawy. You're the only person that knows."

Hearing Zulfiker's name, reminds Naguib of Madiha and Mido.

"I know of Zulfiker, and I know that you have a friendship with him. I also have a friendship with the family of Saad Ibrahim. And they said, you killed Saad?" Khaled clenches his jaws, and after a few seconds, he answers.

"This city doesn't forget anything, and everyone knows everyone's business." Naguib presses his question.

"Did you kill Saad Ibrahim?" Khaled's eyes don't move, and with an icy stare, he answers.

"Yes, I did."

The answer takes Naguib by surprise, but it confirms one thing. Khaled is telling the truth. Naguib thinks about Mido's words. He realises, he cannot take revenge for them. It would be wrong, and he knows, neither Mido nor Madiha, want another death.

"Khaled, this conversation, and your confession has turned my world upside down. I came here with a purpose, but now I cannot kill you. I want to believe you're lying, but my heart tells me, you're not. I don't know what will happen to either of us." Khaled hands Naguib a glass of water.

"Your original wish, to kill me, will come true. You'll not have to wait long." Naguib puts the glass down.

"What's that supposed to mean?" In answering the question, Khaled reaches into his pocket, and he pulls out a strip of pills.

"These are morphine tablets. They're the strongest painkillers on the market. I have an incurable form of cancer, and these tablets allow me to get through each day. But each day, as the cancer gets stronger, and poisons my body, they work a little bit less. And I feel more pain."

Khaled pops a pill into his mouth, and he washes it down with a mouthful of water. Naguib understands the reason for Khaled's skeletal look. He looks away for a second. He wanted to kill Khaled in a quick and humane way. He wanted to minimise the pain. But he can see, this illness is far worse. It's killing Khaled in the slowest and cruellest way it can.

For a moment, Naguib views Khaled as his friend from the old days, and his voice is gentle.

"You look so much thinner than I remember?" Khaled answers.

"I've lost over thirty kilos in eighteen months. This cancer eats you from the inside out, until there's only the shell of a body left. Just enough to bury. Everyone thinks, because I have such a young wife I was dieting, and I was trying to look younger for her. No one, other than you and Zeina know that the cancer is killing me. It's strange to think, you came to kill me, but I think, you came to save me."

All the murderous thoughts that invaded Naguib's mind, leave him, and he asks.

"How long have you got?" Khaled wipes his mouth.

"Three months maximum." Both men sit in silence. Khaled leans forward, and stares at Naguib.

"I'm in no position to ask a favour. But I'm going to ask you for one. It might be my only chance." Naguib takes his hand out of his pocket and rests it on his thigh.

"Ask."

"Naguib, you're my oldest friend. Remember the past if you can. Think back to when we trusted one another." Naguib listens, and when he blinks, Khaled takes it as permission, and carries on.

"Naguib, I live amongst murderers, and men who take pleasure in killing. When I die, they'll feast on my carcass. They'll feast on my wife and children. Please take my family as your own. My wife is beautiful, and in time, my children will come to see you as their father. They're young enough to do this."

Naguib almost laughs, but he stops himself. He cannot believe what Khaled is asking. It feels ridiculous, almost a joke. He had come to kill a man, but instead, there's a chance, he'll walk away with a bride, and more children. Naguib's mind is racing, and he takes time to collect his thoughts.

"Khaled, this is impossible. I can't even believe you're asking me to do this. I have a family and I have children. How can I do this?" Khaled stays calm.

"Your family are in America, and you live on your own. Everything I have I will give to you, and I am a rich man. I know you'll be fair with my children, and I know you'll treat Zeina well. You're the only one I trust. Will you agree?" Naguib scratches his face.

"What about Zeina's own family. Can't they take her?" Khaled grits his teeth.

"Her family disowned her when she married me. They're a very religious family, and they consider me a man with no love of Allah, or morals. I suppose, that's all the outside world sees in me. And I accept it. My own family, as small as it is, wants nothing to do with me. And as you know, my parents are gone."

Naguib's mind is in conflict. One of his key beliefs is. When a dying man asks a favour, you cannot refuse. He needs to buy time, and he wants to get advice.

"May I have a few days to think about it? If I agree there will be terms." Khaled nods.

"Come to the house in two days, but please come dressed in less sinister clothes. Zeina knows my condition, and when I have your answer, I'll know whether I can introduce you to her and the children. As for terms, right now, I'll agree to almost anything. As you can see, I don't have many options."

Walking home, Naguib keeps thinking about the conversation. Despite the enormity of what Khaled is asking, a big part of him is relieved, and he thinks. *'Thank you Allah. I couldn't live with murder.'*

When he gets home, Madiha is awake, and she calls out.

"Naguib, is everything alright?" Sitting on the edge of the bed, he tells her everything that has happened.

"I'm so happy, that you didn't go through with it. I couldn't bear the thought of that. I know in my heart, it would haunt you, and it would destroy you. I hope you've found peace." Naguib stares at his hands.

"I have the answer I was looking for. But it feels like. Every time one question is answered, five more new questions pop into my head." Madiha smiles.

"I will help you as much as I can, to answer the questions." Naguib returns the smile, but he can see that she's troubled. Her eyes are full of tears, and he fears the worst.

"Madiha, are you feeling sick?" Madiha reaches for Naguib's hand, grips it tight, and looks into his eyes.

"I have one favour to ask you." Naguib looks at Madiha's tear-filled eyes.

"Anything you want." A trail of tears run down her face.

"I want to meet Khaled, and I want to forgive him. I must do this. I don't want to go to my grave, with the thought. That I held bad feelings against another human being."

Naguib blinks hard to stop his tears. He cannot believe the sheer size of Madiha's heart. He's read about miracles, but he's sure, he's witnessing one in his own home.

Chapter 21 - Help

The following morning, Naguib wakes up after a deep sleep. He feels refreshed, and for the first time since his conversation with Hassam, he feels calm.

After washing, he makes tea, and he takes a cup into Madiha's room.

"Good morning Naguib. How do you feel?"

"I'm well. And how did you sleep?" Madiha answers.

"Yes, a peaceful rest. And I can see from your face, that you're carrying far less worries. It's made your face look much younger." Naguib nods.

"I slept for a full eight hours, and I didn't wake once. And all thoughts of violence, have left me." She smiles.

"Yes, when you're in the eye of the storm, it's hard to see anything. Your storm has ended for now, but the storm in this country rages on. I wonder when that will end?"

He isn't sure how to answer such a question. He notices that Madiha, often speaks in a poetic way, like a philosopher, or even a priest. He's a practical man, and if something is broken, he fixes it, and he doesn't wait for divine intervention. He answers her the only way he knows.

"Other than to wash, you haven't left this room since you came here. Would you like to sit outside? I can make a comfortable space for you, and the sun hasn't forgotten how to shine on this land." Madiha claps her hands, and her face beams with happiness.

"Naguib, that would be wonderful! Perhaps, we can eat outside? Mido is coming later. Can we all eat together?"

Naguib laughs at the change in Madiha. He watches her transform, from an old woman with not much time, to a little girl, who has all the time in the world.

"Yes, we can do that. In this troubled land of ours, let's find time for joy, even if it's only a day or just an hour."

Naguib spends the next hour tidying. He sweeps the veranda, cleans all the surfaces of dust, tidies the flowerbeds. And he takes a small crate, to use as a footstall for Madiha. He covers the footstall with an old scarf, and when he looks at his handiwork, he smiles.

After laying the table, he brings out falafel, boiled eggs, cheese, and pita bread. Standing back, he feels happy, and he wonders. *'When was the last time I did this?'*

When Madiha sits outside, Naguib looks at her smiling face. He's never seen her in the sunlight. As she sits with her head held high, soaking in the warmth, he sees the beauty that once existed. Her eyes are black, her nose is strong and straight, and although her lips have lost their plumpness, her smile and demeanour are full of grace.

Naguib feeds Madiha, and after three small portions, she stops him.

"That's enough for me. I can't eat big amounts, but it will give me just as much pleasure, to watch you eat." Naguib finishes the food, and then he pours them both a fresh cup of tea.

"Madiha, what do you think I should do about Zeina and the children. Should I let them live here once Khaled dies?"

Madiha thinks about this for a moment.

"Naguib, I just have one question. Do you see Khaled as an enemy or a friend? From what you've told me, you once saw him as a friend, maybe even a brother." Naguib isn't sure and his answer reveals his confusion.

"Yes, we were like brothers once, and I suppose that even with blood relations, you may not talk to each other for years. Right now, I'm not sure how I feel. I know I feel pity because he's dying, and when a dying man asks a favour, it's hard to say no. I understand the dangers for his wife and children, once he's gone. I understand, the fear other men feel for Khaled, will be gone as soon as he takes his last breath. My head tells me to look after Zeina and the children, but my heart still belongs to my wife. I feel, if I take Zeina into my home, I'll be betraying Rashida."

Madiha sits as still as a statue, and she considers his words. Then she answers.

"You still love your wife, just as I still love Saad. But one thing I recognise, is the awfulness of being alone. I've always had Mido, but he's my son, and conversations such as the ones we're having, are difficult with your children." When he nods, Madiha asks.

"What was Rashida like?" Naguib goes into the house and brings out the few wedding photos he has. Madiha stares at them, and then she breaks into a huge smile.

"Oh, my goodness! She was a real beauty. Look at her, she's exquisite." Naguib smiles.

"I fell in love with her the moment I saw her. And I did everything to bump into her, and make it look like an accident. But after a while, Rashida knew, it wasn't an accident." Madiha touches Naguib's arm.

"If Rashida was alive, and Zeina and her children needed help, would she have taken them in?" He knows the answer.

"Yes. At one time, we had eleven people living under this roof. Rashida wouldn't turn anyone away if they needed help." Without taking her eyes of Naguib, Madiha speaks.

"Well, I think you have your answer. You know what you need to do. Zeina must come and stay with you."

Naguib scratches his chin. He still has one big question.

"Should I take Zeina as a wife?" Madiha answers without hesitation.

"No, you don't have to do that. If people ask, you can say she's my dead brother's wife. Your relationship with Zeina doesn't have to be as husband and wife. It can be platonic. Do you know what that means?" Naguib nods.

"Yes, I understand, but Zeina is a young woman. And she'll crave affection, as all young women do. She may not like sleeping alone. What do I do then?" Again, Madiha doesn't hesitate.

"If that's the case, then you must find her a husband. As her brother-in-law, and in the absence of parents, or other family, you're entitled to do that. Does she have family?" He answers.

111

"Yes, she has family, but they've disowned her, because of her marriage to Khaled." Madiha sighs.

"Then all she has is you. You must protect her as you've protected me. One more thing you should know about an Arab woman, maybe all women. Once a woman has a child, she changes. She develops an instinct to protect the child. Women carry children in their womb for nine months. The bond between a mother and her child is the purest form of love. The man, who protects a woman and her children, will gain everything from that woman. He'll even gain her acceptance of a non-physical relationship, because she will see the goodness of the man."

Naguib makes up his mind.

"Zeina, Gamal and Hanan will come to live here. Thank you Madiha."

As they drink their tea, Madiha knows that Naguib hasn't finished, and she asks.

"Naguib, is there something else?" Naguib lights a cigarette.

"Yes. Khaled is a wealthy man, maybe as wealthy as Zulfiker Sakka. I want Khaled to use his money for something good." Madiha wipes her mouth.

"What do you have in mind?"

"I want Khaled to pay for Mido to leave this country, and to be educated. I see a lot of Saad in Mido, and I respected Saad, as I respect you. I want to make sure Mido gets his chance in life." For the first time during the conversation, Madiha's eyes show emotion.

"Will Khaled agree to this?" Naguib stares at her.

"I think he will." Madiha takes hold of Naguib's hands.

"You are a father to many, and you'll be rewarded. If you can do this, I will die a happy woman." Naguib squeezes her hand.

"I will do everything I can."

Chapter 22 - Agreement

Naguib stands by Rashida's grave. He imagines her face, and he speaks to her.

"I hope you can forgive me, for letting another woman stay in our home. I guess you can see I have Madiha living there, but she's different. Zeina is a young and beautiful woman. Did you hear my conversation with Madiha? If you did, then you'll know, it's my intention to look after Zeina and her children. I'll have a platonic relationship with Zeina. I hope this will make you happier. I miss you my love."

He touches Rashida's headstone, says a prayer, and walks to Khaled's house.

It's Friday afternoon, and other than children playing, the streets are empty. It's a day of rest and prayers.

At the front door, Khaled greets Naguib.

"Shall we go to my study?" Naguib follows Khaled up the marble stairs. The two men sit down, and Naguib still finds the situation hard to believe.

Despite his critical condition, Khaled still has strength in his voice.

"So Naguib, you have an answer for me?" Naguib looks at the photo of Gamal and Hanan.

"Yes Khaled, I do have an answer." Khaled waits and after a few seconds, Naguib speaks.

"I'll look after Zeina and your children. But I'll not take Zeina as my wife, but as my brother's wife. She's welcome to stay as long as she wants, but if she wants to re-marry, I'll find her a good husband." Khaled is confused.

"But why won't you take her as your wife. You're a widower, and you live alone. What's wrong with Zeina?" Naguib remembers his words at Rashida's grave.

"Khaled, I was once married to the perfect woman. Well, she was perfect for me. She gave me everything a man could

113

want. I still love her, and I cannot betray her. She was the love of my life, and it would be unfair if I took Zeina as my wife. It would be unfair to Zeina. Because she will feel like she's second best. But I promise, I'll look after Zeina as a brother, and I will love the children as my own." Khaled smiles.

"That's a good reason, and one I cannot argue with, so I'll accept these conditions. But when we spoke before, you said, you had terms. What are they?"

Since he's revealed his heart, Naguib now feels, he can have the conversation with his head.

"There are a number of things. But first, do you remember me telling you, that I knew the family of Saad Ibrahim?"

Khaled nods.

"Yes, I may be weak, but my brain and memory are still strong. So, what has Saad Ibrahim's family got to do with us?" Naguib takes a moment to find the right words.

"At this time, I'm sheltering Saad Ibrahim's wife Madiha. She's sick, and she only has a few months. This came about because I met with Saad's son, Mido. He did me a favour, and I visited them. I saw how they lived, and it was tragic. I couldn't let Madiha live out her last days in poverty. I couldn't see her suffer in this way. I speak to her most days, and I learned about your part in her husband's death. And two of these terms, will compensate the Ibrahim's."

Naguib and Khaled's eyes lock, and they don't lose eye contact for a second. It's a game they used to play when they were younger, to see who would blink first. Khaled blinks.

"Naguib, understand one thing. I didn't want to kill Saad Ibrahim, but if I didn't Zulfiker Sakka, would have killed me. Remember something. In the criminal world, there's cannibalism. And men feast upon other men. Do you understand this?"

Naguib nods, takes a second and answers.

"But all the same, you killed Saad. If you wanted to, you could've got him out of the country. You could've told Zulfiker that Saad found out, or he got a tip from someone, and he fled.

You had options, and you had the power to do that. Real power is to give someone life. But you chose to deny a wife a husband, and a son, a father. Khaled, this is your chance to put things right."

After saying this, Naguib doesn't flinch or blink. Khaled's eyes flicker and for once, he shows some emotions, and his chin quivers.

"Naguib, what are these terms?" Naguib answers.

"First, you'll pay all the costs of Madiha's funeral. In death, her body will rest next to her husband. Second, you'll pay and make all the arrangements, for Mido to leave this country, and to receive an education. You have enough contacts, and more than enough money to make this happen." Khaled sits up.

"Getting Mido out of the country will be expensive. Very expensive." Naguib stares.

"You dare to put a price on this? You dare to tell me. You cannot pay for the cost of a father?" Khaled's eyes drop.

"I'll do it. I need some paperwork, birth certificate, passport photos, and I need him to learn English. My contact at the U.S. Embassy will want to interview him. He needs to show that he can communicate." Naguib nods his agreement.

"I have a friend who can teach him better English. He already speaks some English, because he works as a waiter, and serves foreigners. We'll get him speaking like John Wayne if we have to." Khaled smiles and asks.

"Any other terms?"

Naguib looks out of the window. The wind has picked up and he sees a small whirlpool of dust form, and as quickly, it breaks apart. Naguib looks at Khaled.

"Yes a few more things. The money you took from my son for my passport, you'll send him in dollars. This is the only personal term. The rest is for your children. You'll create bank accounts overseas for your children. Zeina will have complete power over that money. This money will be available to the children when they reach the age, they can attend university. The sum you need to put in is a third of your money, per child, the rest you'll give to Zeina. So, in case of my death, she never needs money again."

Khaled listens, and rhythmically he nods his head in agreement, and then he asks.

"Naguib, you haven't asked for anything. Is there anything you want, or even need?" Naguib purses his lips, and he forces a smile.

"Yes, I want you to create a photo album. Take photographs of you with your children. I want them to remember their father's love."

Khaled cannot hold onto the steel that runs through his veins, and now it turns to blood. His fists unclench, and he brings his hands to his face. But the tears escape, and Naguib walks over.

"Everything will be fine my brother. Your children will know you, and they'll know the good things you're doing. But I have a final request. Yes, it's a request, and it's not a term." Khaled wipes the tears, and he gives a weak smile.

"I hope you're not going to ask me to dance." There's gentle laughter from both men, and Naguib answers.

"No, there's no need for singing or dancing, but something that will set you free." Naguib stares at Khaled and sees his tear-filled eyes. He holds Khaled's hand.

"Madiha asked to speak to you." Khaled's eyes dilate with fear, and Naguib squeezes his hand.

"She wants to forgive you. She doesn't want to die with bad feelings in her heart, towards another human being. She wants to die knowing, she has lived, loved, and she has forgiven."

In front of his eyes, Naguib watches, as Khaled turns from a man of iron to a child, who's in desperate need of help. Naguib offers the help.

"Bring Zeina with you. Let her see the man she married. She can tell your children. Their father was a good man."

Khaled stares at Naguib.

"I wish Hassam were here. I want to say sorry to him." Naguib understands.

"It's too dangerous for Hassam, to return to the city. Inshallah, I'll see him in the future. And if I get the chance, I'll tell him about today, and that you wanted to say sorry." Khaled touches Naguib's face.

"Shukraan my dear old friend, thank you for making me feel human." The two men embrace and Naguib speaks.

"You don't have to thank me. Just do these things, and that will be enough. You have a hard journey ahead of you, and you must walk with dignity and love. It's never easy to say goodbye, but we all have to do it."

Despite pity, and understanding, he and Hassam might be Khaled's only friends. Naguib finds a big part of Khaled's life hard to reconcile, and he wonders. *'How many lives have you ruined? And these people had no choice but to say goodbye to their loved ones.'*

In an effort to be more forgiving, and heed Imam Ali's words, and follow Madiha's ability to forgive. He throws out these questions from his mind. He accepts, no one can undo the past. And he must focus on the future, and the present.

And this time, when he looks at Khaled, he forgives him.

Chapter 23 - Zeina

With his nerves jangling, Naguib follows Khaled into the main room of the house, for his first meeting with Zeina. The children are outside playing with friends, and so this is a chance for them to talk in private, and to get to know one another.

"Zeina, this is my old and trusted friend Naguib."

"As-salaam-alaikum." Although Zeina doesn't say his name, Naguib acknowledges hers.

"Wa-alaikum-salaam Zeina." Khaled recognises Zeina's frosty stare. Although he's discussed these arrangements with her. He knows, her acceptance is going to be difficult. And when he speaks, he doesn't take his eyes off her.

"We all know why we're here. Both of you know, I don't have long. And you're both aware that when I die, my associates will try to carve up my territories. I've decided to give up those territories. My second in command will take over all activities, and on my death, he will respect my family. I am hoping, this will avoid a turf war, or a power struggle. My main concern is you Zeina. And of course, the children. I want to make sure you're safe, and to ensure this safety, Naguib will protect you and the children."

While Khaled speaks, Naguib watches Zeina. She is beautiful. She has piercing black eyes, full lips, and long slender fingers. He watches the tears form in her eyes at the mention of Khaled's death. She lowers her head to hide her tears.

Although she knows her husband's condition is terminal. She still sees it as a bad dream, and she hopes, she'll wake up and find him cured. In a defiant, but calm voice, Zeina speaks.

"I can live on my own with the children…" When she sees Khaled staring at her, her words trail off. She knows, this isn't an option, since Khaled is her husband, and this creates many dangers. Naguib sees her sadness, and he speaks.

"Zeina, you'll live in my house as my sister-in-law, and not my wife. You'll have all the freedom you want. Why don't you give it six months, and if at the end of that time, you want to leave, I'll help you. If that means, you want a husband, I'll make sure he's not after your money. And it will be someone you like, and someone you've chosen. You will not be there as my maid, cook or cleaner, and I will always be fair to your children."

For the first time, Zeina makes eye contact with Naguib, and she asks.

"Shukraan Naguib, will you promise to keep your word?" Naguib stares at her.

"Yes, on my own children's life, I promise." Khaled smiles.

"So, we're agreed?" Zeina nods.

Naguib has a concern, and he speaks.

"Just one problem. This house is twice, if not three times, the size of my house. I'll not be able to fit everything you have here. Please come to my house, and then you can work out what you'll bring with you. Remember you'll have to live a much simpler life than you do now." Without looking at either of the men, Zeina answers.

"I came to this house with one suitcase. My family aren't wealthy. The only thing I had, was me and my looks, but in time, both will disappear."

Naguib smiles, he can see she's a good person. And now he's much happier. Khaled stands up.

"Naguib, Zeina, why don't we step outside, and meet the children while they're playing. It might be easier."

Naguib agrees, and he feels relieved. He felt uncomfortable speaking to Zeina in this room. But the thought of interviewing a seven-year-old boy and a five-year-old girl in this grand space, feels even more uncomfortable.

Outside the house, there are around ten children, four girls who are chatting, and six boys who are chasing a football. When Hanan sees her mother and father, she screams and runs towards them.

Zeina flashes a brilliant smile and runs towards her daughter. She sweeps her up and nuzzles her neck. Hanan giggles and screams with joy, and Khaled smiles.

"She's so ticklish. My God, she makes me laugh all the time. The other day she put my hand on her toes, and then started to giggle, I didn't even do anything." Naguib enjoys seeing this side of Khaled. When they were young, Khaled was the joker, but to Naguib, that was another life.

Zeina walks back to the two men with Hanan on her hip.

"Hanan, this is your Uncle Naguib." Hanan gives a shy smile. She has her mother's beauty and slenderness. Naguib smiles and gives her chin a little squeeze.

"You are ticklish?" Hanan starts to giggle, and the adults join in. She scrambles off Zeina's hip and runs towards her friends, and shouts.

"Hey everyone, come and see my uncle!" Khaled and Zeina know Naguib is a hit with Hanan. Khaled calls to Gamal, and he walks over with his arm over his best friend's shoulder.

"Yes Abbi."

"I want you to meet Uncle Naguib." Gamal stares at Naguib, and sizes him up. Naguib looks at Gamal, and he can see a miniature version of Khaled. Khaled scolds.

"Don't be rude Gamal, speak."

Without formality, Gamal asks the only question that is important to him.

"Uncle Naguib, can you play football?" Naguib has a huge grin on his face. He gets on his knees, and answers in a gentle voice, while looking into Gamal's eyes.

"No, but perhaps you can teach me?" The two boys drag Naguib to the park, and he attempts to play football. He kicks a ball, and when it goes in the wrong direction, the boys laugh. Naguib pulls a silly face, and the six boys run towards him with joy. He has broken the ice with Gamal.

Despite his death standing in the shadows of so much joy, Khaled cannot remember a time he felt so relaxed. He can remember all the perfect moments. Marrying Zeina, their wedding night, and the birth of his children. But knowing that

Zeina and his children will be cared for after his death. This is another perfect moment. He moves closer to Zeina, and whispers.

"There's a lot we forget in life, but we always hold on to the perfect moments, like now. They help shape our hopes and dreams. Naguib is a good man. Don't be scared. My love will always be with you."

Zeina carries on smiling as the tears run down her cheeks.

Chapter 24 - Home

Once Zeina and the children go into the house, Naguib speaks.

"Well, that went a lot better than I thought it would." Khaled agrees.

"Yes. I was concerned because Zeina can be hot headed. But I think she understands the need for this. You were marvellous with the children. They really like you." Naguib smiles.

"I've always found children to be much more straightforward than adults. As long as you don't stop them speaking, they'll always let you know what's important, or at least, what's important to them." Khaled nods.

"Do you think Zeina, and the children will be happy?" Naguib isn't sure.

"Inshallah, I'll do my best to make them happy. But it will be different. It's the personal things that husbands and wives become accustomed to. So, she'll be shy, and she could be embarrassed by many things."

Khaled never thought about this. Although he's home for a few hours a day, by the time he got home at night, Zeina always looked perfect. He never experienced the days when she had a headache, diarrhoea, or stomach cramps. And even if she was suffering, she hid it from him.

Khaled asks.

"You want us to visit your home. I remember it, and you're right, it's smaller than this house. But as Zeina said, her family are very poor, and their home is smaller than yours. But is it because you want me to meet with Madiha?"

Naguib answers.

"Yes, the meeting with Madiha is important, but seeing my house is important too. Zeina has to feel comfortable there."

Khaled nods and speaks.

"I'm worried about the children's friends. They have good friends in this neighbourhood. You saw this with your own eyes." Naguib has thought about this as well.

"I think we have to try and make a clean break. To protect Zeina and the children, we need to start a new life for them. Away from this place, where your associates know you have a home." Again, Khaled nods.

"Yes, the children are young enough to make new friends. And you're right, it's for the best. Break all connections."

Naguib stares.

"Khaled, we need to break the connections from your old life, but not you. You are the children's father, and I will never break that connection. The children will know who their father is, and he loved them. Have you arranged the photographer?"

Khaled is silent for nearly a minute.

"Yes, a photographer has been arranged, he's already started to take some photos. Shukraan Naguib." After another pause, Khaled opens up, and reveals his fear.

"I'm nervous about meeting Madiha." Naguib thinks. *'You should be.'* He doesn't say this, and he lays his hand on Khaled's back.

"It will be fine. You must hear what she has to say, you owe her that."

The two men arrange to meet at Naguib's house the following day. They shake hands and go their own ways.

That evening as Naguib and Madiha eat supper, he tells her about the arrangements.

"When Khaled dies, Zeina and the children will stay with me." Madiha smiles.

"That's very good news. Is Zeina happy to do this?" Naguib swallows his food.

"She's willing, but I suppose she's scared. I've said, give it six months, and if she's not happy after that time, I'll help her to find a home, and if she wants, a husband." Madiha finishes her food.

"That's fair. And is Khaled willing to meet me?" Naguib looks at Madiha.

"He and Zeina will visit tomorrow." Madiha asks.

"Do you think Yousra can do my hair, and put some makeup on me?" Naguib laughs.

"Of course, I'll speak to her later."

He looks at Madiha. He can tell that this meeting will be as hard for her, as it will be for Khaled.

The next morning Naguib is tidying the house, while Yousra is busy combing Madiha's hair. When Yousra puts make up on her, Madiha complains.

"No Yousra, that rouge is too red. I'm not trying to get a husband. Although, I wouldn't know what to do, if I got one. Just add a little colour, so I don't look like you took me out of my coffin."

Yousra giggles.

"You never forget what to do as a bride." The two women laugh at Yousra's suggestive comments.

After Yousra leaves, Naguib helps Madiha into the main room. He's surprised at how little she weighs, and he knows that as each day passes, she's getting visibly weaker. When she sits back, she sighs and catches her breath.

"Shukraan Naguib." Naguib stares at her.

"Madiha, do you need anything?" She looks at him, and when she answers, her voice is weak.

"Just some water, and please stay close to me." Before getting the water, Naguib answers.

"Don't worry. I won't go anywhere unless you ask." Madiha holds Naguib's hand.

After another hour, there's a knock at the door, and it's Khaled and Zeina.

Naguib welcomes them in, and once they cross the threshold, Khaled holds out a package.

"Shukraan Naguib, we've bought you some sweets." Naguib can smell the sweet syrup from the kanafeh. He thanks them, and then he shows them to the front room.

Khaled sees Madiha, and immediately, his heart starts to beat harder and faster. He steadies himself and greets her.

"As-salaam-alaikum Madiha." She nods her head, and smiles.

"Wa-alaikum-salaam Khaled and Zeina." Zeina looks confused at the familiar way that her husband and Madiha speak, but she decides to wait for the explanation.

Khaled shows them both around the house.

"I thought you and Hanan could share this bedroom, and Gamal could have this room." Naguib has earmarked Madiha's bedroom for Zeina and Hanan, and for Gamal, the room Naguib is occupying. Zeina looks at him.

"Naguib, where will you sleep?"

"I sleep in the main room. Don't worry about that, I've been doing this for years, and I'm a very early riser. I'll not be in anyone's way." Naguib smiles, but Zeina is concerned with this arrangement.

"Naguib, this is your house. Why would you live here, like you're visiting?" Khaled agrees, and Naguib answers.

"It really isn't a hardship. The thought of having this house filled with conversation, laughter, and life will make it worthwhile." Zeina smiles, she's starting to understand the depth of Naguib's kindness.

Khaled makes an offer.

"Naguib, I can have another room built for you?" Naguib shakes his head.

"No Khaled, that's a bad idea. It would draw attention to this house. This is not a rich neighbourhood, and people will wonder where I got the money for such a project. Let's not draw attention to ourselves." Although Khaled feels bad, he can see the sense of what Naguib is saying.

In the front room, Madiha is gently snoring, and the three adults sit around her. Zeina asks.

"Naguib, is she your sister?" She wants to say mother, but she doesn't want to insult Naguib, and he smiles.

"No, she's not my sister. She's a friend, and she's down on her luck. I am helping." Zeina is concerned.

"Where will she sleep when we're here?" Naguib looks at Khaled, and Khaled answers.

"I'll explain later. Naguib, can you show Zeina around the neighbourhood while I speak to Madiha?" Naguib sees Madiha raise her finger, and he takes this as a sign to leave her and Khaled alone.

Chapter 25 - Forgiving

Once Khaled hears the front door shut, he turns and faces Madiha, and slowly, she opens her eyes.

"Khaled, would you get me some water." Madiha speaks in a whisper, and Khaled pours her a glass of water. He hands her the glass, and for a brief moment their fingers touch. For him, it's like an electric shock.

She takes a mouthful, and then she hands the glass back to him.

"I suppose, Naguib has spoken to you, and you know why I wanted to meet you?" Khaled nods, and neither of them avert their gaze. Madiha asks.

"Did you know my husband Saad?" Khaled shakes his head.

"No, not personally, but I knew of his politics, and what he stood for." Madiha keeps staring.

"Did you kill him because of his politics, and that it may put your life and livelihood in danger?" Again, he shakes his head.

"No, I had no personal grudge against Saad. As I say, I didn't know him for that. But you might say that others knew him enough, to consider him a threat." Madiha leans a little closer.

"Is there anyone in particular?" Khaled answers.

"Yes, Zulfiker Sakka." Madiha sits back in her chair.

"Yes, if it was going to be anyone, it would be Zulfiker." He waits, and then Madiha asks.

"Did Zulfiker give the order?" Their eyes remain fixed, and Khaled answers.

"Yes." Madiha carries on with her questions.

"What did Zulfiker say. Did he threaten you?" He keeps his eyes fixed on Madiha.

"He said, if I didn't do what he asked, he would kill me and my family."

This answer doesn't surprise Madiha, she was expecting it, and her gaze softens.

"Many lives are lost in our nation. Many families have mothers, fathers, brothers, and sisters who are gone. These are the growing pains of a nation, as it tries to modernise."

He doesn't respond. He isn't sure if she's expecting a response. After a few seconds, Madiha asks.

"How do you feel about Saad now?" He thinks about this, and his answer is honest.

"As I said before, I didn't really know Saad. Sometimes when we kill something, an animal perhaps, please don't think I'm calling Saad an animal. What I'm trying to say is, if we don't know who we're killing, or we know nothing about their family, or their lives, it's easier to kill them."

As much as Madiha tries to understand this, she finds it difficult.

"Is that how a killer sees a victim?" Again, Khaled thinks about this, and again he's honest.

"It's the only way a killer can view a victim."

"So how do you feel now that you've met me?" Madiha stares at Khaled, and he holds her stare.

"Sorry is too small a word for what I feel. I know that my life will end soon, and I accept this. But it's hard to accept, what I've done. I denied you a husband, and Mido a father. What is happening to me is nature, but what I did was a violent and an unnatural act. As I said, sorry is such a small word, but it's what I feel with every part of my heart and soul. I am sorry."

Madiha reaches for Khaled's hand.

"It's easy to forgive someone when they're sorry. I forgive you, and I thank you for seeing me today. Forgiveness is the only real choice we have. I will see Saad soon, and I'll tell him about this conversation."

Khaled holds Madiha's hand, and she grips it with a strength that surprises him. Without losing eye contact, he speaks.

"I will see Saad soon as well. Perhaps you'll let me say sorry to him in person." Madiha answers.

"I would like you to meet him. I think in another life, you could have been friends. Because you and Saad share one common element. Strength of character."

The emotions of guilt and sadness surge through Khaled. And as they hold hands, his heart snaps like a twig, and he starts to cry.

"I will make sure Mido has the best chance possible. I guarantee his education. And to the best of my ability, I'll make sure, he has a good life."

Madiha cups Khaled's chin. She draws his face up, and when their eyes meet, she speaks.

"Then you have fulfilled the role of his father. And I know Saad well enough to say, we both forgive you. When we forgive, everyone is healed."

When Khaled and Zeina return home, and the children are in bed, Zeina asks.

"Khaled how do you know Madiha?" Khaled thinks through several long-winded answers, but in the end, he opts for the truth.

"I killed her husband." He looks at Zeina and her mouth falls open.

"You killed her husband! Why?" Khaled clenches and unclenches his fists.

"I was ordered to kill her husband. If I didn't kill him, the people who ordered me, would have killed me and my family." Zeina's head is in a spin.

"Why her husband, and who ordered such a thing?"

"Madiha's husband was a man called Saad Ibrahim. He was our only honest politician. Other powerful people feared that honesty. They feared what he stood for. Because it was an incorruptible spirit. Some people think, all humans have a price, and once you know that price, you can buy a person. But in the case of Saad, there wasn't a price. Saad would give up his life, rather than, his beliefs. That's dangerous, especially to those, who hold onto power by force, or by lies."

Despite her limited education, Zeina understands what Khaled means. She can also see that Khaled and Saad are similar. It's Khaled's principles, which others fear. She has more questions.

"So, who ordered you to kill Saad?" Khaled wants to protect Zeina.

"The less you know the better it is. All I will say is, the order came from the presidential office. Not from the president himself, but someone very close to him." Zeina's mouth falls open.

"You're joking! The president's office?" Khaled nods.

"Yes." And she shakes her head in disbelief.

"What a country we live in. But why did Madiha want to see you?" Khaled looks at her.

"She wanted to forgive me." Zeina cannot believe his words, and she gasps.

"Forgive you? I couldn't forgive the man who killed my husband." Khaled touches her hand.

"Perhaps you couldn't, but there might come a day, when you would. I learned a very valuable lesson today. I learned the lesson of mercy. To some degree, it takes away some of my fears about death."

Zeina falls to her knees, and she rests her head on Khaled's lap. He removes her headscarf and strokes her long silky hair. Khaled realises, Naguib is right, when he said goodbyes are hard. In meeting Madiha, he also realises, goodbyes are harder for those left behind to deal with life.

Chapter 26 - Deceit

"**Should** we tell Mido about Khaled's involvement? And that he's paying for travel, the passport, and education?" Naguib asks Madiha, but before she can answer, he adds.

"You know Mido better than me. But I don't think he'll accept the money. Not if he knows where it's coming from." Madiha answers.

"You're right. He wouldn't accept it. He'd rather spit at Khaled, before he takes a penny from him." Naguib nods.

"I thought so. So, we only have one choice. We have to lie. But I believe that some lies are worth telling." Madiha agrees.

"Yes they are. That's what we'll do. If pushed for an answer, we'll say, it's your money. Do you agree to this?" Naguib agrees, and they promise to keep Khaled's involvement a secret.

Later that day, Naguib sits with Madiha and Mido to discuss the future. Madiha looks at her son.

"Mido, we have to be realistic. I feel my body getting weaker every day, and I know I don't have long. Sorry if this sounds morbid." Naguib watches Mido wipe his eyes.

"No Ummi it's not morbid, but it's real." Madiha hears the echoes of her husband's words, and it makes her smile. She leans closer to Mido.

"What do you want to do after my death?" Mido shrugs.

"I don't know, carry on working at the restaurant, what else can I do?" Madiha stares at her son.

"Would you like to leave this country, and get an education?" Mido looks at Madiha, and then at Naguib.

"How? I mean, how can these things happen?" Naguib looks at Madiha, and then he answers.

"I can make it happen. My family are in the U.S., and we can do this. We need some documents, so that we can get you a passport, but I also need you to improve your English. I have a friend that can help you with this." Mido is still sceptical.

"Usually families go abroad, and for some reason that's a lot simpler to arrange, than a single man. What will be my reason for leaving the country?" Neither Naguib nor Madiha have an answer. It isn't something they thought about, but then Madiha comes to the rescue.

"We can say, you're the son of Saad Ibrahim, and that your life's in danger. Political asylum?" Mido's eyes move between Madiha and Naguib, and he asks.

"Will an embassy go for that?" They don't know and Naguib answers.

"Let me find out. But in the meantime, I need a birth certificate, passport photos, and for you to start English lessons." Madiha agrees.

"Mido, you'll find your birth certificate in the small suitcase, under the bed." Mido is still uncertain.

"But where will the money come from. It won't be cheap?"

Naguib and Madiha give each other furtive looks, and Naguib answers.

"As I said, my family are in America, and they send me money. It isn't much, but it's enough for what we need." Mido shakes his head.

"Uncle, that's the money your children send you. I can't take that money. It wouldn't be right." Naguib stares at Mido.

"Alright don't take the money. Call it a loan, and when you have the money, pay it back." Madiha stares at Mido.

"Once I am gone, there's nothing for you in this country. You need to get out and have a chance in life." Mido looks at Naguib.

"When Ummi is gone, I can stay with you Uncle. I can pay my way…" It is a half-hearted argument and Naguib smiles.

"Mido, even with your mother here, you wouldn't stay when I asked you. What makes you think, you'd stay now. The other thing is. Why would you want to live with an old man? The best years of my life are behind me. You're young, and you have your life in front of you. And finally, the troubles are getting worse. I read, that these so-called freedom fighters, are not far from the borders of our city. This is no place for the young."

Madiha agrees, and she now throws down the line that clinches the deal.

"This is what your father would have wanted." Mido has no further objections.

"Uncle, when do I start my English lessons?"

Chapter 27 - Bombs

Naguib stares at the newspaper headlines.

"Rebel forces are twenty kilometres from the city. Government forces are fighting a fierce battle, and the President has declared they are close to victory…"

Every day the number of fighter planes flying over the city increases, and every day the sound of explosions gets louder.

In the backdrop of all this violence, the residents of the city try to get on with their lives as best they can. Naguib thinks. *'I bet the president is still shitting on his solid gold toilet, as well as shitting on the people of this country.'*

The economy is in freefall, and prices double, and in some cases quadruple. Naguib notices, shops with empty shelves. And people start to hoard, flour, rice, sugar, salt, and other non-perishable foods.

At least four times a week, electricity supplies shut down, to the point where they go without power for days. Shops selling candles or kerosene lanterns make a small fortune, as they hike up their prices. Yet the lights at the national broadcasting offices never go out, and Naguib wonders. *'Who are they broadcasting to?'*

As he flicks through the papers, there's a knock at the door. It's Nour.

"As-salaam-alaikum Naguib. I have a letter for you, and it's from America."

"Wa-alaikum-salaam Nour, come in and have some tea." They both head out to the veranda, and once seated, Naguib opens the letter and asks.

"Do you want to hear what Anwar has to say?" Nour sips his tea and nods.

"Yes my old friend. I could do with some good news."
Naguib starts to read.

Dear Abbi,

I hope you're well, but I don't know when you'll receive this letter. I read about the worsening problems in our country, and it's frightening to read about the raging battles, on the borders of our city. Every day it seems to be getting worse. I worry and pray for you.

The children are all doing very well, and they're fluent in English. They sound like little American boys and girls. We still speak Arabic at home. I don't want them to forget their language. They're helping Nawal with her English, and she knows enough to go shopping. Her and Veronica, Marcus's wife, have become good friends. I'm happy for her, and she seems more settled.

Farid still wants to stay awake at night. He says, Jadd will visit, and he doesn't want to be asleep when that happens.

The weather is getting warmer. I thought the winter would never end.

My work is going well, and as my English improves, it's getting easier.

The strangest thing happened the other day. I went to the bank to get some money for shopping, and when I asked for my balance, there was a big sum of money in there. Did you have something to do with this? Abbi please don't struggle to help me, I can manage. Let me know what you need, and if I can, I'll send it.

We have some good news. Abdel and Shadia have announced their engagement. They want to marry in one year. They're praying that Uncle Hassam and Aunty Samir will be able to attend. I'm hoping, you'll be able to attend, inshallah.

I've started making enquiries with the local immigration services office, and they have given me some advice. I'm using this, to see how I can bring you to America. I'm sure Abdel is doing the same for Uncle Hassam and Aunty Samir. He asked if you had any news, he hasn't heard from them since arriving in this country. But he understands, that if they've left the city, it would be hard to communicate. If you have any news, please let me know.

I have enclosed a newspaper article about our country. Perhaps Sultan who taught me English, could read it to you. I'm not sure what you know, or what you're allowed to know. Inshallah, this letter doesn't cause problems.

I'll write again soon, and I pray for you every day, please pray for us.

Your loving son

Anwar

Nour scratches his chin.

"I wonder where that money came from. You must have some rich relatives. Inshallah, they'll keep sending money." Naguib folds the letter.

"I don't know of any rich relatives. But it's a good letter, and I'm happy."

Naguib knows, Khaled is responsible for the money. He's glad that he kept his word, and it makes him feel more hopeful for Mido. Nour asks.

"Let me know what that newspaper says. I'd like to know what the Americans are saying about our country. I don't know who to blame anymore, our president, America's president, the Russians, or maybe even the Chinese. All I know. Is we never get the truth?" The two men give each other mocking smiles, and Naguib turns his eyes to the heavens.

With the newspaper cutting concealed in his wallet, Naguib goes to the bus stop. He's visiting Sultan, since this is where Mido is having English lessons, and Sultan can explain what the newspaper says. Sultan's home is out of town and close to the war zone, and it's ten kilometres away.

He hates the motion of the bus, and combined with the choking exhaust fumes, it always makes him feel sick. But it's either the bus, or a ten-kilometre walk.

136

The bus is packed, and people look miserable and hot. Naguib stares out of the window. He sees two children running barefoot through the streets, and poking their tongues out at the passengers, and it makes him smile. The bus stops at a junction, and he and the other passengers, crane their necks to listen to a loud argument. It's between a shopkeeper and a customer. The customer shouts.

"Why is the same kilo of rice, twice what it was two weeks ago!?" The shopkeeper is just as angry.

"Getting supplies delivered is tough, we're paying a lot more for transportation. Come on! You come to my shop every day for the last twenty years! Have I ever cheated you?"

Naguib realises, there's truth in what the shopkeeper is saying. But the customer doesn't have the money, to deal with the massive price hikes. Every week the suffering increases. Naguib understands that over time, all these price increases leave less money in people's pockets. And eventually, their pockets are empty, and they have nothing.

The bus trundles on and the driver announces.

"This is as far as I go." There are two kilometres left, and Naguib asks the driver.

"You go no further, why?" The driver frowns.

"The army stops buses entering the houses near the border. They check everything on the bus, and it takes a long time. It's not worth it, it's just a lot of aggravation, and it screws up my route. Sorry you'll have to walk the rest of the way. I, or another driver, will pick you up from this place. But remember, there'll be no buses after nine o'clock."

Naguib looks at his watch, and it's nearly four. This will be a short visit if he wants to avoid a ten-kilometre walk back. And he thinks. *'I cannot leave Madiha on her own for hours. What if she gets sick? Why didn't I ask Yousra to sit with her? Next time, I'll do that.'*

When Sultan comes to the door, he's delighted to see Naguib. Sultan is an academic, and his whole demeanour shouts scholar. He has long shoulder length silver hair. Although he sweeps it back like a film star, there isn't a trace of vanity. His round wire frame spectacles sit halfway down his nose, and as he speaks, he looks over them.

"Mido is a good student, but we have some pronunciation problems. Arabs have trouble with certain sounds like, P, B, F, and V. It probably means nothing to you, but it can be an obstacle." Mido waves.

"Uncle Naguib, this is a lot tougher than it looks." Naguib smiles and Sultan reassures them.

"Mido is doing well, and he'll be fine. But what brings you here?" Naguib pulls out his wallet.

"I got a letter from Anwar, and he sent this newspaper cutting. Perhaps you can explain it." Sultan's eyes widen with excitement, and he handles the article, with the same reverence as the Qur'an.

"Foreign news! Fantastic! You need to be careful Naguib. Don't let the police catch you with this. If they do, they'll say you're a spy. We'll burn this after reading." And with this warning, Sultan starts to read.

"The Whitehouse's position on the Middle Eastern crisis, is based purely in terms of economic gain. Readers don't be fooled by the rhetoric and clever political speeches. The president's decision to send more troops to the region are an attempt to control the oil. Can the lives of our soldiers be measured in terms of a gallon of gasoline? This is the big question.

We also need to think about the morality of getting involved in other nation's problems, and we need to consider some of the following. Are we being seen as economic imperialists? Are we making the lives of the people safer? And how are we adding to the quality of their lives?

Many think that we need a fresh approach, or as Albert Einstein said. "The definition of insanity is doing the same thing over and over again and expecting different results."

Presidents come and go, and they all try to leave their mark. It's part of their duty, but it's also a part of their ego. But sometimes, we try to scrub out the marks presidents make.

Because we recognise, these as more than simple marks. We recognise them, as scars on humanity.

We need to find a different way. We need to pray for our troops, and the innocent lives that are lost with no consequences.

Finally, I will use another quote that may give hope to an otherwise hopeless situation, and it's by Mahatma Gandhi. "When I despair, I remember that all through history the way of truth and love have always won. There have been tyrants and murderers, and for a time, they can seem invincible, but in the end, they always fall. Think of it, always."

Naguib and Mido stare at Sultan as he translates. In perfect harmony, there is a thought-provoking explosion in their heads, but at the same time, there's a thunderous bang, and it brings them back to their senses.

"What was that noise? It sounded like the roof was caving in?" Naguib shouts over the din, and Sultan shouts back.

"You get used to it. It happens every day." Naguib frowns.

"How do you get used to that?" Again, Sultan shouts.

"Because if you didn't, you'd go mad." Once the aftershock of the explosion subsides, Sultan asks.

"Can you imagine if someone in this country wrote such an article? I'm sure they'd be shot, maybe even hanged, and then beheaded just to be safe." Mido stares at the paper.

"Yes, or they'd end up in the secret police's school of torture and murder." Naguib stays silent. His ears are still adjusting to the din. After a cup of tea, Naguib speaks.

"It's hard to imagine the freedom of the west. We talk about it, but until you read such a thing, you can't imagine it. You think the life we have is normal. But when we read this, we realise how the government strangles our voices." Mido and Sultan reflect on Naguib's words, and when he leaves, Mido carries on with his lessons.

On his journey home, Naguib thinks about the quote from Gandhi. He remembers his conversation with Anwar. He also thinks about the explosion, and he realises. That the physical damage done by a bomb is immediate, but the way people get used to the horrors, does far more damage. It wrecks a person's idea, of what is normal.

Chapter 28 - Farewell

The day of Mido's departure is drawing near, and he spends his remaining time at Naguib's house. He sleeps on the floor of Madiha's bedroom. During those nights, mother and son stay awake, and sometimes they talk for hours. Madiha is in a reflective mood. Before speaking, she stares at Mido.

"When I first saw your face, I couldn't believe I produced something so perfect. You were the most beautiful baby in the world." Mido laughs.

"All mothers think that of their babies." Madiha cannot accept this.

"No, I don't think so. Do you remember the woman that lived across the road from us? What was her name?"

"You mean Mrs Almasi?" Mido answers and Madiha's eyes light up.

"Yes Mrs Almasi, how did you remember that? God, I wonder what happened to her." In silence, they both recall memories of their old neighbour. Mido asks.

"What about Mrs Almasi?" Madiha picks up the thread of their conversation.

"Well, her little boy was not an attractive baby. When you two played together, it was like watching two different species." Mido laughs and splutters.

"Ummi, you can't say that. That's awful." Madiha giggles.

"No, listen, and I'm not trying to be wicked. But one day we were having tea, and she said to me, I hope Lateef, oh yes that was his name, Lateef. She said, I hope Lateef has brains. I nearly choked on my tea, because she was saying, well he doesn't have looks. In my head, I kept thinking of the name Lateef, because that was my uncle's name. And I know it means, one of a kind. All I kept thinking was. He's certainly one of a kind."

Mido bursts out laughing, and Madiha puts her hand over her mouth to suppress her laughter. Once they stop, Mido wants to know more.

"Ummi, what was Abbi like? My memory of him is like a dream, and I cannot always remember. Sometimes it's clear, and at other times, I can't see anything. Do you know what I mean?" Madiha sighs.

"Yes, I know what you mean. It's like a picture that keeps fading in and out, like you have bad eyesight." Mido nods and Madiha carries on.

"First of all, I'll say, that as you get older, you look more like him. You're a lot taller than Saad, but you have so much of him in you. Your voice, the way you question things, your kindness, and how much importance you place on family." This didn't give Mido the answers he's looking for.

"No, what I mean is. What was he like as a man?" Madiha thinks about this for so long, Mido thinks she's fallen asleep. When he looks at Madiha, her eyes are wide open. And when she sees him staring, she speaks.

"Your Abbi was a man of enormous principles, and his principles ruled him. You know that he trained as a lawyer, and I think that training made him see people, as a vital part of the justice system. He also thought that governments were answerable to the people, and not the other way round. Some called him idealistic or a dreamer, but that's what I loved about him. Your Abbi wasn't a perfect human being. His beliefs and ideas would consume him, despite what others thought. He didn't care what others thought. He knew that many considered his ideas impossible, and that he was mad for thinking, that a perfect society could exist. But he couldn't let go of an idea, if he felt it was right, and in those moments, he didn't think of others. At times, he had what people call, tunnel vision. But in the end, his principles cost him his life."

Mido listens to every word, and then asks.

"Did he love us? Did he love you and me?" Madiha doesn't hesitate.

"Yes, of course he did. Mido you must never doubt his love. The first time he saw you, he was overwhelmed. You were born late at night, and at home. He picked you up, and he stood by the window in our bedroom. He showed you to the stars, and he said. You will always be loved. And then he held you in his arms, and he breathed you in. That was the only time I saw him cry." Mido wipes the tears from his eyes.

"Am I anything like Abbi in character?" Madiha reaches for his hand.

"Yes, and with the right education you'll finish what he started. But I want to give you one piece of advice. And these were the very words, I said to your Abbi, but perhaps he wasn't listening. Choose your battles well. Remember, some things are worth fighting for, while others aren't. There's no shame in walking away, if it allows you to come back, and finish the battle later. Do you understand?" Mido answers.

"You mean, don't be stubborn?" Madiha stares at her son.

"Yes, I guess that's what I mean, but there's a saying by Aristotle, a Greek philosopher, and it sums up your father's desire for this country. *"The only stable state is the one in which all men are equal before the law."* It's good to have principles. But understand that others may not share them with you. Your Abbi wanted to reform this country, but his actions made our leaders even more paranoid. And they became even more power hungry. Your Abbi could have taken smaller steps, and in time, it would've made a big difference. Despite that, he was a good man, an honest man, and a man who treated everyone with respect."

Mother and son carry on holding hands, and when Mido hears Madiha's peaceful breathing, he gazes at her face. She's fast asleep, but she's smiling.

Mido sits up and he stares at her until daybreak, and he doesn't take his eyes off her. He knows, once he leaves, he'll never see her again, and unlike his father, he doesn't want her image to fade.

Madiha is too weak to see her son off, and she speaks to him for the last time.

"This is all I can give you for your journey, and for when you make a new home." She slips off her wedding ring, a pair of pearl earrings, and a gold bangle.

"Your father gave me the bangle when you were born. And my mother gave me the earrings, on my wedding day. And this is my wedding ring. Maybe you can trade these things, they have some value. I have one more thing to give you, please fetch my suitcase." Mido brings the case.

"Look inside, and at the bottom there's an envelope, open it." Mido opens the envelope, and inside are a dozen photographs in sepia tones.

"These are your memories of your Abbi and me. They were taken when we were young, and some, were taken after you were born. If you find that the pictures in your mind fades, then these will remind you of your family. Look after them."

Mido stares at the photos, and in one, he sees an elegant woman holding a toddler, and a smart man wearing a western suit. They're both gazing at their child. The love that flows out of this picture overwhelms Mido, and he's in agony. It's Abbi and Ummi, and he is the centre of their world.

Mido holds onto his mother, and he struggles to let go. Yousra sits in the corner of the room weeping, and Naguib finds it hard to keep his emotions in check.

"Come on Mido, we must leave, or we'll miss the boat." Madiha pushes Mido back a little, and she cups his face.

"When I see your father, I'll let him know what a wonderful man you are. I love you and I'll watch over you." She kisses him and gives him a final hug.

The journey to the docks is silent, and when he has to say goodbye, Mido chokes.

"Shukraan Uncle Naguib. Thank you doesn't feel like it's enough. You've given my mother dignity, and you've given me hope. All I can offer is my thanks and my prayers."

Naguib stares at Mido.

"That is enough. You deserve life, and you deserve a life with hope. In the memory of your mother and father, do something that will make them proud. You don't need to thank me, thank yourself for being a good man."

The two men embrace, and swiftly they turn and walk away from one another. This is the only way they can escape the pain.

Mido slips Madiha's wedding ring on his smallest finger. He promises. *'I will never take this off. Next time we see each other, look for this ring. You may not recognise me, but I hope you will. I will always recognise you.'*

As Naguib makes his way home, he keeps thinking about the youth of his nation. He sees that little by little, they will all leave, until all that remains are children, the elderly, and the weak. This is a dying country, and he sees its lifeblood draining away, because of greed and power.

The next morning Naguib prepares breakfast, and he walks into Madiha's bedroom with a tray.

"Good morning Madiha, your breakfast is ready."

Madiha usually gives Naguib a cheerful answer, but this morning there's only silence. The hairs on the back of Naguib's neck stand up, and he knows, Madiha is dead.

He puts the food down, and he goes to her bedside. She looks happy and in a dreamlike state. He sees her smile, and he speaks to her.

"Did Saad come for you in the night?" Although there's no audible answer, he hears her voice in his heart.

"Yes, and we're together again. Shukraan Naguib, shukraan…" Madiha's words fade, but they are forever a part of Naguib's living memories.

Chapter 29 - Beginnings

Naguib sits with Khaled in his study, and after Zeina brings them tea, the two men talk.

"Madiha died yesterday…" Naguib can think of nothing else to say. Khaled is upset but not surprised.

"Was it peaceful?" Naguib nods.

"Yes, very peaceful. She looked like she was having a good dream when her heart stopped. And Mido has left. Thank you for everything you've done Khaled." Khaled's face turns serious.

"My friend, it was as we agreed. I'm happy to have made at least one life better." Naguib nods. Khaled puts a tablet in his mouth and then takes a mouthful of tea.

"Naguib, I don't have very long now. I'm taking these tablets as if I were eating peanuts. The cancer is now affecting my liver, and I'll be going into hospital this Saturday, three days from now. Will you take me to prayers on Friday?" Naguib looks at Khaled.

"Yes I will, and we'll take Gamal with us." The two men sit in silence, and to break the sheer weight of despair, Naguib speaks.

"I'll get a new bed and mattress, so that Zeina and Hanan don't have to sleep on Madiha's old bed." Khaled asks.

"Let me do that please." Naguib agrees.

"So, are Zeina and the children ready to move in on Saturday?" Khaled nods.

"Yes, they're packed, and they're ready." Naguib stares at Khaled.

"How long have you got?" Khaled looks at his hands.

"Maybe a month, but I've asked the doctors to stop my medication." Naguib is shocked.

"But you will suffer, and you will be in pain. Why!?" Khaled looks out of the window, and then he faces Naguib.

"Naguib, I am not a good man. I have made many people suffer. I have stolen lives with the drugs I sold, so it's a sort of justice that I'm now dependant on drugs. But at a certain point, I realised, I needed to suffer. I needed to feel what I've done to others. So, when the almighty asks. Do you know what you've done? I can say with honesty. Yes."

Naguib finds this hard to accept.

"But Khaled, you've done good things as well. There's no need for suffering." Khaled keeps his eyes locked on Naguib.

"It's a choice I've made. In balancing my life, I realise, the bad outweighed the good many times over. If nothing else, I want my last moments to be ones, where I'm not hallucinating, because of morphine. I want to be awake until my last breath. I want to clearly see, the faces of my children, and my beautiful Zeina."

Naguib doesn't have anything else to say. He looks at Khaled and sees the devastation of this illness. He sees a man who once weighed a healthy eighty-five kilograms, now reduced to around forty-five, or the weight of a twelve-year-old child. Cancer has stripped Khaled of everything, and all that is left, is a devastated shell. For Naguib, Khaled is a mirror image of what is happening to his country. The government are like the tumours in Khaled's body, and the freedom fighters are the parasites who feed off the tumours.

At Friday prayers, Naguib speaks to Imam Ali, and Khaled sits through the prayer. He's too weak to make too many movements. Naguib stays at Khaled's house that night, and the next day, they pack a car, with Zeina and the children's belongings. Before going to Naguib's house, they stop at the hospital. The hospital is expecting Khaled, and once he's in bed, Zeina asks.

"Naguib, I will stay here. Could you please take the children?" Naguib asks.

"Shall I come back for you later?" Zeina shakes her head.

"No, come back for me in the morning, I'll be fine." The children say goodbye, and whisper in Khaled's ear.

"Abbi, we'll visit you tomorrow, and we'll tell you about our new house." Khaled smiles, and with his bony fingers, he holds them and showers them with kisses. He then turns to Gamal.

"Gamal, look after your mother and sister, and always listen to Uncle Naguib and your mother. Study hard at school, never tell lies, and never get in trouble with the police. Will you do this for me?" Gamal holds onto Khaled's neck.

"Yes Abbi, I'll do everything you tell me." Khaled kisses Gamal and keeps repeating.

"Good boy, good boy…"

In the early hours of the morning, just as the calls for Fajr prayers starts, Khaled opens his eyes, and looks at Zeina.

"Was I good to you?" She holds his face.

"Always. You saved me, and my heart is always with you." Khaled speaks in a whisper.

"Since meeting you, my day starts with you, and my nights end with you. I've loved you from the moment we met."

Khaled smiles and squeezes Zeina's hand. It's his last ounce of strength. His head sinks against the pillow, and he is gone.

Naguib arrives at the hospital early. He walks to Khaled's private room, and he sees Zeina standing outside. When he looks at her, he sees dark circles around her eyes. The door of the room is open, and inside is an empty bed. Zeina speaks.

"Khaled died as the sun rose, his heart stopped."

Naguib puts his hand on her shoulder, and she leans against it for comfort. Although she thinks, she has no more tears left, Naguib's comforting hand finds another reservoir and she start to cry. Zeina dries her eyes, and she looks at Naguib.

"We have to start again. Many things end, but we must look for new beginnings. That's how we survive."

Chapter 30 - New

Despite the tragedies in their lives, life continues, and they do their best to adjust. Yousra misses Madiha, and despite a combined age of over one hundred and twenty years, there was a teenage charm to their relationship. They often made each other laugh.

Having Gamal and Hanan at the house is something new, something joyous, and it fills the house with happiness.

Every day Yousra visits Naguib. She loves seeing Gamal and Hanan, but she wants to make sure Naguib isn't suffering. Yousra is blunt, and she doesn't understand subtle language. And when Zeina is out of earshot, she speaks to Naguib.

"Naguib, you've been through a lot, why don't you take Zeina as a wife? She's beautiful." Naguib smiles, but his answer is as blunt as Yousra's question.

"That's not the deal I had with Khaled. He was my brother, and I can't marry my brother's wife."

He doesn't want to go into more details. Yousra's sighs, and she accepts part of Naguib's answer.

"He wasn't your real brother, so I don't know what the problem is." Naguib gives Yousra a stern look, and she sighs.

"Alright, but when you're old, and only have a few marbles left in your head, you'll say, I wish I'd listened to Yousra."

Naguib laughs.

"When I have a few marbles left, I might not remember who you are?" Hussein has joined them and is enjoying the banter.

"I try to forget Yousra, but it isn't easy when she shouts at me." Yousra smiles and pretends to slap her husband.

"Without me you'd never eat properly. I'm the one who should try to forget. All the work you make me do. Even a murderer can get out of jail, but no, I'm doing a double life sentence." The three of them laugh.

On hearing their laughter, Zeina stands by the door, and gives them a shy smile. She asks.

"Can I make tea for all of you?" Hussein smiles at Zeina.

"Yes, let's have tea. And where are these children. I've heard so much about them, but where are they?" Zeina speaks to the children, and they come out. Five-year-old Hanan runs straight into Yousra's arms, while seven-year-old Gamal stands by Naguib's side, and Naguib introduces them.

"Children this is Uncle Hussein, and he is Aunty Yousra's husband." Hanan's eyes widen with surprise, and she cries out.

"Aunty, you didn't tell me you had a husband!" Everyone on the veranda, except Gamal starts to laugh. Yousra squeezes and hugs Hanan from sheer joy. Hanan giggles and speaks.

"Aunty, why didn't you let me come to your wedding?" Still grinning, Yousra answers.

"Because when I got married, even your mother wasn't born. I didn't know you then, but if I had known you, I would have invited you."

Hanan smiles and carries on with her questions.

"If you get married again, can I come to your wedding?"

The adults are enchanted, and Hussein answers.

"Yes darling, if Yousra marries again, you can come, and you can take my place."

Hanan claps her hands with joy. Hussein now turns his attention to Gamal.

"So Gamal, what do you enjoy doing?" Gamal steps in front of Naguib and says with confidence.

"I like football." Hussein raises his hands and shouts.

"Oh my goodness! I also love football! It's the best game in the world." Gamal walks over to Hussein.

"Uncle Hussein, can you play football?" Hussein purses his lips.

"Yes, I can play, but I haven't played for many years. But I guess I can still be a goalkeeper." Gamal is delighted.

"I have a ball. Can we go and play?" Hussein thinks about this.

"I tell you what I'll do. Tomorrow, I'll take you to meet other boys, and they'll play football with you all day. Will you be free tomorrow?" With excited eyes Gamal nods, and then asks.

"Uncle Hussein, can I ask you something?" Hussein reaches for Gamal's hand, and smiles.

"Anything you like my boy." Gamal steps closer and runs his small fingers over Hussein's arm.

"Why are your arms so hairy? I haven't got any hairs on my arm." Zeina exclaims.

"Gamal don't be rude!" Hussein smiles and speaks in a gentle voice.

"Zeina its fine, don't worry. Well Gamal, let me tell you. When you are very brainy and wise, hair doesn't grow on your head. That's because the brain is working so hard, it pushes all the hair out of your head. But hair needs to grow, and if it can't grow on your head, it must grow somewhere else, like your arms. So, the reason I have such hairy arms is because, I am clever and wise." Gamal's eyes widen with amazement, and he turns to Zeina.

"Ummi, is that true? If I become clever, will I have hairy arms?"

Zeina kneels next to her son. She looks at Naguib and Hussein and gives them both a slight bow, and then turns to Gamal.

"Yes Gamal. If you are as clever as Uncle Hussein, you will have hairy arms, and if you show kindness, you will be like Uncle Naguib. You are lucky to have so much love, and you must listen to your uncles."

The two men smile. Zeina is showing them a huge amount of respect, and they know it.

Despite the humour brought about by childish wonder, Yousra wipes away a tear. The adults stare at one another, and although they have experienced losses, hardships, and general unfairness of their country, in that moment they feel blessed.

151

They also know that life has a way of balancing itself out, and a way of taking a person from despair to feelings of hope.

Chapter 31 - War

*"**Freedom** Fighters are within ten kilometres of the city border. The president has declared that the army will crush these rebels…"*

As Naguib reads the bulletin, he realises. That in the last two months, the army has lost another ten kilometres of ground. He's scared, and he thinks. *'Why is the president declaring they're going to crush the rebels. He's lying. My God, what a deluded man.'*

As this thought sinks in, he doesn't know which regime is better. The current president, or the leaders of the freedom fighters. To him, they're both bad at running a country.

Zeina and the children are now a part of Naguib's life, and the children make new friends. They adapt well, and they never mention the privileges they enjoyed when Khaled was alive. They are as comfortable playing in the dusty streets, as they are in a well-manicured park.

Within a few weeks, Zeina adjusts to her new surroundings, aided hugely by her friendship with Yousra. Also, Naguib's life is a lot closer to her humble beginnings, and this makes the transition a lot easier. Although he never asks, she cooks, while he does most of the cleaning. He is determined to make sure, she doesn't see herself as a servant, or worse, as a wife, with none of the love a wife can expect.

The children spend part of their day with Yousra. She loves having them over, and somehow Hussein has become the young boy's goalkeeper. And during this time, Naguib sits on the veranda, and reads the newspaper, but today, he nods off.

Zeina is busy preparing the evening meal, and there's a knock at the door. She puts her headscarf on, and when she opens the door, she's confronted by a man with mad eyes. At first, he scares her, and she suppresses a scream. The man looks exhausted. His clothes and face are grey with dirt and dust, and parked next to him, is a wheelbarrow full of books. Her eyes widen, and despite feeling scared, she asks.

"As-salaam-alaikum, can I help you?"

"Wa-alaikum-salaam Miss. I think I must have the wrong house. I'm sorry." Zeina stops the man.

"Who are you looking for?" The man stares at her with tear-filled eyes.

"I'm looking for Naguib Ghali. Miss, do you know him?" Seeing the terrified look on the man's face, and streaks where his tears have run through the dirt on his cheeks, Zeina answers.

"Sir, please wait, I'll get Naguib." She runs to the veranda.

"Naguib, please come to the door, there's someone who needs your help! He looks desperate." Naguib jumps out of his chair and runs to the door, and when he sees Sultan, he is horrified.

"Sultan, what's happened?" Sultan gasps.

"Naguib, please let me have some water. I've pushed this wheelbarrow all the way from my house…" Sultan collapses before finishing his sentence. Zeina runs to the kitchen and gets a pitcher of water and a glass.

When she gets outside a crowd has gathered, and Naguib has Sultan's head on his lap, while a passer-by fans his face. Naguib holds Sultan's head higher, and Zeina starts to give him water. As the cold refreshing liquid lands on his parched tongue, Sultan's eyes open wide, and he looks wild. He grabs the glass and Zeina's hand, and gulps down the water. The passer-by is worried.

"Slow down, you'll be sick if you drink that fast." Sultan cannot hear the passer-by and pleads.

"More water, please more water." Zeina gives Sultan another glass, and after finishing this, he passes out.

By now, Yousra knows something is happening outside Naguib's house, and she screams.

"Hussein wake up! Go and help Naguib! There's something wrong!" Hussein is having a nap, but the panic in

Yousra's voice, makes him jump. Dazed and only half-awake, he shouts.

"What, what's happened woman?" Yousra stares at him and shouts.

"I don't know! Just go and help Naguib, there's some trouble. I've got the children here!" Hussein runs out of the house, and all the time, he barks at the crowd.

"Move out the way! Move, come on, get out of my way!" Within thirty seconds, Hussein is kneeling next to Naguib.

"Naguib, what's happened?" Without looking at Hussein, Naguib answers.

"I'm not sure. But this is Sultan, he's an old friend. He was Anwar and Mido's teacher. I don't know what's happened to him. But help me, and let's get him inside." Naguib turns to Zeina.

"Can I use Gamal's bed?"

"Of course, Gamal can sleep with me." Naguib and Hussein lift Sultan and carry him into the house. After putting Sultan on the bed, Naguib goes back outside, gets the wheelbarrow, and pushes it to the veranda.

When Naguib enters Gamal's room, he sees Zeina washing Sultan's face with a wet cloth. Hussein leans against the doorframe and asks.

"Naguib did he say anything? What's his story?" Naguib stares at Sultan and answers.

"I don't know Hussein, he didn't say, but he looked terrified. Let him rest. Once he's awake we'll find out more." Naguib turns to Zeina.

"Thank you for letting Sultan use Gamal's room. And thank you for taking care of him." Zeina looks surprised.

"Naguib there's no need to thank me. Anyone would have done the same." Hussein stares at both of them.

"Zeina, Naguib, the children can stay with us until you get this sorted, it's no problem, we love them staying." Naguib looks at Zeina for permission, and she answers.

"Shukraan Hussein. That will be a great help, they might get scared. But are you sure you don't mind?" Hussein answers.

"Not a problem. But do me a favour. Call me when Sultan tells his story. I'm dying to know what he has to say." Zeina smiles.

"Of course, as soon as he wakes, I'll let you know."

Sultan sleeps for over three hours, and after sunset, he wakes up. Naguib hears the bed creak.

"Sultan, let me help you." Naguib wraps his arm around Sultan, and almost carries him into the front room.

"Sultan, what's happened?" Sultan asks for more water, and once he finishes, he breaks down and starts to cry. Zeina looks at Naguib.

"Let me get Hussein, he might be able to help." Naguib nods and sits next to Sultan, and he leans against Naguib for comfort. When Zeina and Hussein enter the room, Sultan feels he owes everyone an explanation.

"It's all gone, all of it, gone. My home, my neighbours, all bombed, everything smashed to pieces. There's nothing left. The bastards destroyed everything!" Sultan holds his hands over his face and sobs, and Naguib speaks.

"It will be alright my old friend, I am here."

Witnessing the scene, Hussein's heart aches. He can see the absolute misery of a man who has lost everything. He realises, it's more than possessions. It's the destruction of a life. A life with colour, sound, and voices. And all of it gone, in the blink of an eye. With despair in his voice, Hussein speaks.

"Sultan, please eat some food. And when you're stronger, we'll see what we can save. You'll need your strength." Sultan dries his eyes.

"Is there somewhere I can wash? I'm sorry for the mess I've made with my dirty clothes." Naguib squeezes Sultan's shoulder.

"Dirt we can clean. But as Hussein said, you'll need your strength. Zeina, could you please boil some water, I'll get soap and a towel, and I have clean clothes. Have a wash, eat, and then get some sleep. In the morning we'll see what we can do."

Naguib helps Sultan to his feet, hands him the clean clothes, and shows him where he can wash.

In the front room, Hussein is slumped in a chair, and when he sees Naguib, he asks.

"Where did he live?" Naguib is lost in his own thoughts, and after a while, he answers.

"Where did he live? Well, he used to have a house on the border, about ten kilometres west. It's on the edge of the desert. He had a wife, but she and the baby died during childbirth. That little house was his sanctuary. It's where he lived with his wife, and he never changed anything. He once said to me. If my Rania visits, I want her to recognise everything. We grew up as neighbours. He was a scholar, and a good boy, and he's an even better man. After Rania's death, he lived like a hermit, and one day I saw him, and he looked half-dead. Rashida and I looked after him, and we got him back on his feet. My Anwar was his first student. Since then, he has taught hundreds, maybe even thousands. He's a good man, and he doesn't deserve this. This bloody war doesn't give a damn about innocent people!"

The room is silent. Naguib's words resonate like a call to prayer. Hussein walks over to Naguib.

"Let me know what you need. The children can stay as long as it takes, and if you're struggling for space, I have a room I can clear out and turn into a bedroom for Sultan. Whatever help you need, we're here." Naguib grips Hussein's hand with both of his.

"Shukraan Hussein."

When Sultan re-enters the room, he's clean, and he smells of soap. He looks human, but his eyes are faraway and confused. They're reliving a tragedy. Naguib sees the pain, and he asks.

"Sultan, please sit down, and eat." Sultan's voice is thick with emotion.

"I tried to clean my clothes, but I ran out of water, I'm sorry." Naguib grits his teeth, and words start to fail him. Zeina answers.

"Sultan, please don't worry about the clothes. Just eat a little. Would you like some more water?" Sultan nods.

"Did you see my books? I brought my books with me." Zeina reassures him.

"Yes Sultan, I've cleaned all the books in the wheelbarrow, and they're all in your room." Naguib eats with his head bowed, and Zeina notices tears falling onto his plate.

Sultan apologises.

"I'm sorry, but I'm not very hungry. Just water please. Please forgive me, I'll go to bed." Zeina stands up.

"Let me take you to your room. I'll show you where I've put your books, and I'll bring you some water." Without another word, Sultan goes to bed. Naguib stops eating, washes and goes out onto the veranda. He lights a cigarette and stares at the night sky. It's peaceful.

Zeina comes outside.

"Sultan is lying down. Naguib are you alright?" Naguib flicks his cigarette.

"Yes, I'm fine, but how much more can the people of this country take?" It's a big question, and Zeina reminds Naguib of her words after Khaled's death.

"We have to start again. Many things end, but we must look for new beginnings. That's how we survive."

Naguib asks.

"Zeina, where do these words come from?" Zeina answers.

"These were my father's words, after both my brothers died of typhoid."

Chapter 32 - Remains

For the next two days, the mood is sombre. The children stay with Yousra and Hussein. Zeina visits the children, and she stays for hours. She's happy that Gamal and Hanan see this as a holiday. She wants to protect them.

When the children go out to play, Yousra asks.

"How's Sultan doing?" Zeina thinks about the question, and after finding the right words, she answers.

"For the last two days, he seems to be lost. But what worries me more, is how little he eats. I don't know what Sultan looked like before. So, I don't know if he's changed, but he reminds me of Khaled's thinness, over the last few months. It's as if his skull, and the shape of his bones are revealing themselves. Does that make sense?" Yousra nods.

"Yes, it does. Has he said anything to you or Naguib?" Zeina rotates the bangle on her wrist.

"Well, only to thank me for the food, and for washing his clothes. If nothing else, he has great manners. Sometimes he starts to say something, but I think it must be so tragic, he can't make himself say the words. It's as if, by not saying it, it won't be real. I did that when Khaled started to lose weight, and his illness was visible." Yousra says a little prayer, and then asks.

"Has he spoken to Naguib?" Zeina answers.

"They sit on the veranda, and whenever I go out to give them tea, they're silent. I don't know what they're thinking, but I haven't seen them talking. The mood in the house is very depressing. Thanks for having the children." Yousra touches Zeina's arm.

"That's not a problem. Although I'm not sure who's the bigger child, Hussein, or the children. And now he wants to buy goalkeeper gloves." Zeina gives a little laugh, and then she becomes thoughtful. After pouring a cup of tea, Yousra asks.

159

"How's Naguib, how's he taking this?" Zeina puts her cup down.

"Not well. Naguib is often serious, but sometimes he laughs, and that sound is worth waiting for. It fills the house. But in the last two days, he hasn't laughed. Also, on the night of Sultan's arrival he cried." Yousra is shocked.

"Naguib shed tears?" Zeina nods.

"My mother always said, that when a person sheds silent tears, their heart is breaking." Yousra agrees.

"Yes, I'd say that's true. Naguib has been through a lot, and sometimes when we're doing that, we don't see what it's doing to us. These tragedies touch all of us, and Naguib has experienced much sadness, maybe too much for one person. It feels endless."

The two women sit in silence, and while they sip their tea, Zeina asks.

"Do you know if Naguib has a favourite food? I can make it for him, it might help?" Yousra is thinking hard.

"You know, I have no idea. I've been his neighbour for many years, and I used to talk to Rashida, but I never asked this question. You'd think that in thirty years, you'd know a bit more about your neighbour." There's a look of regret on Yousra's face. Zeina touches her arm.

"Yousra, you and Hussein are like family to me. You're the best neighbour anyone can ask for." Yousra's cheeks flush red, and she speaks.

"Give Sultan time, he'll talk when he's ready."

While Zeina is with Yousra, Naguib and Sultan sit on the veranda, and for a long time they sit in silence. Sultan hesitates, but on the fifth attempt, he speaks.

"Naguib thank you. I don't think I've thanked you for looking after me." Naguib gives Sultan a gentle smile.

"Thank me for what. I've only done, what you would have done for me. Did you think I'd turn you away?"

Sultan smiles, it's his first smile since arriving at Naguib's house. And he answers.

"No, I didn't think you'd turn me away, but this is the second time in my life you've helped me. I didn't want you to think, that I always need rescuing." Naguib looks at the flowerbeds.

"You see those flowers. If I didn't water them every day, they'll wither and die, and so, I water them. Humans need to look after humans, the same way I look after the flowers. Looking after a person isn't a question we debate. It's something we do on instinct. In over fifty years we've known each other, this is the only time you've come to me for help. The first time I decided to help you, and you repaid me in more ways than you can imagine. You helped Anwar, and because of that help, he and his family have a good life in America. Sultan, I've only sheltered you. Tell me, how I see the old Sultan, the one with humour and great stories? When I see that Sultan, that's when I'll know, I've helped you."

Sultan weeps silent tears, and after wiping the tears from his eyes, he speaks.

"It's not the house, and it's not the material things. But it's the sheer waste of lives. That house held many memories, it's the memories, it's…" Sultan doesn't finish his words and Naguib speaks.

"Memories are in your heart. We carry them wherever we go. Have you ever been shopping and suddenly a memory came back to you? Something you see, or something you smell, reminds you. It happens to me all the time. Memories exist outside of four walls. They're a part of us, and they exist wherever we are."

For the first time in two days, Sultan looks into Naguib's eyes without the veil of sadness. He asks.

"What should I do Naguib?" Naguib now finds the practical answers.

"First, let's go and say goodbye to your neighbours. Second, is there anything you need from your old house? If there is, let us go and get it. Sultan, you have to start again, you have to have a new beginning."

Although he condenses the words, Zeina taught Naguib this lesson. Sultan agrees.

"Very well Naguib. Let's do that. There aren't many things, just some old photos of Rania, that's all." Naguib smiles.

"Will we need your wheelbarrow?" Sultan gives another smile.

"No, the wheelbarrow won't be needed. I don't know why I dragged that thing ten kilometres, I wasn't thinking straight."

Naguib touches Sultan's arm.

"The troubles we face can make us do strange things."

The next morning Sultan, Naguib and Hussein set out for the old house. They take the bus as far as it will go, but they still have to walk over three kilometres. Every day the danger zone is widening.

As they near Sultan's house, they stop dead in their tracks. The destruction is overwhelming and complete. The three men cannot believe their eyes. It's a mass of bricks, concrete, and broken furniture. And then, they start to see the bodies. For some, only an arm, a leg, a torso, or a face is visible. Some are fully exposed, but what breaks their heart, is that of a mother trying to shield her two children with her arms. All three are dead. For three days, these bodies have been rotting. This was once a happy neighbourhood, where children played, people talked, and there was life, but now, it's a tomb.

Naguib knows why they're there, and he turns to Sultan.

"Do you recognise your home?" Sultan answers.

"Yes, it's the one with the wooden pillar, which is still standing." As they walk to the pillar, the smell of rotting corpses mingles with the open sewers, and it overwhelms their senses. They hold handkerchiefs over their mouth and nose, but the thick, almost physical odour, claws at their throats.

In the middle of the devastation, they experience a miracle. On the pillar, and still hanging in a picture frame, there's a photo of Rania. Sultan takes the picture out of the frame and looks at Naguib and Hussein.

"Let's leave this place. There's nothing here, there's no life, this place is dead."

Through clenched teeth, Hussein hisses.

"Where's the bastard army? Why are these bodies not buried?" Naguib puts his hand on Hussein's shoulder.

"They'll be buried. Inshallah, they'll be buried."

Before heading home, the three men visit the local police station. At the desk, the harassed and overworked police officer tries to help them.

"I know what's happened, and we're hoping to get men out there in the next two days..." Hussein yells.

"Two days!? That means the bodies will be lying in the heat for a total of five days. These people are Muslims! Their bodies can't be left for so long, it's not right."

The officer turns on Hussein and shouts.

"I know this, and I am a Muslim! But the military has said this is a danger zone. How did you get there?"

Naguib realises this question could get them all in a lot of trouble, and he tugs the back of Hussein's shirt. Hussein understands and shuts up. Naguib answers.

"Sir, we were passing the area. We're builders, but once we saw what happened, we left straight away. We didn't see any soldiers." The Officer accepts the answer, and his response is calm.

"You have to avoid the area, otherwise you'll be arrested. We'll do everything we can. If you want to volunteer, come back in a few days."

The three men leave the police station and take the bus home. They remain silent for the entire journey, and they all try to deal with the horrors they've witnessed.

That night Naguib and Sultan sit on the veranda, and Sultan pleads.

"Naguib, I need to teach, it's all I know. And if my teaching allows one child to escape this hell, then I'll die a happy man." Naguib nods.

"Let's see what we can do. You can start with Zeina's children." Sultan stares at the stars.

"My God what have we done to this country? I know we struggle, and at times, we are scared, but we were never as scared as we are now. People can't live in constant fear. I remember reading a line by Plato. *"Courage is knowing what not to fear."* But now, we don't know what to fear, and we fear everything."

Chapter 33 - Teaching

Naguib, Sultan and Hussein, along with fifty other civilians, volunteer to clear the area around Sultan's home. The army and police, provide another fifty men and supervise the operation. Sultan finds the senior police officer and asks.

"Sir, my home was here, and these were my neighbours. Sir, if I find something that belongs to me, may I take it? I'm not stealing." The police officer asks.

"What sort of things?" Sultan looks at the officer.

"Photos of me and my wife, and any salvageable books, I am a teacher. That's all, nothing of value to anyone else."

The police officer is a kind man.

"When you find the things you want, put them next to my car. Let me check them, and as long as it doesn't look like you're looting, which I doubt, you can take them." Sultan shakes the officer's hand.

"Shukraan Sir, may Allah bless you." The police officer smiles, walks away, and barks orders at his men.

Recovering the remains of dead bodies is harrowing, and the stench is far worse than before. Despite the men wearing masks, it's excruciating. The bodies have been in the baking sun for six days. And the smell is a combination of putrefied rotting flesh, human waste, rotten eggs, rotten cabbage, and a strong garlic like odour. When the men move a body, insects scurry away. While these insects are nature's clean up team, it makes the men's flesh crawl. The men also wear gloves, to protect them from the toxic chemicals the body releases after death. From a distance, it breaks the men's hearts, but as they get closer, they feel revulsion. Some men cry as they carry out the work.

First, they have to recover the visible remains, including those of women and children. Afterwards the army starts to remove the debris, and this is a slow process. When they expose another body, the men lift the remains, bag them, and put them on a truck.

The work goes on for two weeks, but the increasing shellfire makes it too dangerous, and they evacuate the area.

Sultan is sure they haven't recovered all the remains, even some of his closest neighbours are still missing. He says a silent prayer. *'Inshallah, you're all staying with family, and you're not under the rubble.'*

In the end, they manage to recover, three more photos, and a dozen books. But the most important thing for Sultan. Is the chance to say goodbye to his neighbours, and to pray for their souls.

It takes Sultan nearly two months to adjust to his new surroundings. He suffers with bad dreams, and sometimes they turn into nightmares. Zeina often sits in his room and fans him. Sometimes she hums a tune to sooth him, in the same way she sings lullabies to her children, to help them sleep.

Slowly Sultan appears to be his old self again, but for the rest of his life, he carries a deep unhealed wound. Naguib had known the young, vibrant, and humorous Sultan, and he can see that less than half his vigour and strength has survived. He puts part of the change down to old age. But in his heart, he knows, Sultan will never be the same again, since grief and loss has robbed a big part of his character.

As they sit on the veranda, Naguib asks.

"When do you want to start teaching? Hussein told me that he has the space for a classroom, on the roof of his house. He has a large piece of tarpaulin, and it will shade you and your students from the sun." Sultan is in a thoughtful mood.

"I'll need something to write on, a blackboard if we can get one. I'll also need, some chalk, pencils, exercise books, and a few other things?" Naguib looks at Sultan.

"Make a list of the things you need, and I'll make sure you get it. A blackboard might be difficult, but what if we paint the bricks black, would that work?" Sultan thinks about it.

"I suppose it would, I don't see why not. Let's try that first. Naguib, I don't have much money, but please take it. I need

166

to do this. Sitting around doing nothing, is turning me into a vegetable. Sometimes we have too much time to think." Naguib agrees.

"Yes, you're right. It's both a blessing and a curse to have brains that remember. Don't worry about the money. There are many children in the neighbourhood, who could do with the extra help. I'm sure their parents will give what they can. We'll manage."

Naguib, Hussein, and Sultan build the classroom. They secure the tarpaulin to the wall with wooden batons, and Naguib builds a frame and secures the tarpaulin to it. The neighbours bring things that might be of use, including an old rug that has seen better days. Yousra stares at it with a frown.

"Why are you bringing that flea bitten thing into my house? Hussein answers.

"It's for the classroom." Yousra shakes her head, and then inspects the rug for a full ten minutes. When she's satisfied that there are no bugs living in it, she gives her begrudging approval.

"Alright, take it to the roof, but don't touch anything in the house with this piece of junk."

After three days of sifting through rubbish, the charity of neighbours and anyone willing to help, the classroom is ready.

It's a large space, and it takes up half the roof, or around twenty square metres, enough for fifteen to twenty students at a squeeze.

The adults gather on the roof. Sultan is humbled by the occasion, and with his chin quivering, he speaks.

"I'd like to live here, and I'd like to make this space my home. I should always be here for the students. Anyone wishing to learn should never have to look for me." With raised eyebrows, Naguib looks at the others.

"Sultan, this isn't meant to be a permanent room, there's a tarpaulin roof, and it'll keep the sun off you, but that's it. There's one solid wall and two canvas sides. It's more like a tent than a permanent structure." Sultan looks at Naguib.

"Our Bedouin brothers live in tents, why can't I?" Naguib doesn't have an answer.

"Very well, but I'll have to make all the sides covered, and with something a little stronger. I'll also have to add a flap, so you can open and shut it. It will keep out flies and mosquitoes." Sultan listens, and nods.

"Shukraan Naguib. Hussein, Yousra, do you have any objections to me living on your roof. I'll pay you rent. Please don't answer that while I'm standing in front of you, think about it and let me know." Hussein already knows the answer.

"When you first came here, I said, you could stay with us, and I haven't changed my mind. I just didn't expect you to live on the roof like a flying gypsy, but if you're happy to do this, we're happy to call this your home. Please don't worry about rent, get yourself sorted."

Sultan smiles.

"I want to thank all of you for your generosity. Your kindness breaks my heart, but some heart breaks are good."

This is Sultan's new home, a makeshift Bedouin tent on the roof of Yousra and Hussein's house. Everyone helps to make it as cosy as possible. There's a small bed, a desk, a chair, a bookshelf, and the threadbare rug for the students to sit on. On the bookshelf are the photos Sultan managed to recover. He positions them in a way, so that he can see Rania when he's in bed. Every night while he sleeps, Rania watches over him.

During the day, he teaches the children. He starts with Gamal and Hanan, and sometimes he teaches adults, since many want to learn English. For them, it's a possible escape route. There are no fixed fees, and people give whatever they can. Sultan gives the money to Yousra, who at first refuses it, but realises, it's easier to accept it. Then she gives the money to Naguib, and he uses it to buy what Sultan needs, and gives Sultan the change, along with a made-up excuse.

"One of the parents gave me this money to give to you. I can't remember the name, but she said her daughter, or is it her son, is enjoying school."

Sultan teaches everyone who comes to him. He doesn't discriminate, and he welcomes anyone who wants to learn.

On clear and quiet nights, Sultan sits on the roof gazing at the stars. Neighbours who sit on their roofs to feel the cool evening air, wave to him. The people in the neighbourhood call him the Bedouin teacher, a title he carries to the end of his days.

On those starlit nights, Sultan speaks to Rania.

"My beautiful Rania, I will see you soon."

Chapter 34 - Living

The pattern of everyone's life in this war-torn country, changes on a daily basis. As more people are affected, they become better at enduring the horrors of their world. But in equal measure, their celebration of good news, has a life-giving force, and they find happiness in simple acts of kindness.

Very few go unscathed. Whether it's the sudden death of a loved one, or a separation, due to their departure to a foreign country.

Naguib reads the papers when he can get them. But the propaganda spouted by the official lines, is very different to the realities he and others face.

People use more water for mixing the flour for bread, and less oil for cooking. Every day the size of the meals shrinks. Children and the elderly suffer the most, as they become prone to sickness.

Naguib holds Gamal's hand, and he thinks. *'He's small for seven, his wrists are bony, and I can feel his ribs.'* When he looks at the other children, he realises that in comparison, Gamal is a healthy size. Many, who are older, are smaller, and they cannot run for long. Naguib worries for the children's health, but he's powerless to do anything.

Every day Zeina's confidence grows, and with Sultan living on the roof of Yousra and Hussein's house, she often sits with Naguib on the veranda. The more she speaks to him, the more she starts to have feelings for him.

Naguib is always kind, and he has a good sense of humour. He's polite and respectful, and he never does or says anything, to suggest, he has feelings for her. But Zeina needs to know.

"Naguib, tell me about your wife. What was Rashida like?" Naguib smiles.

"I always thought she was beautiful. But then, if a wife is beautiful in the eyes of her husband, it makes things a lot easier. Would you agree?" Yousra nods.

"Yes, I would. If a husband thinks that, it's bound to help the relationship." They both laugh, but she wants to know more.

"I mean, what was it about her that was beautiful? A woman can have days when she feels horrible, even ugly, so what made her beautiful on those days she felt bad?"

Naguib thinks about this for a long time. No one, not even he had asked himself that question.

"That's a tough question, is there a prize if I get it right?" Zeina flashes a smile.

"If I think you've got it right, I'll make fresh tea." Naguib scratches his unshaven chin.

"Don't get me wrong. We argued just like all couples do, and one time she went to her parents. Because I upset her so much. Her father brought her back and said to us. Never go to sleep on an argument. Always make peace, otherwise you'll take the argument into tomorrow, and the day after. And if this carries on, you'll only find mean things to say to each other. We listened, and that night, we promised, before going to sleep, we would always make up. Let me tell you, that was a stupid promise. Because some nights, we didn't sleep. We just spoke and tried to fix the problem. But after a while, we started to realise, we were arguing about unimportant things. The more we realised this, the less we argued, and our love grew. I'm not saying we didn't love each other before. What I'm trying to say is. We learned to love each other as we once did. I always thought she was beautiful, but as we grew older, there was something else in her beauty. Perhaps aging made her the person she was capable of being. When we're young, we often think with the strength in our bodies. But I think as we age, we think with our heart, and this creates an almost angelic quality to a person. So, for me, Rashida became a living angel."

Naguib falls silent and stares at the night sky.

Zeina is in awe, and after a while, she asks.

171

"Do you think Khaled found me beautiful?" Naguib smiles.

"I know he did. I could tell by the way he looked at you. But you must know this, and he must have told you?" Zeina toys with her bangle.

"I do know, but I'm uncertain, and sometimes, it's nice to be reminded."

Naguib has an uneasy feeling about where this conversation is going, and he wants to stop it going any further.

"Zeina, there's no doubting your beauty. You stand out like a red rose in a field of white roses. But I'm not your husband, and I can't talk to you as a husband can. I can talk to you as a friend."

Zeina lowers her head. She's embarrassed. And she realises, she's been so transparent. But she's also determined to evoke feelings in Naguib. Maybe not this evening, but at some point, in their lives together.

The following day Zeina has tea with Yousra, while Sultan teaches the children. This shared time, is now a part of their daily routine. And despite the age gap, they speak as equals. Her conversation with Naguib has been on her mind, and she stayed awake until the early hours thinking about it. Yousra senses the uneasiness.

"Zeina what's wrong?" Again, Zeina feels embarrassed, but she needs to get an answer that makes sense. After all, she's young, and the oestrogen that runs through her body, fuels some of her thinking.

"Does Naguib ever talk about being lonely?" Straight away Yousra's instincts kick in, but she also remembers the conversation she had with Naguib, about taking Zeina as his wife.

"He hasn't said anything to me about loneliness." Zeina asks another question.

"Has he ever mentioned me?" This is a broad question and Yousra asks.

"In what way?" Zeina's cheeks flush red, and once her face cools down, she answers.

"In the way, a man may show interest in a woman, when he wants a wife."

Yousra's instincts are right. She knows that Zeina and Naguib's friendship has grown, but she also knows that Naguib sees Zeina as a sister, or maybe a daughter, but not as a wife. She wonders whether she should tell a white lie or the truth. She opts for the truth.

"You know that Naguib is still in love with his wife?" Zeina nods, and after a few seconds, she answers.

"I know that. But she's no longer here. I am, and we have to keep living." It was more of a plea than an answer, and Yousra moves a little closer.

"I understand what you're saying. I also feel that life should go on, and that you don't pin all your love on someone or something, that isn't capable of loving you back." Zeina agrees.

"That's right. So why does he still live in the past?"

Yousra thinks. *'Only Naguib can answer this question.'* Although she doesn't know the answer, she tries.

"Naguib is a man of strong principles, and I guess he believes marriage is for life. Even if one person in the marriage is missing. He doesn't wholly live in the past. Look at everything he does. I just think there's one element of his life that he's not prepared to change. Call it blind loyalty, or just pure stubbornness. Naguib is a good man, we can all see that. And you're a young woman, with the needs of a young woman, and today I can see that." Again, Zeina's cheeks flush red.

"Yousra, do you think Naguib could ever love me?" Yousra smiles.

"I think Naguib already loves you, just not the way you want him to. Love comes in many forms. It can be the love of children, a partner, siblings, parents, family, and friends. Remember, whenever you are with a person who cares for you, and wants to protect you, love is already there."

Although this answers Zeina's question, it doesn't fill her with joy. It manages to confuse her a little bit more.

"Do you think he could ever love me as a wife?" Yousra senses the confusion.

"Ever is a long time. A lot may change during that time. Yes, people can learn to love in a different way, but the way we love someone, is often determined at the start of the relationship. It's true that friends can become lovers, and lovers can become friends. Remember one major hurdle to all of this. Is age. Naguib is nearly twenty years older than you. At this stage of a person's life, just getting out of bed can be a struggle. Do you want to confront that, and how will that make you feel? You see Naguib now, and he's still strong, but in ten or twenty years from now. How will you feel then?" Zeina's answer is immediate.

"I'd rather have Naguib for ten or twenty years, than another man who treats me bad. His age isn't a problem for me." Yousra realises that Zeina has real feelings for Naguib, feelings a wife has for a husband.

"Give it time, things may change, but you must be patient. It's not even a year since you came to live with him, and I can see that you have a good friendship, build on that. Wait for him to say, I didn't see you all day, where have you been?" Zeina smiles.

"He already says these things to me. What should I make of it?" Yousra pours a fresh cup of tea.

"If he has already said those words, then he's already thinking about you as being a part of his life. Time will tell if he'll do anything about it. Build on this and build a strong friendship. Understand something, being friends is much more important than physical love. If you're lucky, physical love lasts for thirty minutes, but then there's over twenty-three hours left. And those twenty-three hours can only be filled with friendship, so you'd better be friends. Naguib is at the stage in his life, where liking someone, is far more important than taking them to bed."

Both women chuckle and Zeina speaks.

"Yousra, you know a lot about life, and without insulting you, a lot about men." Yousra sighs.

"To know life, you must live it, and you have to pay attention. As for men, well, with five sons and a good husband, I know a little about men. But you know, just when I think I know

174

Hussein he can surprise me. Playing football at his age, what next?" Yousra starts to laugh and Zeina joins in.

Chapter 35 - Birthday

Hanan is approaching her sixth birthday and she cannot contain herself.

"Uncle Naguib, I'm going to be six, I'm going to be a big girl." She smiles with glee, and she reveals gaps at the front of her mouth, where she's already lost four of her milk teeth. Naguib holds her close as she sits on his lap.

"What would you like for your sixth birthday?" Hussein, Yousra, Zeina and Sultan stare at her with sparkling eyes, as they wait for her answer.

"I don't want a husband." The adults roar with laughter and Naguib gives her a big hug.

"Fine, we won't get you a husband. So, we all know what you don't want, but what do you want?" Again, Hanan starts to think, and after ten seconds, she speaks.

"When Sultan teaches me, he tells me stories about a place called university. He had lots of fun there. I want to go to university, but I think it's a school for grown-ups, but I want to go." Sultan beams with happiness.

"My dear girl, there're many more lessons you have to learn, before you can go to university. But if you'll let me teach you, I'll make sure you go. Not yet, but when you're around nineteen." Hanan can count to a hundred, and she starts to count aloud and then exclaims.

"But I'll be an old woman by then!" The adults laugh and Hussein adds.

"My God, if nineteen is an old woman, that makes us a bunch of fossils."

In the end, they settle for two storybooks and a doll.

The day of the birthday arrives, and the children gather on the roof. Half a dozen children sit on the rug, and Sultan reads them stories from the book he bought for Hanan. It's an illustrated book of stories by Hans Christian Anderson. Sultan reads a page, and then turns the page around so the children can see the pictures. They're captivated, and as he finishes one story, they shout in unison.

"Another story Uncle Sultan, please, another story!"

The adults enjoy themselves, and Zeina smiles throughout the storytelling. She's never experienced such a moment in her life. She had gone from being a girl, to being a woman, as soon as her menstrual cycles started. This was the custom for most girls from poor families. But she didn't want that life for Hanan.

Towards the end of the birthday celebrations, they hear the whine and roar of jets. And when they look up at the sky, they see four planes.

There's a long-range aircraft with an American flag. It has two fighter planes flanking it left and right, and another at its rear. The four airplanes fly in this formation and head out towards the desert.

They're all scared, and people start to scramble to safety. Mother's grab their children, and they run into the house. The men stare at the planes, and Sultan speaks.

"That's not an attack. It looks like they're escorting the big plane. I wonder where it's going." Neither Naguib nor Hussein answer, since they don't know what to make of it. Once the planes are out of sight, they see hundreds of faces looking to the heavens. With a smile, Hussein whispers.

"I hope it's our bastard president leaving the country!" Naguib and Sultan smile, and the three of them speak with one voice.

"Inshallah."

The following day, while Naguib sits on the veranda there's a knock at the door, it's Nour.

"Salaam Naguib, I have a letter for you from the U.S. It looks like, it was posted over a month ago. Sorry but it's out of our control." Naguib invites Nour into the house.

"Salaam Nour, come in and have some tea. It's not your fault. You can only deliver what is there." Zeina makes tea, and the three of them sit on the veranda, and Naguib reads the letter.

"Dear Abbi,

I hope this letter finds you well, and that you're eating properly. The children are happy, and I can say, they're as much American as the two blue-eyed, blonde-haired boys, Daniel, and Ben, who live next door.

I got a promotion at the school since Marcus retired, and I now take care of the maintenance as well. It pays a little bit more, and so I've enclosed twenty dollars with this letter.

Nawal has a job at a local grocery store. A Pakistani family owns it, and they're Muslims. They speak a little Arabic, and so they talk to Nawal in broken Arabic, but mostly English. It makes me laugh when I hear the conversations.

Farid likes the photo you sent, and he keeps it in a picture frame in his room, he doesn't want to share Jadd with anyone. But I'll get a copy made for the family room. Rafa and Salma are doing great, and Rafa has started senior school. She's proving to be a very good student.

I had a visitor recently, his name is Mido Ibrahim, and he told me how you helped him and his mother. It made me feel so proud.

I'm still trying to see how we can bring you to America, but the biggest problem is proving your birth. I think Abdel is facing similar problems with Uncle Hassam and Aunty Samir, but we'll keep trying.

I recently passed my American driving test, and now I am looking to buy my first car. This country is full of cars. I went car shopping with Marcus, and he keeps talking about good gas mileage. I'm not sure, I know what he means. I'll find a good car, and I'll send a photo of us sitting in it.

The cold weather is starting again. This is a strange country. In New York, the summers can be as hot as back home, and the winters are colder, than anything you can imagine.

The children send their love. That is a common saying in America, and they tell me, they miss you.

178

I've put another newspaper cutting for you. Perhaps Sultan can read it. From what I've read, there seems to be a bit of calm, but it's hard to tell what that means to real people.

I remember when I worked with the army as a mechanic, calm meant, vehicles not coming back from patrol damaged. But on my way home, I could feel the tension on the streets. In America, we don't know how much tension there is on the streets.

I'll stop for now, but please tell me if you need anything, and as always, I'll do my best to get it to you.

Please pray for me as I will pray for you. Inshallah, I will see you soon.

Your loving son

Anwar

Nour finishes his tea.

"It's a good letter, and it sounds like the family are doing well. But I don't know if I could let my wife work with strangers. If you need help to convert the twenty dollars let me know. I know a good man, and he'll only take five percent commission, that's very cheap."

Naguib knows it's cheap, and he agrees to use Nour's contact. He thinks about the twenty dollars, and he realises, it's about a month's wage for the average person in the city. Naguib wonders how he can put it to good use.

With the newspaper clipping in his pocket, Naguib visits Sultan. While there's a recess, and the children go home to eat, the adults follow Naguib to the roof. When Sultan sees them standing in front of him, he jokes.

"Naguib, Hussein, Zeina, Yousra, what brings you all here, and what do you want to learn?" Naguib smiles.

"Just for you to tell us what this American newspaper is saying. Anwar sent it with a letter."

Sultan is excited, and his eyes widen.

"Oh my God, foreign news! Maybe we'll learn the truth."

179

The adults sit on the rug like eager students ready to learn, and Sultan reads and translates.

"*In a recent press statement, The Whitehouse has stated that the Middle Eastern crisis is at a stalemate. The Government and the Freedom Fighters have entered talks, with a view to power sharing, and future democratic elections.*

The Whitehouse has sent Henry Adelstein as a peace envoy to the region. Mr Adelstein has a long and distinguished career in areas of diplomacy, and he is a judge at the Supreme Court. In a recent interview, he was quoted as saying.

"*The American people may view this conflict as a long-distance game of chess, and that the game has no bearing on their lives. The truth is. It does. Thousands of men, women and children have lost their lives, and thousands more are in danger. Communities are being decimated, and societies in the region will suffer for generations to come. Peace in this region will benefit all of us. There will be less immigration to American shores, and this will stop, or at least reduce the civil unrest in the U.S. Peace in this region, means peace between different beliefs, and this will result in global peace. We owe it to mankind not to stand by and watch another bloodbath. I would like to remind both sides, that they're fighting for the same country, and they should look to rebuild their nation, rather than destroy it.*"

Our prayers are with Mr Adelstein and that he succeeds in his mission.

Readers, the real question is how achievable is peace? And, how achievable are democratic elections, in a country where the current president has ruled for decades, as the life appointed leader. It's not easy to let go of power, and it's even harder to let go of absolute power. This man has ruled with an iron fist, is he willing to loosen his grip?

Currently the U.N. is working with local agencies to ensure essential supplies reach the worst affected areas. At the end of this article, you can find an address. Please send your donations, whatever they are. We have been assured it will get to the people who need it most.

If our Middle Eastern brothers and sisters get a chance to read this article, please know that our thoughts and prayers are with you all."

The adults are amazed and Naguib looks at Sultan.

"So that was the big plane, it was carrying this Adelstein man." Hussein interrupts.

"Adelstein sounds like a Jewish name, is he a Jew?" Sultan answers.

"Yes, Henry Adelstein is Jewish." Hussein is horrified.

"Why would the American's send a Jew, to negotiate peace in a Muslim country? Have they lost their minds?" Sultan stares at Hussein, and there is a flicker of anger in his eyes. Then, he faces them all, and he speaks.

"Henry Adelstein fled Germany with his family during World War II. During that war, six million innocent Jews were slaughtered. He knows more about the horrors of war, than most people, and he understands our suffering. His words bear that out. If he cannot negotiate peace, no one can."

Everyone falls silent, and Naguib agrees with Sultan.

"I don't care if he's a Jew, an idol worshipper, or a monkey. If he can bring peace and give us back our families, I thank Allah for this man."

Naguib's words silence all of them, and in their own way, they all say a prayer.

Sultan asks Naguib to stay when the others stand up, and once they leave, he speaks.

"This news won't bring back the dead, but it gives hope to the living."

Naguib and Sultan embrace and as they do, they both whisper in each other's ear. "Inshallah."

Chapter 36 - Ceasefire

Within a few days, news of the ceasefire sweeps across the city. Some confuse this with permanent peace, and they start to sing and dance in the streets. Others, who understand, realise, it's just a pause, and they're more sceptical.

In this case, Naguib leans towards scepticism. But his view, comes from the many losses, he and others have endured. And the violence inflicted on the people, by their leader. Throughout his life, he's seen his countries leader's choose violence, rather than kindness. While all of this causes doubt, he keeps an open mind, and he looks forward to a better future.

He sees this ceasefire as an argument between two surly children, and it needs an adult to settle things. From personal experience, he knows that trying to settle an argument, often creates another one. It's only when both sides understand and accept what they've done wrong, that an argument can be settled. He cannot imagine his countries arrogant president, ever admitting to anything. He feels that this new calm is temporary, and that it could escalate into a bigger fight.

All the same, people come out of their houses, smile, chat, and enjoy the feeling of not having to look over their shoulder.

Sultan gives the children a day's holiday. He sits with Naguib and Hussein at a café. They enjoy the relaxed atmosphere. They see people greeting each other with warmth. Hussein is in a thoughtful mood, and he speaks.

"You forget what it's like just to be normal, and to live without fear." Naguib nods.

"Yes, it's wonderful to see this. This is how life was. Even though things were bad, there was something good in the strong leadership of the president." Sultan smiles.

"I suppose you're right. He was unjust and brutal to those who opposed him. Look back in history, and you'll see, that all our leaders have behaved this way. I wonder if something like democracy can work in a country like ours. Democracy works when people are educated enough, to make an intelligent choice. I don't know if that intelligence exists in our country. Where there's a lack of understanding, you go with the strongest or loudest. Sometimes, it doesn't even matter what they're saying."

This goes over both Naguib and Hussein's head, and Hussein asks.

"So, what would happen with democracy?" Sultan looks at Hussein.

"Well, we get to choose our leaders." Hussein is staggered.

"How would we know which is the right leader, I mean they're all crooks. They're all lining their own pockets." Sultan laughs, and then answers.

"Perhaps the person we should choose, is the most reluctant candidate, and not the one whose eyes are on power. Our country still has good men, but the true political giants are dead, or they're overseas. I get the feeling. This country has corruption running through its veins. Even if someone starts out with good intentions, it never lasts, and they become distorted by money." Naguib doesn't agree.

"If we believe this, then there's really no hope for us." Sultan thinks about his own words.

"You're right Naguib. I am being very negative, and that's never helpful. For a body to heal we must remain positive, and I guess it's the same for a nation."

After a few hours at the café, Naguib decides to visit Rashida's grave, while Sultan and Hussein return home.

As he stands in front of the headstone, he speaks to her and reads Anwar's latest letter.

"Anwar and Nawal have settled in New York. It sounds like a tough life, and they're both working. But I think, we now have American grandchildren."

As he sits on a step at the cemetery, he stares at the letter. To his surprise, a soldier sits next to him. Naguib offers him a cigarette.

"As-salaam-alaikum young man, are you visiting family here?" The soldier takes the cigarette.

"Wa-alaikum-salaam. And thank you for the cigarette Sir. Yes, I'm visiting my mother, she's buried near the back wall, but when I saw you, I thought I'd speak to you. It's been a long time since I spoke with someone that didn't look like a soldier." Naguib asks.

"Where have you come from?" The soldier inhales the cigarette, and after exhaling, he speaks.

"I've come from the front, where all the fighting is taking place. Half my battalion got leave, and the other half will get leave when I, and others return." Naguib takes the packet of cigarettes out of his pocket. He offers them to the soldier and the soldier smiles.

"It's alright sir, I have money. I just wanted to speak to someone. I haven't spoken to any civilians, since arriving back a few hours ago."

Naguib stares at the soldier and asks.

"What's your name?"

The soldier stares back, and Naguib recognises the penetrating sadness in the soldier's eyes. Sultan had shown the same despair after losing everything. He forces himself to hold the stare, and the soldier answers.

"It's Karim, and what's your name Sir?"

"I am Naguib, but please, you don't have to call me sir. I'm not a soldier, I'm just an old carpenter."

Both men light another cigarette and Naguib asks.

"So, where's your family home?"

Karim's eyes well up, and Naguib is about to apologise for the question, when Karim stops him.

"Naguib, no need to apologise. My home was bombed and there are no survivors. My father, my younger brother and my older sister are gone. They're buried in another part of town, and I'm trying to find out where they are. My mother died ten years ago, and that's why I've come here. I'm hoping that she'll be able to help."

Naguib sits in silence and listens. He learns that Karim's home was in the same district as Sultan's.

"Go to this police station. I've written down the address. Ask for this police officer, I've written his name as well. Tell them about your family and your address. The police will have names of those who died. The police at this station, were responsible for clearing the area. They'll know where your family are."

Karim stares at Naguib.

"I knew my mother would help. I think she sent you to me."

Naguib touches Karim's arm.

"If she sent me, I'm happy, and I'm glad that I could help you."

Naguib waits, and then he speaks.

"If you don't mind me asking, but what's it like on the front, and who's winning?" Karim points to the pack of cigarettes, and Naguib pushes the packet over to Him. Karim inhales, blows out the grey cloud, and then he answers.

"I no longer believe in heaven or hell. Because the battlefield is hell. Imagine if you can. The worst possible nightmare, and add gunfire, heat, people dying next to you, while choking on their own blood. Then you'll get an idea of the front."

Naguib clenches his jaws, as he chews over Karim's blunt and graphic description. He decides to ask no further questions. Karim gives a tight-lipped smile.

"I'm sorry, I wasn't trying to scare you. But it's beyond dreadful, and it can break a man. Who's winning? According to the president, we're winning, but it's strange that I'm trying to kill someone from my own country. If I did that at any other time, I'd be a murderer. Naguib no one is winning, as a country, we're all losing."

Naguib touches Karim's arm, and he sees his chin quiver with emotion. Before Naguib can say anything else, Karim stands to attention, and speaks with as much confidence as his shaking voice allows.

"Shukraan Naguib, stay safe and well."

Without another word, Karim walks away. Before Naguib can say goodbye, Karim has turned the corner and is gone.

Naguib sits motionless. He's unsure if the conversation with Karim took place, or had he imagined the whole thing. As he looks at the ground, he sees the impressions left by the army boots, and he realises.

"This horror is real. I didn't dream it. It's real."

Chapter 37 - Marriage

Naguib stares at the photos of Abdel and Shadia's wedding. While everyone is smiling, there's an element of sadness in the images of Abdel. According to Anwar's letter, he hasn't heard from Hassam and Samir in two years.

Naguib starts to fear the worst for his old friend, but for the time being, he puts the thought to the back of his mind.

He looks at the photos of his grandchildren. Although Rafa is only twelve, she's taller than Nawal. In the photo, Rafa is wearing a headscarf, and she's starting to look like a woman. Ten-year-old Salma still has her girlishness, but she's the same height as her mother.

Then Naguib stares at eight-year-old Farid. His beaming smile could light a stadium. He can see, Farid looks healthier, taller, and stronger than Gamal, despite being roughly the same age. Naguib runs his fingers across the images and blows his grandchildren a kiss.

He then turns to the photo of Anwar and Nawal. The faces staring back, worry him. When he sees Anwar with grey hair, and dark circles under his eyes, Naguib sighs with sadness. He knows Anwar carries the guilt of leaving his father behind.

Naguib wishes he could hug Anwar. He wants to tell him things will be fine. Just as he used to do when Anwar was a boy. Out of desperation, he speaks to the photo. "Anwar, it isn't anybody's fault. We all tried our best, and that's all anyone can do. My son, enjoy life."

Zeina comes out on the veranda and sees Naguib staring at the photos.

"I heard you talking. Was that you Naguib? Did you get another letter?"

Hearing Zeina's voice, Naguib's imagined conversation with Anwar ends. He looks at her, and he hands her the photos.

"Oh, they're beautiful. Who's getting married?" Naguib answers.

"Abdel Elneny is marrying, my daughter in laws sister, Shadia. She's been educated in America." Zeina looks at the photo of the bride.

"She doesn't look like an Arab woman. I thought she was a westerner." Naguib nods.

"Yes, I can see that. But I guess wherever you are, you take on some of that place."

Nour the regular postman, is on a day's leave, and Naguib is unable to share this letter with him. But sharing it with Zeina, is a nice change.

"Anwar has sent some money. Is there anything you, Gamal, and Hanan need?" Zeina looks surprised.

"Naguib that money is for you. You know I have my own money. Is there anything you need, some new clothes, sandals, just something for you?"

Naguib thinks about this, and thoughts of Hassam and Samir come back to him. He looks at Zeina and answers.

"There is something, but it isn't clothes or sandals. Mind you, if I do this thing, I may need new clothes, and maybe a stronger pair of sandals."

Zeina keeps staring at Naguib. She waits for a better explanation, and when there's only silence, she asks.

"Naguib, tell me, or do I have to force it out of you?" Naguib laughs.

"Sorry, but what is going through my mind. Is something you may not like. In fact, it might be something no one likes."

Again, Naguib is silent, and Zeina looks puzzled.

"Well, with that answer, I still haven't got a clue. So, are you going to tell me what you want to do?"

Naguib smiles, but then his face is stern.

"I want to travel down South. The groom in the photo is the son of Hassam Elneny. Hassam, Khaled, and I have known each other all our lives. Abdel, Hassam's son hasn't heard anything from his parents in over two years, and neither have I. If Hassam and his wife Samir are alive, I need to show them these photos, and I need to get a letter from them to their son. Abdel is probably going out of his mind with worry." Zeina is terrified.

"Naguib, the roads out of town, for hundreds of kilometres aren't safe! Why has Hassam not come back to the city?"

Naguib understands Zeina's concern, and the same thoughts about safety have crossed his mind. He puts the doubts to one side, and answers.

"If Hassam comes back to the city, he'll go to jail, and he won't survive that ordeal. He will die in that torture chamber, just like thousands of others, who walk through those doors." Zeina understands, but for her, it's just too dangerous.

"Why don't you wait, until all of the talks between the president and the freedom fighters are finished?" Naguib has thought about this as well.

"This might be my only chance. While the politicians talk, no one fights, but if the talks go wrong, the fighting will restart. I think if that happens, the two sides will fight to the end."

In the papers, they read that the peace negotiations were going better than expected. They saw a photo of the president shaking hands with the leader of the freedom fighters. The politicians agreed to extend the ceasefire by five weeks, to allow both sides to agree a new power sharing, and democratic process.

Zeina realises that she cannot talk Naguib out of this. But then she takes the bold step, and she reveals her heart.

"Naguib you can't do this on your own, you have to take someone with you. The most important thing for me is, I have feelings for you, and I cannot lose you."

Zeina's head drops with embarrassment. Naguib lays a gentle hand on her arm.

"I'll find someone to travel with me. Zeina, I have feelings for you as well, you cannot live this close to someone without feeling something. My fear is, my feelings aren't the same as yours, but we can have this talk when I return."

At that point, Zeina wants Naguib to sweep her into his arms and kiss her, but he doesn't. Instead, he gets up and leaves the house.

Naguib knocks on the Kulthum's door, and when Yousra answers, she notices that he's looking down the street.

"Naguib is everything alright?" Naguib faces Yousra.

"Salaam Yousra, yes everything is fine, but I need to speak to you, Hussein and Sultan. Can you come to my house later this evening, after the children are asleep?"

"Yes, of course. About nine?" Naguib nods, and he leaves without another word. That afternoon Naguib goes shopping. He buys a bedroll, a torch, a large box of matches, strong sandals, and a water canteen. He also buys dried meat and fruit, enough for a six-day journey. Although he isn't sure, how long it will take. And finally, he purchases an oilskin rucksack.

When he gets home, Zeina has prepared the evening meal. Once they sit down to eat, Naguib can see, she's keeping her distance. He realises, he's hurt her feelings, and when the children go to bed, he smiles and speaks.

"Zeina, please don't be angry. The atmosphere in this house is much nicer when you're happy." Zeina flashes him a smile, and despite feeling rejected, she can see the warmth in his eyes. She knows he means well, and she hands him some bread.

"I've asked Yousra, Hussein and Sultan to come over. They'll be here in about thirty minutes, let's sit outside."

On the veranda, Naguib shows them the letter and the photos. At the mention of Hassam's name, Sultan's eyes light up.

"Is that old fox still alive?" Naguib answers.

"I hope so. The police were going to put him in jail, so he and Samir fled the city. In all that time, his son Abdel hasn't heard from him, and I need to trace him. I need to show Hassam these photos, and I must get a message to Abdel. I want to give Abdel some definite news about his parents. Before Hassam left, he came to see me. He told me he is going to stay with his brother Ismail. I know where Ismail settled. I just hope he's still there. I know it's near the southern borders of our country, so I'm going there first."

190

Hussein spits out his tea.

"You want to travel down South, near the border!? Are you mad!? That's at least three days journey, and that's if you have transport. Naguib don't do this!" Naguib stays calm, and he looks at Hussein.

"I have to do this. I have no choice." Hussein laughs.

"Of course you have a choice. Don't go. I can't see anywhere in the letter, where Abdel asked you to do this. If he'd asked, then I'd say. Maybe you don't have a choice."

Naguib turns to all of them.

"It's bad enough not being able to see your loved ones. And there's some relief when you get a letter, but not to hear anything for two years. That could drive you insane." Hussein nods his agreement, and then warns.

"I understand what you're saying, but this is a treacherous journey. You're not a young man anymore, and you want to do this on your own?" Naguib looks down at his feet.

"I know the dangers, but during this ceasefire it might be my only chance. And I wasn't thinking of going on my own?" Feeling a little relieved, Hussein asks.

"Well, that's one thing we're agreed on. So, who will you take?" Before Naguib gets the chance, Sultan answers.

"I'm going with Naguib. Hassam was an old friend of mine as well." Yousra puts her hand over her mouth, and then she pleads.

"Sultan, you can't leave the school! What about your students?" Sultan smiles.

"We'll be back before the politicians reach an agreement. We have to work to that timeframe, so that we can avoid any danger. I estimate that we'll be gone for one month. It shouldn't take longer than that. The children will enjoy the holiday. Naguib is right. While there's a ceasefire, our journey should be trouble free. After all, we're two Arab men visiting family, what's so strange about that?" Sultan smiles at Yousra, and Hussein starts to laugh.

"You're both as mad as each other! That's a tough journey for two men half your age. My God, you're a couple of geriatric boy scouts." Naguib fixes his eyes on Hussein.

"Hussein, you can say what you want, and I'm not offended. I'm very grateful to have a friend who cares so much, shukraan. My friend, I have to do this, and all I ask of you. Please help Zeina and the children while I'm gone."

Hussein is humbled into submission by Naguib's words, and Yousra answers.

"Of course, we'll help. There's no question about that. And Hussein will help organise what you need, including transportation." Hussein nods.

"Yes, I'll help. I know some traders who travel down South. They take supplies, clothes, and many things, and sell them to the locals, who can't get these things where they live. For a price, they'll take you. They return once they sell everything, it's about a two-to-three-week turnaround." Naguib gives Hussein a smile and reaches for his hand.

"Thank you my friend. That sounds perfect, and I have the money. I just need one more thing, a camera. I want to take photos of Hassam and Samir to send to Abdel. Can you get me a camera?" Hussein answers.

"Yes, I can do that." Sultan looks at Naguib.

"I know how to use a camera, don't worry that will be my department. I also know the geography of our country, so I'll know if we're going in the right direction. I won't let you down Naguib." Naguib nods his agreement.

"I know you won't, and that's why I didn't object. But we'll need some things for you, for the journey ahead." Yousra sighs.

"I'll pray for both of you until the day you return." Hussein touches her shoulder, and when he speaks, his voice is soothing.

"We'll all pray for your safe return."

They all sit in silence and listen to the noises coming from the neighbourhood. They hear muffled conversations, laughter, and the occasional raised voice.

Hussein makes the travel arrangements and gets a camera. He then speaks to Naguib and Sultan.

"In two days, my contacts Tawfik and Ezzat will meet you on the edge of town, on the desert road at sunrise. Tawfik is Ezzat's father. They're honest traders, and they can be trusted. I've paid them for your transport, and in eleven days or so, they'll bring you back. I also have this camera. It has film inside, but the shopkeeper said. There's no flash, so you must take all your pictures during the day. I managed to get two more things which might be useful, a compass, and binoculars."

Sultan is delighted.

"A compass!? I've always wanted a compass, shukraan Hussein." While Sultan inspects the Leica 35mm camera, compass, and binoculars Naguib speaks to Hussein.

"Hussein, I didn't want you to pay, give me ten minutes and I'll give you the money back."

Hussein stops Naguib.

"Naguib, it was my pleasure, and I don't want the money back. I wish I could do more, but I'm not as brave as you are. So please, let me do this little thing. Let me be a small part of your adventure."

Naguib stares at Hussein.

"Hussein, you're a very brave man. You're a man who keeps his sense of humour in troubled times, and that takes courage. You're loyal, and there's nothing more anyone can ask." The two men shake hands and then embrace.

Sultan walks over to them and announces.

"This camera is great, and the compass is excellent. I'm sure we'll make good use of the binoculars. So, we're all set."

Naguib answers.

"Yes, we're ready. Inshallah, the journey will be a safe one." The three men repeat the word.

"Inshallah."

The night before travelling Naguib opens his old suitcase, and at the bottom, there's the gun Hassam gave him. He wraps it in a bundle of rags, and he puts it at the top of his oilskin bag. He settles down to sleep, but he remains wide-awake until it's time to leave.

Zeina prepares breakfast, and in silence, she watches the men eat. As they're about to leave, she speaks to Naguib.

"Please be careful. I want to see you back here. I've never asked you for anything, but today I'm asking for one thing. Please come back."

Naguib squeezes her arm and stares into her eyes.

"Inshallah."

Chapter 38 - Desert

The men stand next to an old canvas backed truck. It's loaded to the rafters with clothes, shoes, make up, books, and many other things. It's a mobile convenient store.

Tawfik folds his prayer mat, and then he speaks to Naguib.

"This truck may look old, and that's good. Because people don't question you, when they see this old thing. But the engine, it purrs like a kitten."

Naguib looks at Tawfik and wonders. *'Is he Hussein's brother?'* The similarities are remarkable, even down to the nicotine-stained teeth. Naguib asks.

"Where will we sit? The cabin is too small for four men?" Tawfik grins.

"I've made a space for you in the back of the truck, you'll be comfortable there." Naguib and Sultan follow Tawfik, and when he lowers the tailgate, they see a small space. There is just enough room for two people to sit, topping and tailing. Sultan scratches his chin.

"Well, it will be cosy, that's for sure. But this is better than trying to make it on foot, or on the back of a camel." Tawfik smiles, but within a second, his face is serious.

"Are you carrying a gun?"

Naguib nods and Tawfik speaks.

"Give it to me. It's acceptable for a trader like me to carry a gun. If soldiers stop us, and find a gun on you, it could be a big problem. The soldiers expect to find a gun on me, to protect my merchandise, and my life against bandits."

Naguib takes the gun out of his bag and hands it over. Sultan stares in amazement. In the back of the truck, Sultan asks.

"Naguib, you have a gun? What were you going to do with a gun?" Naguib stares at Sultan.

"Yes, I have a gun. And what do you think I was going to do with it. Swat flies? Look, I want to make sure, you come back in one piece. I couldn't stand the thought of anything happening to you. Let's call it insurance and leave it at that."

Although Sultan shakes his head in disbelief, he is grateful. He touches Naguib's arm and smiles.

As the engine roars, both men look in the direction of the city, as it starts to wake up. Slowly the truck pulls away. As it drives along the smooth tarmac, Naguib's head falls forward, and he falls asleep.

Two hours into the journey, the road becomes uneven, and with a jolt, Naguib wakes up. His mouth is bone dry, and his tongue feels like a stone made of sandpaper. Due to a lack of sleep, his eyes sting. When he looks at Sultan, he sees him with a scarf around his mouth and nose. It makes him look like a bandit, and he's looking at the desert through his binoculars. He feels Naguib stirring.

"Salaam Naguib, looks like you needed that sleep." Naguib points to his mouth, and then he takes a huge swig of water. He holds the water in his mouth, and allows his tongue to soak, and for the saliva to return. After a minute, Naguib answers in a rasping voice.

"I didn't sleep last night. My God, this is uncomfortable, and my mouth feels as dry as the desert." Naguib takes another mouthful of water, and Sultan laughs.

"When you were asleep, your mouth was open. You need to put the scarf around your face. It will stop the warm air drying your mouth. I guess we'll stop soon, and then we can stretch our legs, and straighten our backs."

Naguib sits up. He leans against the side of the truck, and after looking around, he asks.

"Sultan, have you seen anything interesting?" Sultan lets the binoculars dangle from his neck.

"On the outskirts of the city, I saw some burned-out army vehicles, and then sand for miles. I saw a camel train. I think if you go back a thousand years, the lives of those on the camel train would be exactly the same. I saw an African Golden Eagle,

I must have watched it circling the sky for twenty minutes, but it never came down. It's a beautiful and majestic creature."

Naguib listens to the wonderful way Sultan describes things. He understands why Sultan's young students are mesmerised when he speaks to them, or he tells them stories. Naguib asks.

"Did you see any troops?" Sultan takes a sip from the canteen.

"I did, for the first ten kilometres. The soldiers stay close to the borders of the city. I guess they won't be fighting over the desert unless they find oil. So far, it's been a quite journey, inshallah it will stay that way." As Sultan finishes his sentence, the truck slowly comes to a halt.

Tawfik and Ezzat walk to the back of the truck, and Tawfik smiles at his passengers.

"Let's stretch our legs. It's already been a long day." For the first time, Naguib and Sultan, see Ezzat. When they left at sunrise, they barely made out his features. In the daylight, they see a tall awkward looking boy. He is sixteen or seventeen, with a large face, and uncoordinated limbs. His hair is a mass of curls, a monobrow separates his forehead from the rest of his face, and the angle of his chin and jaw are so sharp, it resembles the edge of a knife. Then they see his eyes. They are almost feminine, with long lashes that any woman would be proud to own.

Ezzat speaks.

"We share the driving. I drive for three hours and then Abbi drives. Otherwise, it's very hard on the legs, or at least one leg." Tawfik smiles and then he speaks to Naguib and Sultan.

"Would you like to share some food with us? It's just dried meat and fruit, and some water?" Naguib and Sultan agree. As they eat, Tawfik asks.

"You're visiting family?" Naguib nods and Tawfik carries on.

"Where we're going there's only one town, and most people live out of town. There are many Bedouin tribes, and when you give them the family name, they'll be able to take you to your family. Be careful, there are many crooks in the desert, just as many as the city." Sultan asks.

"Is there someone we can trust to help us?" Tawfik swallows his food.

"Yes, my contact Sadiq is an honest man, and I'll introduce you to him. Pay him something, even a small amount just to show good will." Naguib asks.

"How much do you suggest?" Tawfik thinks about this.

"If you give him two week's wages, he'll be your guide and protector. But please don't give any more than that, otherwise it will cause me a problem in the future." Tawfik smiles and Naguib nods his agreement. Sultan asks.

"How many hours before we stop for the night?" Ezzat answers.

"We'll stop just before sunset. We try to get on solid ground, less sand, and more dirt. It's not wise to travel at night. The headlights from the truck can attract the wrong type of people."

Tawfik now looks at Naguib and Sultan.

"Ezzat speaks the truth. Bandits would love to get the things in this truck, and they'd have no problems killing us for it. Before we all go to sleep, I'll give you your gun. I have one piece of advice. If it comes to it, shoot first and ask questions later. Inshallah, it won't come to that."

Back in the truck, Sultan stares at Naguib and with astonishment, he speaks.

"I cannot believe Ezzat is Tawfik's son. They look like two completely different people. There are no similarities at all. You'd expect a father and son to share something." Naguib chuckles.

"He must take after his mother." Sultan grins.

"Yes, I guess he must. But whoever he takes after, he needs to grow into that face of his. Because right now, his face doesn't suit him." Naguib roars with laughter.

For the remainder of the journey Naguib and Sultan spend time staring out of the truck, napping or just deep in their own thoughts. Sultan asks.

"Could you live like a Bedouin?" Naguib thinks about this, and answers.

"I've always lived in the city, or at least very near to one. I don't know if I could live the way they do, but I can see the attraction of such a life. You know, the quiet and the solitude. Sometimes, when you live so close to each other, as we do in the city, you want some peace. No car horns, screaming children, or dogs barking. But I think it might drive me mad, to live with so much quietness, and no one else around. Also, it seems so impractical. What if you needed to borrow a cup of sugar?"

Sultan bursts out laughing, and after thirty seconds, he stops. With a grin, he asks.

"A cup of sugar! Naguib, is that your biggest headache?

Naguib smiles.

"Well, there are many things, not just sugar. Look at all the things in this truck. Out here, they can't get anything. Of course, it's impractical to live like that."

Once the humour subsides, Sultan speaks.

"I agree with you. But using a cup of sugar as an example was very funny. The other thing that could drive you mad, is the endless kilometres of sand. You look at the horizon there's sand. Then you get beyond the horizon, and there's more sand. And the quietness makes you think, this place is haunted."

Naguib smiles.

"Yes, but there's also the continuous heat, it's inescapable. In the city, you can stay out of the heat and Sun, but here it's everywhere. You can't get away from it." Sultan asks.

"Have you ever imagined what it must be like to walk on snow?" Naguib remembers Anwar's letters.

"I've never imagined it, but Anwar described it to me. It sounds as hellish as being stuck in the heat. I think for humans there's a perfect temperature. For me, it's during November and December. I love that time of the year."

The men carry on chatting, and every now and again Sultan puts the binoculars to his eyes. But within seconds, he removes them, and announces in a sarcastic tone.

"It's just another shifting sand dune, nothing else."

During a period of silence, Naguib feels the weariness return and he drifts off again. Sultan keeps staring through the binoculars, and then he sees something that startles him. He gets on his knees, and he cranes his head towards the sky. He gasps, and then he shakes Naguib. Naguib panics and exclaims.

"What is it?" Sultan removes the binoculars and hands them to Naguib.

"Look at the sky, to the right. The eagle, it's back."

Naguib holds the binoculars to his eyes, and as he focuses, he sees it swoop, turn, and head towards him. Even from a distance, the wings look wide and powerful. He's sure he can see the eagle's eyes glint. And as he stares, the bird flies away. Naguib removes the binoculars.

"That's magnificent! I've never seen such a thing, what a beautiful creature." Sultan's eyes widen.

"I told you. Did you know that some of them have a two-metre wingspan? That's taller than any man I've ever met." Naguib is astonished.

"My God, a bird with wings taller than a man. If you ever came face to face with that bird, it would scare you to death." Sultan nods and carries on watching.

Just before sunset, the truck pulls off the road, and onto a flat piece of land. When Naguib and Sultan look at the ground, they see the bones of dead camels and other animals. The Sun has bleached the bones white, and the sand has smoothed them. Tawfik walks to the back of the truck.

"We'll camp here for the night." Sultan stares at the skeletons and exclaims.

"Here, in this animal graveyard! With all these dead creatures?" Tawfik answers.

"Yes here. It's the perfect spot, and a place very few will visit. Sultan, remember something, the dead can't harm us, but the living can."

That night as they lie-down, Sultan points to the sky and speaks.

"Can you see how clear the sky is, and how wonderful the stars look. They shine a lot brighter in the desert than they do in the city. I don't think I'll ever forget this vision. It's wonderful."

Naguib asks.

"How many stars do you think there are?" Sultan laughs.

"I don't know. I don't think we will ever know. But I'd say trillions, but it could be a lot more than that." Naguib asks.

"How is a star made?" Sultan wants to give him the astronomical answer, as he knows it, but decides to make up a story.

"Stars aren't made, they are born. Whenever someone on Earth dies, his or her soul is reborn as a star. You can call it, the natural order of things."

Naguib knows this isn't true. It sounds like something Sultan might tell the children, but he likes the answer, and he doesn't question it.

"Do you think my Rashida is a star?" Sultan smiles.

"Yes of course she is." He points to the sky.

"You see those two stars next to one another?" Naguib nods.

"One of them is Rashida and the other is my Rania. I think they're talking to one another, and their saying. Why are those two old fools sleeping in the desert?"

Both men laugh, but then they hear Tawfik.

"Quite please. Let's not attract unwanted guests."

On the second day, they stop five times. Twice to change drivers. But the other times, they wait for the radiator to cool down, and top it up with water. This cost them nearly three hours of driving, and Tawfik shakes his head with disappointment.

"We'll not arrive until midday tomorrow. I was hoping to arrive in the morning. I get most of my customers between sunrise and midday." Naguib asks.

"Will you be able to introduce us to Sadiq when we get there?" Tawfik nods.

"As soon as I see Sadiq, I'll make the introduction. Just one more thing, make sure you keep your belongings with you.

And make sure, you stay alert. Although we're all from the same country, the Bedouin people see us as outsiders."

On the second night, gusts of wind swirl the sand around them. Despite this, Naguib and Sultan fall into a deep sleep.

During the night, Naguib wakes up. He rubs his eyes, stares at the sky, and speaks to the two stars pointed out the night before.

"Rashida and Rania, if you can hear me, please look after us." Sultan hears Naguib, but he doesn't interrupt him. Instead, he repeats the words in a whisper, as if they're a prayer.

Chapter 39 - Bedouin

Naguib looks around at what he thinks, is a derelict and deserted village. Tawfik announces.

"This is the place, we made good time." Naguib is astonished, but his voice remains calm.

"This is the town? I can see twelve buildings, and some broken walls. Is this all there is?" Tawfik notices the disbelief in Naguib's voice, and answers.

"Yes, this is it. It's more of a depot for merchants. There's a market for traders like me, and there's a camel market that gathers once a month. The biggest building you see, the one with two floors, that's the mosque. From the outside, it doesn't look great, but go in and have a look. It's beautiful, like an oasis. The building nearest to the mosque is a school, and the other is a clinic, but they deal with minor problems. If you get a serious illness, you have to travel to a city. The building about fifty metres from where we're standing, is a café, and they have one or two rooms for hire. The rest of the buildings are for storage. But on market days, this place is heaving with people."

To Naguib, the place looks abandoned, and the buildings look beaten up by the weather. Many look fragile, as if a violent sandstorm could easily turn them into another sand dune.

Ezzat has moved the truck to a building with a canvas awning. From this position, they'll sell their goods. Ezzat walks back to the others.

"Why don't we go to the café, the tea is very good." Sultan is delighted.

"Let's go, I haven't had a cup of tea since we left the city."

When the waiter at the café comes to take their orders, Tawfik greets him.

"As-salaam-alaikum Tameer, it's good to see you. We'll have tea, and whatever food you have. Enough for four people. Also, have you seen Sadiq?"

Tameer returns the greeting, and replies.

"Sadiq is due back in a few hours. He was here this morning, and I'm expecting him back, just before sunset." Tawfik thanks Tameer and turns to the others.

"It's a shame I missed Sadiq this morning, he would've sent messages to the Bedouins. And I would've had my first customers today. Well, you can't rush in this place. We might as well enjoy the afternoon. Let's eat, drink and get some rest." Sultan asks.

"The rooms you mentioned, can we ask about it? I would like to lie on some kind of mattress. The desert floor isn't bad, but the cold creeps into my bones." Tawfik laughs.

"Yes, spending nights in the desert is hard. I have a thermometer in the cabin of my truck. I bought it in a souvenir shop. The daytime temperature has been around forty-three Celsius, but at night, it drops to about five." Naguib pats Tawfik's back.

"Sometimes, not knowing is better. You should've waited until we got back to the city before telling us." They all laugh.

As they sip the tea, Naguib and Sultan notice the mint flavours, and it has a refreshing quality. Even after one cup, the dryness in Naguib's mouth is gone. Then Tameer brings out farrasheeh bread, and a stew made with goat's meat. After the dried meat and fruit, Sultan is overjoyed.

"It's worth doing this journey just for this meal. My God, this is delicious." The men tuck into the food and Tameer brings out more tea. Naguib turns to Tameer.

"Tameer, I was told that you have some rooms we can use?" Tameer answers.

"Yes, I have two rooms and they're both available. Will you need both rooms?" Naguib looks at Sultan, and Sultan answers.

"No, we can share a room, leave the other for Tawfik and Ezzat." Tawfik grins.

"We usually sleep near the truck, so that things don't get stolen. Please don't worry about us." Sultan is satisfied.

"All the same, we'll share a room, if that's alright?" Tameer agrees.

"Of course, I'll get the rooms ready."

The room is in a small box shaped structure, with a narrow door, and two small windows. It resembles a house a child might draw. Inside, there are two thin mattresses on the floor, a chair, and a small table, with a pitcher and a bowl to wash in. And hanging from the ceiling, is a kerosene lamp. Naguib turns to Sultan.

"Well, what do you think?" Sultan raises his eyebrows.

"It's basic, but after two nights on the desert floor, this is a palace." Naguib agrees.

They put their belongings in the room, lock the door and head back to the café. As they drink more tea, Naguib and Sultan stare at the setting sun. In the amber glow, the sand dunes silhouette the landscape. In the distance, they see a lone camel and its rider disappear over the horizon. Then the night sky begins its star show, and with the fading light, the show becomes more spectacular. As he stares at the sky, Hussein speaks.

"Did you know, there're people who believe God is an architect, and he designed everything?" Naguib knows what an architect is. Since Anwar wanted to study architecture when he was a boy.

"But an architect builds buildings, and buildings have straight edges. The sky has no straight edges." Sultan nods.

"Yes, you're right, and in nature you'll never find a straight edge. A tree and its leaves, a river, a camel, leopard's spots, humans, and all the other animals, nothing has a straight edge. Nothing is the same, but we still believe God makes us. I believe that man is the only creature, who creates straight lines. Personally, I think straight lines and walls, keep humans from thinking outside of those borders. But the few who escape this thinking, are labelled mad."

While amazed by Sultan's knowledge, Naguib's thoughts are far simpler. He isn't aware of what others believe, but he did believe, that most people have the same needs. All Naguib can do is agree.

"Perhaps you're right, but right now I'm wondering if Sadiq will arrive tonight." Sultan is about to respond when they hear a deep voice from behind them.

"I am Sadiq, as-salaam-alaikum."

Chapter 40 - Camel

Naguib and Sultan jump out of their chairs, and spin round. Standing in front of them is a Nubian dressed head to foot in black. His face shines, but until he comes into the light, they cannot make out his features. He is as black as the night.

The two men stare, and Naguib answers.

"Wa-alaikum-salaam Sadiq, please sit with us." With an even pace, Sadiq walks to the other table and picks up a chair. His every move is elegant, and he doesn't waste an ounce of energy. Once he sits near the lamp light, they see his face. It is strong and broad, and there are wisps of grey hair knitted to his eyebrows. It's the only sign of age. His eyes are black, and when he stares at Naguib and Sultan, they have a feeling, he's searching their souls.

"Tawfik told me, you want to find a member of your family." Naguib answers.

"Yes and no. I'm looking for an old friend, who I consider as family, but we're not blood relations. His name is Hassam Elneny, and his brother is Ismail Elneny. Ismail, has lived in this area for most of his adult life."

Sadiq sits motionless, and the only movement he makes, is to bring the cup of tea to his lips. Then he responds.

"I know the man you speak of. I know Ismail. He's a good man, and someone I've done business with." Sultan asks.

"What kind of business?" Sadiq stares.

"Buying and selling of livestock, legitimate business. We're not all bandits." Sultan realises that he might have offended Sadiq, with the directness of his question.

"Sadiq, I meant no offence. In the city, the term I've done some business, conjures up all sorts of thoughts. I wasn't questioning you. Please forgive me if I have offended you." For the first time Sadiq smiles and he answers.

"No offence taken. I have one question. Have you two ever ridden a camel?" Naguib asks.

"No, but why is that important?" Sadiq gives them an even broader smile.

"This isn't the city. You can't get a taxi or a bus. Ismail Elneny lives a Bedouin life. He lives in the desert, and the only way to reach him is by camel. It's a day's ride." Naguib scratches his chin.

"No, we haven't ridden a camel. Can you teach us?" Sadiq nods.

"Yes, I'll do my best. I will teach enough for the journey, and some things, you'll learn along the way. I can get two decent camels, and I have my own. Do you have money?" Naguib pulls out the money he's set aside for Sadiq.

"This is for you, and for your help. Let me know what else you need for the camels." Without taking his eyes off Naguib, Sadiq takes the money and speaks.

"This is enough. I don't need any more. But I'd ask you to take a gun with you." Sadiq parts his robe to reveal a traditional Bedouin dagger, a shibriya, not a curved dagger, but one with a straight blade. And on the other side, there's a revolver. He draws the robe together and continues to drink his tea.

Sultan wants to know more about their guide and asks.

"Sadiq we would be honoured if you would eat with us?" Sadiq accepts, and while they eat, Sultan asks.

"Where are you from Sadiq? I mean, where's your family from. Mother and father, and what are your roots?"

Sadiq's eyes soften, and he reveals a smile with so much warmth and grace, Sultan is sure, he's in the presence of an old Nubian King.

"Sultan, this is what I know. My great grandfather was brought to this land as a slave from Sudan. He married my great grandmother, who was also a Sudanese slave. He worked for a Bedouin sheik, and by the time my grandfather was born, slavery was abolished. And my grandfather, was born a free man. The sheik my grandfather worked for, lost all his sons in a war. Heartbroken, he took my grandfather as his son, and he gave him what I now own." Sultan smiles and asks.

"And your father, he married a Sudanese woman? He didn't want an Arab wife?" Sadiq purses his lips and looks into Sultan's eyes.

"Yes, and I also married a Sudanese woman. Slavery was abolished long before I was born, but people still see us as slaves. It is better for us to stay with our own people. Sultan, the culture of slavery created a need to dominate others, seen as inferior. This has existed in our country long before the current president, so don't be surprised by the president's actions. I think the way my people are viewed, will continue to exist, and it might take an act of God, to change people's thinking."

Sultan realises, Sadiq has incredible knowledge and wisdom. If ever a royal and wise lineage existed, it existed in the man who sits in front of him. Sultan gives Sadiq a little bow.

"Inshallah, people will change. Inshallah, we will see people as neither inferior nor superior, but as equals." Sadiq gives a graceful nod, and in that moment, he is their friend.

Naguib sees, Sadiq is an honest man, and a man he can trust. But he's worried about riding a camel, and with hesitation, he asks.

"So, can you give us riding lessons tomorrow?" Sadiq laughs.

"Yes I can, but please don't be offended if the locals gather to watch. Watching grown men, who have never been on a camel, will be entertainment for them. Don't get upset. Please take it with good grace."

The following morning, they wake at sunrise. They have breakfast at the café, and while they drink tea, Sadiq arrives with two camels. Naguib and Sultan have seen many camels, but they have never mounted one. Sultan looks up at the camels' face and asks.

"Sadiq, are these giant camels? They seem a lot bigger than the ones I've seen before." While Sadiq and the locals laugh, Naguib becomes anxious, and he hopes, he won't make a fool of himself.

Sadiq approaches the seated camels with confidence. Then he faces Naguib and Sultan, and he gives them instructions.

"The first thing you must remember is. Stay calm and loose. A camel will feel your tension, and this can distress the camel. When a camel becomes tense, they're unpredictable. Remember, camels are very calm by nature. Always approach a camel from the side, and when you get close, talk to it. Talk in a gentle voice, but not with fear. Now, I will mount the seated camel, and while I do this, I'll give more instructions. Listen."

Sadiq speaks to the camel. "Relax, that's it, relax."

As he mounts the camel, he looks at Naguib and Sultan, and he carries on with the lesson.

"Throw your leg over the middle of the hump, and in a quick and even movement, mount the camel. Don't make erratic or rough movements, just a simple smooth mount. Lean backwards as the camel starts to rise, and then lean forward when it starts to stand on its front legs. Adjust your weight to help the camel. Once the camel knows you're being kind, it will be kind to you. Hold the reins tight, but don't pull hard, and don't kick the camel. If you can do this, the rest is easy."

Sultan stares at Naguib and whispers.

"It's much easier in theory. I never thought I had a bad memory, but I can't remember anything Sadiq said." Sadiq dismounts the camel and repeats his instructions, but this time he looks at both men in turn.

Naguib offers to go first, but his first attempt isn't successful. He forgets to lean forward when the camel gets onto its front legs. And with the change in direction, he falls off the camel. As he lands on the soft sand, he hears laughter. He stands up and walks back to the camel. Sadiq smiles.

"Naguib, you made one simple mistake. Remember to lean forward when the camel gets onto its front legs."

Naguib dusts himself down and tries again, and this time he gets it right. As much as the crowd laughed, they now cheer. Sadiq gives further instructions.

"It will be more comfortable if you cross your legs. It will spread your weight more evenly on the camel. This isn't a horse. You'll have to adjust to the camel. The camel won't adjust to you. They'll also follow my camel, so don't worry about controlling it. Relax and breathe as I lead the camel."

Naguib forces himself to calm down. He takes deep breaths through his nose, and exhales from his mouth. While he does this, Sadiq leads the camel and Naguib starts to enjoy the ride.

Sultan learns from Naguib's mistake, and successfully mounts the camel on his first attempt. Two young boys lead the camels out, and for half an hour Naguib and Sultan ride along the nearest dunes. They are ready.

Within two hours of their lessons, the three men set out across the desert. Sadiq leads and they follow. They know they will ride for at least eight hours, and they will do the entire journey in one go. They will only stop for a call of nature. Otherwise, they will eat and drink while riding.

As he rides through the desert, Naguib marvels at the peacefulness. Sometimes the sand cascades away, under the weight of the camel and its rider. He notices, the sand has an almost liquid appearance, in how it moves and shifts.

He's astonished at the sheer scale of some of the tallest dunes. There are many, which are taller than any building he has ever seen. It's a mountainous scene, but here, the mountains are on the move. Every now and again, he sees sand rats burrowing to get out of the sun. The sun shines bright, and the heat is fierce. Naguib pulls his scarf around his face, and only his eyes are visible.

It's a hard and exhausting ride, and when they stop, and dismount. Sultan complains.

"I don't think I can feel my legs anymore. My God, to think we have to do that journey again."

After dismounting, Sadiq walks over to them.

"Considering this is your first camel ride, you did well. We'll walk the rest of the way. It's about a kilometre, and it will give you a chance to get the strength back in your legs."

The men take the opportunity to relieve themselves, and then they start the final part of their journey.

In the distance, Naguib makes out the camp. He can see a large square tent, but on either side, there are smaller ones.

This is a far cry from the city, but Naguib knows why he is there. He has to get answers.

Chapter 41 - Reunion

When they're within twenty metres of the large square tent, around ten children come running out to greet them. They leap for joy when they see Sadiq, and they run towards him.

"Salaam Uncle Sadiq!" They surround him, and a little girl of five or six grabs his hand, and she walks with him.

The first person Naguib recognises is Ismail, and the vision hits him like a bolt of lightning. Ismail left the city when he married his Bedouin bride Mervat. Naguib walks briskly towards Ismail.

The two men embrace, and when they pull away, Naguib stares into Ismail's eyes.

"This is beyond my wildest dreams. I hoped to see you, but I never thought I would."

Ismail wipes away a tear.

"Naguib, there were many days I thought about the times we were children. I wanted to go back to the city, just to visit, and to see the old life. But there's always something to do. Children, work, life, and before you know it, it's been forty years." Naguib gives Ismail a tearful smile.

"Yes, time goes very quickly. It only seems like yesterday that I was looking at the raven-haired man wearing a western suit. I always wished I could be like you."

Naguib introduces Sultan, and immediately Ismail's face breaks into a smile.

"Sultan! Oh my God, I remember you! Always with your head in a book. Why are you here."

Sultan hugs Ismail and answers.

"I came along to make sure Naguib keeps out of trouble, and to protect him." The three men laugh.

Naguib asks.

"I have to speak to Hassam and Samir, are they here?"

There is sadness in Ismail's eyes.

"Yes, but you may not recognise Hassam. First, get washed, my grandson Bassem, will show you where you can wash. I'll have Hassam and Samir brought to my tent. They live in another tent. Bassem will bring you back."

On hearing the warning about Hassam, the hairs on the back of Naguib's neck stand up. After washing and cooling down, Naguib, Sultan and Sadiq follow Bassem.

Inside the main tent, there's a large square space. Sultan stares at the luxurious and colourful rugs, which cover this space. Surrounding the rugs there is seating, and Ismail sits at the centre of the tent. Sitting, or rather slumped next to him in a wheelchair is Hassam. Chills run down Naguib's entire body, and he forces his legs forward.

When Hassam sees Naguib, he smiles, but only with the left side of his face. A familiar voice speaks from behind a curtain. It is Samir.

"He recognises you." With these words, she breaks down in floods of tears, and Mervat comforts her. Nervously, Naguib asks.

"What's happened to him?" Sultan knows the answer.

"Hassam has had a stroke. It's a sudden interruption in the blood supply to the brain. He's lucky to be alive." Ismail nods.

"We got him to a doctor, and he said the same thing. He also said, as long as he didn't have another stroke his condition wouldn't get worse, but it won't get better. With support, he can walk, but it's a struggle, since only one side of his body works. My brother was never a small man, but it takes some strength to support his weight. Tawfik the trader got this chair from the city hospital. It stops Hassam from being bed ridden, but beyond the camp, and on the sand, it doesn't work."

Naguib asks.

"Can he talk?" Hassam answers.

"Yes…a little." Like a drunk man, Hassam's words slur. Naguib falls to his knees in front of Hassam, and he holds both

214

his hands. He feels the powerful grip from his friend's left hand. Naguib looks into his eyes.

"My old friend, what's happened to you?" Hassam smiles and keeps squeezing Naguib's hand, and he sheds a silent tear. Naguib gently wipes the tear away, but in that moment, his heart breaks.

As they eat, Naguib watches Samir feed Hassam. He realises, this has aged her as well. When she left the city, she was a healthy woman in her early fifties. But looking at her now, he would swear, she looks like a woman of seventy. Although she wears a headscarf, he can see a few strands of hair, and they're as white as milk.

After the meal, Ismail asks.

"So, what brings you all the way out here?" Naguib hasn't forgotten why he travelled this far, but with what he'd seen, his immediate thoughts were for Hassam..

"I have some news about Abdel." Samir's head whips in Naguib's direction, and Hassam exclaims.

"Abdel, where is he?" Naguib smiles.

"Abdel is in America, and he's married. He married Shadia, my daughter in laws sister." Ismail claps his hands.

"Naguib! That makes us family now! We will show you how Bedouins celebrate such an occasion." Still staring at Hassam, Naguib speaks.

"I have some photos in my bag, and two letters from Abdel." Samir is frantic.

"Naguib, please show me!"

Naguib pulls out the photos and hands them to Samir. Hassam and Samir pour over the images and weep. With his voice shaking, Hassam asks.

"We keep these photos?" Naguib answers.

"Yes, they are yours." During the meal, Hassam, and Samir stare with loving eyes at the images of their son, and his bride.

Later that evening Naguib, Hassam, Sultan, Ismail, and Sadiq sit outside by the campfire. The men drink tea and watch the night sky. While there's silence, Hassam speaks.

"Good to see you Naguib." He pauses for breath, and summoning all his strength, he carries on.

"I tried to escape jail, but I'm in prison. There's always justice."

The men remain silent and Naguib reaches for Hassam's hand. While the two friends sit holding hands, Hassam remembers the days when they were young. When they were healthy, and when they thought, old age or sickness, would never catch them.

With the news of Abdel, Hassam is determined not to let his condition defeat him. His willpower is strong, and there's a visible change. Each day Hassam becomes a little bit stronger.

During the day, the men sit in the tent and talk. Samir joins them when she finishes her chores, and it's during this time, Naguib asks.

"Why didn't you write to Abdel?" Samir answers.

"We wanted to. Every day we wanted to, but we didn't want to say, Hassam was ill. We know our son, and we know, he would've come back from America. And we didn't want that." Naguib nods.

"I understand, but I think we should send him some news. Perhaps, you wouldn't mind if we took some photos of this place. Of you and Hassam, of Ismail and Mervat, and the children. Let's show Abdel and his wife, that you're living well. We can say, it was impossible to get a letter to them." Sadiq offers help.

"I go freely across the border, and I have many contacts. I'll ensure delivery of the letter. If you put this address on the letter, I'll also make sure the replies get back to you. As for Hassam's health, I would say. Water down the truth, so Abdel doesn't worry." Sultan adds.

"And I'll take photos of Hassam's left side only. Samir stand near him on the right, so that it casts a shadow on his face. Abdel will be happy to see this."

In this way, they take photos, and somehow Sultan turns into the great photographer.

"No, that smile looks unnatural. Why are you screwing up your face? It looks like you've tasted something bad! Be more natural, soften your face, and smile." Even Hassam finds these instructions funny, and whispers to Naguib.

"How many faces does one person have?" Naguib laughs.

To his disappointment, Sultan uses the whole reel of film, and asks.

"Naguib, do you think someone at the camp has any film?" Naguib stares at Sultan in disbelief.

"Film, are you mad? This may be the first time they've seen a camera. Camel shit, yes, plenty of that. As for film, I don't think you'll find that here." Sultan laughs.

"I hope these photos come out well. I want to see them, but I know we'll have to wait until we get back to the city."

Sultan helps to write the letter. It's a long letter, and he writes ten pages. It gives details of Hassam and Samir's journey out of the city, and of their new lives as Bedouins. And on each page, there's something, which tells Abdel how much they miss and love all their children. Finally, they promise to write again and to send photos.

When the letter reaches Abdel, it frees his heart of anxiety, and it allows him, to get on with his life.

In the four days that Naguib and Sultan stay at the camp, Hassam's mind and body finds new strength.

Sultan and Sadiq become lifelong friends, and for the remainder of their lives they write to one another, as often as they can. Sultan always starts his letters with, "My Dear Sudanese Sheik." Being alone and without family, Sultan visits Sadiq at least once a year, either during the festival of Eid al-Fitr, or Eid al-Adha, and he stays for a month. The two men ride for days to visit Hassam, and others that Sadiq knows. Sultan does this for many years, until he's unable to travel the distance. But by then, he has an adopted family of his own.

On the sunrise of the fourth day, Naguib sits with Hassam, and Hassam asks.

"Pass me that stick." Naguib picks up the long shepherds' crook and hands it to Hassam. Hassam then asks.

"Help me up and let us walk."

Naguib's eyes bulge with fear. He wraps his arms around Hassam's waist. Slowly and with all his strength Naguib hauls Hassam out of the chair. Hassam grips the stick with his good hand, while Naguib supports the right side of his body. Everyone at the camp, including Samir watches.

Samir's eyes stream with tears at what she is witnessing, and she tells herself. "I am going to get my husband back."

At first, Hassam and Naguib take small tentative steps, but then they look like two friends with their arms around one another. And slowly, it looks like, they're taking a stroll. Hassam turns his face to Naguib.

"Thank you for setting me free. We are family, but we have always been family." Naguib doesn't take his eyes off Hassam and answers.

"Brother, we build our own prisons, and we have everything we need to set ourselves free. You have set yourself free. All I did was to help you out of that chair."

Hassam laughs, and it's the most heart-warming sound. It's a roar, and it resonates and bounces off the rocks, until everyone at the camp hears him. Out of sheer joy, all the people start to make the shrill howling scream of ululation, and it echoes across the desert. For the Bedouin, they've just witnessed a miracle.

In the years that follow, Hassam learns to walk again, and with Sultan's advice, he changes his diet. He eats mostly fruit and vegetables, and occasionally he eats meat. His body becomes leaner, and he can support his own weight.

Samir often sits and watches her husband walking with the children at the camp. It's a lopsided walk, but still, it's a walk. Some days she walks with him, and although public shows of affection between men and women is frowned upon, they're forgiven. And they walk, with their arms around one another.

In the back of a tent used for storage, sits an old wheelchair. It gathers dust and eventually, cobwebs cover it. This man-made device with its straight edges, which can only travel over smooth ground, is no longer able to confine Hassam. He is more than the wheelchairs limited capabilities. And now, he is free, to see beyond the horizon.

Chapter 42 - Return

The return journey is much smoother, since Tawfik has taken the time to fix the trucks radiator. Also, the truck is empty, and this allows Naguib and Sultan to stretch out.

On the second night in the desert, Naguib sits bolt upright. The sudden movement wakes Sultan, and with fear in his eyes, he whispers.

"What is it? Is it bandits?" Naguib rests his hand on Sultan's shoulder.

"No, I had a dream. It was so real, it shocked me." Sultan sighs with relief.

"A dream? My God Naguib, I nearly pissed myself." After rubbing his sleepy eyes, Sultan asks.

"What was this dream?" Naguib hesitates, and Sultan moans.

"For God's sake, I'm awake now. Just tell me." After some hesitation, Naguib speaks.

"In my dream, I was kissing a woman." Sultan yawns, and after wrapping the blanket around himself, he asks.

"What woman?" Naguib answers.

"It was Zeina." Sultan turns and faces Naguib.

"Even you know what that means. You're in love with her, and I hope for your sake, she's in love with you." With these words, Sultan shuts his eyes and goes back to sleep.

Naguib looks up at the stars. He sees the two stars next to each other. As he stares at them, one shines brighter than before. He doesn't know what it means, and he keeps staring until exhaustion overtakes him, and he falls asleep.

They arrive back in the city, early on the third day. They've been away for twelve days in total, and as they enter the square. They see and hear, the hustle and bustle of a working metropolis.

Sultan and Naguib walk to the newspaper seller, and they read the headlines.

"The ceasefire is to be extended so that power sharing negotiations can continue. The President and the leader of the Freedom Fighters are said to be making good progress."

Below the headlines is a photo of Henry Adelstein. He has his arms around the shoulder of the president, and the head of the freedom fighters. But both men stand as stiff as a waxwork. Seeing the photo, Sultan's eyes widen.

"Inshallah they'll make some progress. But looking at this photo, they look like two sulking brothers caught red handed, and neither one will admit that they broke a precious ornament." Naguib laughs.

"Perhaps you're right. Let's go to the photography shop on our way home. I'd like to see your photos, rather than these bloody crooks."

After the solitude of the desert, the noise and smell of the city assaults the two men's senses. As they walk, Naguib sniffs the air, and he speaks.

"This city smells sick." Sultan nods.

"Yes it does. After the clean air in the desert, it makes you wonder how we survive in this place."

They drop the film at the shop, and then turn for home. At Naguib's front door, Sultan speaks.

"Shukraan Naguib. As much as you needed to take this journey, so did I. It has helped me more than you can imagine. It has made me love my country again. I think you have affairs of the heart to attend to. Good luck my friend." Sultan gives a boyish grin, and the men embrace.

When Naguib enters the house, the children are the first to see him. With uncontained excitement, they run into his arms. Hanan clings to him and Gamal holds his hand and shouts.

"Ummi, Uncle Naguib is home!" Zeina scurries from her bedroom, and on seeing Naguib, she flashes a radiant smile, and then breaks down in tears. Hanan leaps from Naguib's arms and runs to her mother.

"Ummi Uncle Naguib is not sick, he's alright, please don't cry."

Zeina holds onto Hanan for comfort. Naguib walks over to Zeina and lifts her chin. With gentleness, he rests his open hand on her cheek. Zeina places her hand on his, and she looks into his eyes.

That evening, there's a celebration on the roof. Sultan is in a jubilant mood. He tells them of what they've seen, the eagle, the camels, and how the Bedouins live. Then he tells them about the single most beautiful thing he's ever seen.

"And if you think the stars look good from this roof top. Then you should see them under the desert sky. It will take your breath away." Yousra asks.

"How was Hassam? That was the purpose of your visit." Naguib answers.

"He's been very ill. He suffered a stroke and wasn't in a good way. The stroke left the right side of his body paralysed. The photos of Abdel and his bride did a lot to heal him, and by the time we left, he was twice as strong as when we first got there."

Naguib doesn't mention that he played a big part in his friend's recovery, but then he isn't aware, that he had. Yousra asks.

"Are you satisfied, and has your restless thoughts left you?" Naguib answers.

"I was never restless. For me it was more of a duty. I had to do this for Abdel. Abdel never asked anything of me, but he did a lot for my family, I couldn't see him suffer. In showing Hassam pictures of his son, I am sure it gave him a reason to get stronger. Just knowing that things could get better has helped me." Yousra adds.

"Inshallah." In unison, all of them repeat the word.

Once they're home, Zeina offers to make tea. Naguib agrees, and the two of them sit on the veranda. For the first five minutes, they don't say a word. Zeina fears the worst, but then Naguib opens his mouth.

"Zeina, I want to say I do have feelings for you. We've lived in the same house for nearly three years. I know that we're considerate and respectful, and that's a good thing. There are many reasons, why I tried to avoid this subject, but I feel you need to know what they are. First, and the most important thing for me is. I did love my wife, and I loved her with all my heart. I'm sorry for saying this, but a part of me will always love her. But if this journey showed me one thing, it was, time passes very quickly. And before you know it, we've spent many years just looking back, and not looking forward. In the desert your face came to me in a dream, and I realised, you were a part of my future. But only if you want that."

Zeina gently touches Naguib's arm. He acknowledges her touch. To him, it signifies her willingness to be a part of his life. He smiles and carries on.

"There's also my age. I am almost twenty years older than you. But then I thought, so was Khaled, and that wasn't a problem. I may live another twenty years, or if I'm lucky, another thirty. Only Allah knows the answer to that. I'm not as worried about the end, as I am about the life in between. My health and my ability to be a husband will diminish. After seeing Hassam, this was clear. There's also the question of Gamal and Hanan. They know me as Uncle Naguib, and I don't want them to know me as anything else. I don't want them to take my name, and I want them to remember their father. The final thing. My own children. I need to let them know that we've had this conversation, and I need to be honest with them. I don't want them to think, I've betrayed their mother."

Zeina keeps her hand on Naguib's arm and then she asks.

"Naguib, how long has it been since Rashida passed?"

Naguib looks at Zeina's hand resting on his.

"It's been eight years."

Zeina looks into Naguib's eyes.

"You're a good man, and eight years is a long time to grieve. No one will think anything bad about you, not after all this time. Or is it because you don't like my cooking?"

Naguib laughs and Zeina smiles, but then her face becomes serious.

"Your last point was the most important one. You must write to Anwar and see how he feels. Gamal and Hanan will be fine, they're young, and they already see you as a big part of their lives, just as I do. But you must put your mind at rest, and you must ask your own children. Find out, what they think." Naguib asks.

"Are you scared of their answer?"

Zeina looks at Naguib.

"Yes, I am, because a lot depends on their answer, and I can see that. I'm hoping your children will feel as I feel. That everyone deserves happiness. They left this country, so they and their children can be happy. And I'm hoping they'll understand, their father deserves happiness as well."

Naguib sees something new in Zeina. He sees a woman with values and wisdom. He asks.

"Is there anything else?" Zeina answers.

"Yes there is. You've mentioned age, but you also remembered that Khaled was the same age as you. Understand something. I have suffered the death of my husband, as you've suffered the death of your wife, and my family shunned me when I married Khaled. Some things in life age us beyond our physical years. It's possible that I've caught up with you in age. If I was just looking for a husband, then I think you would have helped me to find one. I have money, and I think for many men, this would be an attractive proposal. I'm not looking for just any man. I'm looking at you Naguib. Because you're the right man."

At that moment, Naguib wants to kiss Zeina, but he doesn't, since he needs to hear from Anwar. However, he wants to show how he feels, and he takes Zeina's hand and gives it a gentle kiss.

While Zeina feels joy with the kiss, she's anxious about Anwar's response.

Naguib writes to Anwar. He talks about Hassam and Samir, about his journey with Sultan, and everyday life. Then he writes about Zeina. He explains how she came to stay with him after Khaled's death. Finally, he tells Anwar that he wants to marry Zeina. The letter allows him to cleanse his mind, but it also allows him to visualise a future, and he feels a sense of relief.

He stands outside the post office for over thirty minutes. He struggles to go in, and to send the letter. He knows, this is a pivotal moment.

At the counter, he speaks to the man serving him.

"Salaam, how quickly can this letter get to America, and can it be guaranteed?" The man answers.

"Salaam Sir, it's just a letter, nothing valuable?" Naguib answers.

"Yes, it's just a letter." The man weighs it and speaks.

"Standard first class will get there in two weeks. You're lucky, we couldn't give that kind of assurance a month ago. But since the talks, it should be alright."

Naguib hands over the money for postage, thanks the man and walks out.

A month passes and Naguib's mind is in turmoil, but then he thinks. *'You're being an idiot. It's only been four weeks.'*

Although he showed Zeina the letter, he now does everything he can to avoid her, until the answer comes. Zeina asks him.

"Naguib, have I done something wrong?" Naguib confesses.

"No, you haven't done anything wrong, but I'm nervous about the answer." Zeina asks.

"And if Anwar says no?" Naguib answers.

"Then we'll have to rethink what we do next. Maybe we run off together, and we live the life of a Bedouin." Zeina laughs.

"I'm not sure I want to do that. Walking to an oasis every day to get water, I prefer to use the tap." Naguib laughs.

On the eighth week after sending his letter, there is a knock at the door, and it's Nour.

"Salaam Naguib, a letter for you, and it's from America."
Naguib hesitates.

"Shukraan Nour. Sorry but I can't invite you in, I have to
go out." Nour smiles.

"It's alright, I'll call back later." Naguib shuts the door
and stands face to face with Zeina.

"I'll make tea and bring it out to the veranda. Would you
like some food?" Naguib shakes his head.

"No, just tea." Zeina's hand trembles as she pours the tea.
She forces herself to stop shaking just to avoid spilling the drink.

Naguib stares at Zeina and when she sits down, he starts
to read.

"Dear Abbi,

*I was overjoyed to receive your letter. I shared it with
Nassef, he's been visiting the U.S. on a conference from work,
and he was delighted at what we read.*

*Do you remember I once said? I am not an improvement
on you Abbi, and all that is good in me, came from you and
Ummi? That is still true.*

*When Nassef and I read about what you've been doing.
How you set aside your differences with Khaled, and sheltered
Zeina, Gamal and Hanan. We couldn't believe that this is our
father. I have to say, this is truly amazing. Maybe you see this in
a movie, but you never think, this person is your father.*

*I have not forgotten what you did for Mido, and now for
Abdel. I spoke to Abdel, and he was in tears when he got the
letter from Uncle Hassam and Aunty Samir. But they were tears
of joy and relief.*

*And of course, you should get married, you won't get any
objection from me and Nassef, all you will get is our prayers. See
the photos of Nassef and me. We are giving you the thumbs up.
This is an American tradition, and it means, satisfaction or
approval. Although you never need our approval.*

*Nawal is overjoyed, and the children are happy, and they
hope to see their new grandmother soon.*

226

I have put a hundred dollars in this letter. It will pay for some of the wedding.

Despite some levels of improvements to our country, there are many warnings about going back, even for a short visit. The government confiscate the passports of those who return, and one or two who sought asylum were imprisoned once their plane landed. I don't think the situation will improve anytime soon. It is unlikely that we will be able to attend your wedding. I will not lie to you, bringing you to America is still proving difficult. It's the same bureaucracy. It will prove even more difficult to bring Zeina and her children, but I won't give up.

As for us, we're all well. I am struggling to make sure the children speak Arabic at home. I use you as motivation and tell them. If you forget Arabic, how will you speak to Jadd and your new grandmother, and that seems to work.

I've put a few photos of the family, and a newspaper cutting about the asylum seekers who are now in jail.

Please send me photos of your wedding. We would all like to see them. Could you please ask if we can call Zeina, Zeina Ummi? If she objects, we'll find something else, but something respectful.

I'll write again soon. The children, Nawal, Abdel, Mido, Nassef and I send our love, and our eternal gratitude. Enjoy your wedding day and enjoy life. If anyone deserves to enjoy life, it's you Abbi.

Please tell me if you need anything, and, as always, I will do my best to get it to you.

Please pray for me as I will pray for you, inshallah I will see you soon.

Your loving sons

Anwar and Nassef

Naguib and Zeina sit in silence, and they take in the contents of the letter, and the enormous change this will make to their lives.

Naguib looks at Zeina, with tear-filled eyes. Zeina gets on her knees, and she holds his face in her hands.

"I will be a good wife." Naguib holds her face, and he speaks.

"And I will be a good husband."

With these words, Naguib kisses Zeina. Their love pours out, and during that kiss, their tears entwine, but they are tears of joy.

Chapter 43 - Joy

Naguib and Zeina dry their eyes, and stare at the photos. Zeina cannot contain her happiness.

"We have to tell Yousra, Hussein and Sultan." Naguib agrees.

"But don't say anything straight away. I have an idea. Let's take the letter, the photos and the newspaper clipping. Sultan will of course read the papers to us. Then we'll show the photos. Finally, I'll get Sultan to read the letter. It will be a surprise." Zeina giggles. It is something she hasn't done in a very long time.

She can see how serious Naguib can be, but this is the first time she sees his playful side.

That night after Sultan reads the article, the usual debate starts. Hussein leads.

"Still the politicians are talking, and now they're imprisoning people who come back to the country. That will make more people leave. For every good idea, they ruin it with ten shit ideas. And it's always the shit ideas that become law." Sultan is waiting for his chance.

"At least when they're talking, they're not fighting. Naguib what do you think?"

It's rare for Naguib to get involved in these conversations, since he enjoys listening, but tonight he is quieter than usual. He turns to Sultan and asks.

"Sultan, will you do something for me. Please read the letter from Anwar to everyone." Sultan asks.

"Are you sure?" Naguib nods and hands the letter to Sultan. Zeina moves closer to Yousra and links arms.

Sultan reads, paragraph one, two, three, four, and then paragraph five starts with.

"And of course, you should get married."

229

There's wide mouthed silence, and then Hussein shouts.

"What, get married? Who are you marrying?" Zeina squeezes Yousra's arm. Yousra turns to face Zeina, and when their eyes lock, Yousra gives Zeina a massive hug. Hussein is still waiting for an answer.

"Naguib, who are you marrying?" Yousra pulls away from Zeina, and she shouts.

"He's marrying the goat from down the road. If you were a detective, nothing would get solved. Who do you think?" For a few seconds Hussein remains puzzled, and then he sees the grin on Zeina's face.

"Zeina! Of course, who else could it be?" Yousra raises her eyes to the heavens and speaks.

"At last, yes of course Zeina." Hussein claps his hands with joy, and then does a little dance while waving his hands in the air.

Sultan walks over to Naguib.

"So, the dream came true?" Naguib smiles and answers.

"Yes, I think it did."

Yousra is in high spirits, and without letting go of Zeina's arm, she asks.

"Have you set a date?" Naguib stares at Yousra, and then switches his gaze to Zeina.

"We haven't set a date. Perhaps this is something you and Zeina can organise?" Yousra is ecstatic, and she gives a little scream.

"Yes, of course, that would be wonderful. Leave it to us, but you must speak to Imam Ali. I will do the rest." Sultan asks.

"Who are you inviting?" Naguib answers.

"All of us of course, Gamal and Hanan, Nour the postman and his wife, and anybody else you have in mind." In a sheepish voice, Sultan asks.

"Can I invite someone?" Naguib and all the others are amazed at this request. Naguib asks.

"Who would you like to invite?" With a shy voice, Sultan answers.

"I'd like to invite Sadiq. If you agree." Naguib smiles.

"Yes of course, but will he come?" Sultan answers.

"I'll write to him tonight. I will give it to Tawfik to deliver. I hope he'll come." Naguib squeezes Sultan's shoulder. Sultan is excited at the prospect of seeing Sadiq again, and he speaks with enthusiasm.

"All of you just wait until you meet him. He's a great man, and so dignified. I think you'll like him."

In the middle of the backslapping and congratulations, Zeina speaks.

"I'd like to invite my mother, father and sister, if I can." Naguib feels ashamed. He knows so little about Zeina's family, and yet she is going to be his wife.

"Of course, you must invite them. I'm sorry I didn't mention them." Zeina smiles and then turns back to Yousra. In the back of Naguib's mind another thought lurks. *'I hope they don't let her down.'*

That night when Gamal and Hanan are asleep, Zeina comes to Naguib. He holds her all night, and when they wake up, they're still holding each other.

After breakfast, Naguib decides to visit Imam Ali. On his way to the mosque, he stops at Rashida's grave, and he speaks to her.

"I'm guessing you know the news. If you're angry, please give me a sign. Let a bird shit on me, or I catch my toe on a loose paving stone." He pauses for a moment and with sadness, he speaks again.

"I hope I was a good husband, and I hope I was a good father." He pats Rashida's headstone and walks to the mosque.

Imam Ali is pleased to see Naguib, and even happier to hear the news.

"It would be an honour to marry you and Zeina." However, Imam Ali sees the confusion in Naguib.

"Naguib what's on your mind?" Naguib answers.

"On my way here, I stopped at Rashida's grave, and I spoke to her." He repeats his words. Imam Ali smiles.

"Naguib, you have nothing to fear, you haven't done anything wrong. You've lived your life well, you've honoured your wife, and you've taken care of all your duties."

Naguib then asks.

"And what about Zeina, and the rules for a woman?" Imam Ali thinks about the question, and then answers in a more serious tone.

"Today, I'll use my knowledge of the Qur'an. And in it, there is the Iddat period. This is four months and ten days, and a woman must wait until this period is over, before she marries again. If the woman is pregnant during this period, she must wait until the child is born. Zeina has been a widow for over three years, and you my friend, lost Rashida more than eight years ago. In the eyes of Allah, neither of you have broken any rules." Naguib looks at Imam Ali.

"I understood that during this period, the woman must not leave her house, but Zeina did." Imam Ali is a little annoyed when he answers.

"The worst kind of religion is when people decide for themselves, what's good and what's bad, and how rules should be applied. But you're right. However, there are conditions to this. If the woman is in danger, then she can spend the Iddat period somewhere else. Zeina was in danger, and as far as anyone knows, the danger may still be there. Khaled's old enemies may still hold a grudge."

Naguib is satisfied with this answer, but he still has a question.

"Despite this, there's still a part of me that feels guilt. Why?" Imam Ali reaches for Naguib's hand, and smiles.

"That part of you is your own goodness. But ask yourself one question. If Rashida outlived you, and you died when she was young enough to remarry, would you have objected?"

Naguib thinks about this and answers.

"No." Imam Ali looks at Naguib.

"Then she wouldn't object either. When two people are in love, they often become the same in their thinking. If you agree that Rashida should remarry, then her answer to you is. You

232

should also remarry." Naguib gives Imam Ali a sad smile, wipes his mouth, and answers.

"Shukraan." Imam Ali then becomes business-like.

"Just one small thing, I need the wedding dates as soon as you have them. You know my diary is full. I'm a very popular man."

Naguib laughs and as he walks home, he thinks. *'An Imam with a sense of humour. I wasn't expecting that.'*

Chapter 44 - Parents

Zeina is dreading seeing her parents. As much as she loves them, they didn't stand by her when she needed them. She speaks to Yousra.

"Should I go and see my parents?" It's a tough question, and Yousra reveals something of herself.

"What I'm about to tell you, is only known to Hussein and my sons. I am an orphan, and my parents died when I was a baby. In this country, people don't want female orphans. Everyone wants a boy. I had no choice when it came to parents, but you do. But there's another choice, and it's happiness. If your parents have caused you so much pain, then the simple answer is. You're better off without them." Zeina's mouth gapes open in wonder.

"Yousra, I had no idea you were adopted. I know we've never talked about parents, but for me, it was a painful subject." Yousra smiles.

"I've never known anything different. I don't know what it feels like to have parents. In many ways, when Hussein married me against his parents' wishes, it was the first time I knew love. Hussein had to teach me, how to love. When my children were born, I knew I could love. Good parents, and I hope I've been one, never give up on their children."

Zeina sits a little closer to Yousra and holds her hand.

"We will be sisters." Yousra squeezes Zeina's hand.

"Then I'll be the older, short, fat, ugly one." Zeina gasps, and when Yousra laughs, Zeina speaks.

"You're none of those things. You're the beautiful one." Yousra pushes Zeina and laughs.

"I was a beauty once, but after giving birth to five boys, my hips, and other things just do what they want. I no longer have any control over them." They both laugh and Yousra goes to a drawer and pulls out a photo album.

Zeina is astonished when she sees pictures of a young Yousra.

"My God you are beautiful." Yousra touches the photo.

"Hussein is a good man, and his love made me beautiful."

The two women stare at the photo. It is of Yousra and Hussein, and they are no more than twenty-one. The way Hussein has his arms around Yousra is daring for its time, but it shows how much he loves her.

Yousra snaps herself out of her daydream and speaks.

"Now, if you ask me, which you have. I'd say there's no need to involve your parent's. Have they ever seen their grandchildren?" Zeina stares at her hands.

"No. I took them when they were babies, and they wouldn't even come to the door." Yousra is livid, and she spits out her anger.

"They don't deserve you. They don't deserve any invitation, other than to their own funerals. If you invite them, I'll be mad with you. As for your sister, invite her, but if she's made of the same stuff as your parents, I wouldn't bother."

That makes up Zeina's mind, and then she says.

"But that will mean I'll have no one from my side of the family." Yousra looks amazed.

"Naguib hasn't got a bus load of people from his side. He doesn't have anyone. Think about it, you have Gamal and Hanan, and you said five minutes ago, that we're sisters. So, you have a lot more coming from your side than Naguib." Zeina starts to laugh.

"You always talk sense. Thank you Yousra." Yousra feigns exasperation.

"With five sons, and a husband who would say, that the murder victim was poisoned, when he has a knife sticking out of him. I need to talk sense." Zeina laughs until tears stream down her face.

Later that evening Zeina waits until the children are in bed, and then she speaks to Naguib, about her conversation with Yousra.

Naguib responds with caution.

235

"I'll only use these words once. When we're married, I won't say this again. Unless I have to." Zeina waits and then she laughs.

"Naguib, sometimes your answers are long, when they could be short, and they're short, when they should be long. Are you going to finish your sentence?" Naguib laughs.

"What I was going to say was. When you get to my age, you sometimes don't give a damn about those, who don't give a damn about you. I agree with Yousra, but these are your parents. I cannot criticise them, and many might say, we're going against tradition. What I can say is. You would have to shoot me first, before I treated my children, or grandchildren like that. Unthinkable."

Any shred of doubt now leaves Zeina. It's true that in some respects, they're going against tradition, but her parents didn't give their blessing to her first wedding, and they had never seen their grandchildren. Zeina decides her wedding will be with those who want to be with her. She realises, life is simple, and all she has to do, is avoid the things that make her miserable.

They decide, the day of the wedding will either be the 10th or 11th of December. According to Yousra, these are lucky days. Sultan adds his knowledge to this.

"Yousra, you are right. Ten in numerology is a divine number. Ten means, a return to unity. The number ten denotes the completion of a cycle. The number eleven is a master number, and it has huge spiritual significance. Good choices, where did you learn numerology?"

Hussein stares at his wife, and he wonders how she knows such things. She looks at both Sultan and Hussein, and she answers.

"I don't know numerology. What is it? I suggested those days because the weather is nice."

Naguib, Sultan and Hussein roar with laughter.

A week before his wedding Naguib stands by Rashida's grave. The mental anguish and pain, makes his heart pound. He wipes his eyes, and he speaks to Rashida.

236

"My love, I'll not visit you again. Inshallah, I'll see you one day. For now, I must work on my life with Zeina. Coming back to see you every week, feels like cheating. I know it isn't, but for this to work I need to stop. Please remember that you'll always be a part of me, and that part lives in my memories. And until I die, those memories will remain."

He plants immortelle's, which he picked from his flowerbeds. He hopes, they'll continue to grow.

During the walk, Naguib sees something he hasn't seen since his time in the desert. Sitting on the roof of the mosque's minaret is an eagle. The eagle looks directly at Naguib, spreads its wings, and then it flies away. He knows he will see the eagle again, but for now, it's waving goodbye.

Chapter 45 - Wedding

Naguib spends his final few days as a widower, with Sultan and Hussein. And to everyone's delight, Sadiq turns up with his two teenage daughters. Thirteen-year-old Alek, and fifteen-year-old Emithal. They begged their father to let them see the city.

The two girls pamper Zeina, and they adorn her arms and hands with henna tattoos. Zeina claims them both as sisters.

Hussein is in awe of Sadiq. He's never seen such a statuesque figure, and with so much nobility. As they walk the streets, people move out of the way when they see Sadiq. Hussein whispers to Sultan.

"He's everything you said he was. It's as if his ancestors are alive in him." Sultan nods.

"Yes, you're right, but underneath, there's a huge heart. I saw this at the Bedouin camp. The children in that camp love him, and children make friendships with their hearts."

The night before the wedding, the men talk, while they eat and drink. It isn't the marriage of a young man, and so there aren't the usual revelries, which go with such an occasion. Naguib knows, some might object to the marriage, but he's not worried. Since he has the blessing of his children and his friends, and they think, it's the perfect marriage.

Hussein asks.

"Naguib, do you want more children?" Naguib hasn't thought about this.

"If Allah wills it, then let it be. I would worry about having children at my age. You know, if I had a child now, by his or her eighteenth birthday I would be close to seventy-five. God forbid they want to play football." The men laugh, and Sadiq speaks.

"As we get older, we may not be able to teach the physical things anymore. The only thing we can teach, is how to think. Naguib, you can do this at any age."

Naguib reaches for Sadiq's hand. Sadiq leans forward and grabs the hand with friendship. Naguib looks into Sadiq's eyes.

"Shukraan my friend." Sadiq smiles and bows his head.

Alek and Emithal want to sleep on the roof, in Sultan's classroom. They stare at the city until the last shop closes its shutters.

Zeina and Yousra carry on talking, and Zeina asks.

"Are we doing the right thing? I don't mean marrying Naguib. I know in my heart that this is the right thing. But in breaking with tradition, are we breaking the laws of our faith?"

Yousra answers.

"I only remember one quote by our holy prophet. *"Kindness is a mark of faith, whoever is not; has no faith."* You and Naguib are oceans of kindness. There's nothing in your actions, which goes against those words. You have nothing to fear. I wish I had Sultan's brains, I'm sure that man's head is heavier than ours. He has so much knowledge." Zeina asks.

"If you had Sultan's brains, what would you say?" Yousra answers.

"I'd probably quote some great lines from a book, but then I've only ever read the Qur'an. But what I'd say is. Every generation does things a little different to the last one. It doesn't mean something is wrong. It just means that there's a reason for change. When people question how things are, it can make the world a better place. Did you know that few women of my generation can read or write? Hussein taught me those things. In doing this, he gave me a better life. Look at the world we live in. There are women doctors, scientist, and all sorts of things. Women are half the world, but if you stop them from learning, then the world only has half the intelligence, and not all it deserves."

Yousra stops talking. She isn't sure how to end the conversation, and she feels embarrassed.

Zeina stares at her, and marvels at her words.

"Yousra you may have only read one book, but you have more wisdom than someone who has read many, and they learned nothing." Yousra holds Zeina's hand.

"Don't worry what people think. If people have nothing better to do than talk about you, then take it as a compliment. You know in your heart that this is right, and you know that you're not breaking any rules. Live well and live with kindness in your heart, if you can do this, you'll be a better Muslim than many who claim to be one." The two women embrace.

Nikkah, the wedding ceremony is a very simple affair. The guests gather and Imam Ali reads from the Qur'an, and Naguib and Zeina exchange vows.

Sitting to their left is Yousra, and on her lap is Gamal and Hanan. She holds them in a loving embrace as she cries tears of joy.

Chapter 46 - Life

Fourteen years have passed since Naguib and Zeina's wedding. In that time, Rafa and Salma have married, and Farid is still studying. Gamal is at university in America, studying to be a lawyer, and Hanan hopes to follow her brother. But she wants to study medicine. Every day she waits for the post, and news of her exam result. Zeina speaks to her.

"Just relax. It won't get here any quicker because you're standing by the door." She gives Hanan a hug. Naguib asks.

"Shall we take a walk to the college. Let's see if there's any news."

Hanan gives a little scream of excitement, and within two minutes, she's waiting by the front door. She pops back in the house and calls out to Naguib.

"Come on Abbi let's go." Despite Naguib's request, the children start to call him Abbi as soon as Naguib marries Zeina. At first, it startles him, but slowly he accepts it.

Hussein and Yousra are still the same, but Hussein is in poor health. Over time, he loses all his teeth, and then he suffers a massive heart attack, after which he's never the same. He now shuffles where once he almost bounced down the street. He often falls asleep during a conversation, and Yousra places a blanket over him. She kisses his forehead. Sitting near him, she reads one of the many books, Sultan now owns.

Sultan has replaced the makeshift shelter on the roof with a genuine Bedouin tent. Sadiq sent this to him, along with the most beautiful rug imaginable. Sultan has also set up a telescope so that he can watch the stars. Yousra complains.

"I have no room for hanging my washing." It's a half-hearted complaint. Since she cannot imagine her and Hussein's life without Sultan.

Life in the country is now as stable as it has ever been. The talks between the president and the leader of the freedom fighters broke down. The military organised a coup and they took over. During the trouble, the president was killed, and his family exiled. The Presidents family didn't suffer, and it was reported that they were multi-millionaires, and lived a good life, between Paris, London, and New York.

Zulfiker Sakka tried to flee the country with his family. He was arrested at an out-of-town airstrip. It was rumoured that the plane was full of cash, gold, and jewellery. He died in jail after he was found guilty of two charges. Corruption, and perverting the course of justice.

After many years of military rule, the country is holding its first democratic election, and Mido Ibrahim returns to be part of the new nation. He studied at university and received a doctorate in political science. The new government welcomes him back, and he joins the ranks as an under-secretary. His first personal journey after returning is to visit Naguib.

As he enters Naguib's house armed police patrol the area. As soon as Mido sees Naguib, he hugs him.

"Uncle Naguib, if I cry it's because I'm happy." They speak for many hours, and when Naguib tells him about Sultan, Mido exclaims.

"Is Sultan far?" Naguib answers.

"No, he's next door." When Sultan arrives, he almost runs to Mido. The two embrace and for the next five minutes, they have a rapid conversation in English. Sultan then turns to everyone and speaks.

"Well, Mido's English has improved. Not ten out of ten yet, but it's not bad, he'll need to practise a bit more." Mido laughs and the guard standing in the room looks embarrassed. After all, Mido is his boss.

When it is time for Mido to leave, Naguib holds his hand and looks into his eyes.

"Your mother and father would be proud of you. I am proud of you. Look after this country." Mido embraces Naguib, and then turns to Zeina.

"Aunty Zeina, please take care of these two men, they mean the world to me." Zeina nods.

"I'll do my best Mido, you have my word."

Two weeks before Hanan's twenty-first birthday, a letter arrives. Hanan stares at the letter. When she sees that it's from the college, and addressed to her, she runs to the veranda.

"Abbi, Ummi I have a letter." Zeina takes food off the stove, and she rushes out. Hanan stares at them.

"I can't open it. I'm too scared." Naguib smiles.

"If you don't open the letter, you'll never know what it says." The three of them sit down. With trepidation, Hanan tears the edge of the envelope. Inside is a neatly folded piece of paper. She unfolds it and reads.

Zeina stares at Naguib. She doesn't recognise the look on Hanan's face.

"Well, say something Hanan. What's happened?" Hanan has a sad look on her face, and then she burst into tears. Zeina kneels at her daughter's feet.

"There's always next year." As they hug, Hanan pulls back.

"Ummi, I have the required grades, and I've been accepted at the same university as Gamal. I'm crying because I don't want to leave you and Abbi." Now Zeina starts to cry and Naguib comforts both of them.

Until the day of Hanan's departure, she spends most of her time at home. She memorises the smell, the air, her mother and Naguib. She sits in silence while they eat. She wants to remember everything that is special to her.

On her last night, Naguib speaks to her.

"Hanan, do you know who your real father is?" Hanan nods.

"Yes, I do. His name was Khaled Sharif, and he was your friend." Naguib nods.

"Yes, that's right. He was my friend. I want you to remember him." Hanan holds Naguib's hand.

"I don't remember much about him, other than him tickling my feet. I know he loved me, but he wasn't here, and I know he didn't have a choice. But you were here, and you could have chosen not to be. All my memories of childhood revolve around you and Ummi. That makes you my father in equal terms to Khaled Sharif. I don't remember calling Khaled Abbi, but I'll always remember calling you Abbi."

Naguib hugs Hanan with all the love of a father.

After Hanan leaves, Zeina and Naguib are at a bit of a loss. Naguib can't remember the last time there were only two people in that house. It feels strange, and the walls echo with fifty years of memories.

One night as Naguib and Zeina sit together, Naguib makes an announcement.

"I was thinking, maybe we should adopt a child." Zeina is shocked.

"Why did you have that thought?" Naguib answers.

"I've never known a time when this house was so quiet." Zeina pouts.

"Don't you like my company anymore?" Naguib laughs.

"No, it's not that. I love your company. I was just thinking, we have money, and I would like to use it well. I want to give somebody else a chance. Look at Mido, look what a chance did for him."

Zeina remembers Yousra's humble beginnings, and she agrees.

"It's a wonderful idea. Find out what we need to do." Zeina moves closer to Naguib and holds his hand.

"I always knew you were a good man. The more time I spend with you, the more you amaze me." Naguib squeezes her hand and kisses her.

It's a hot day and Naguib is returning on the bus, after four long hours at an orphanage. Sitting on the bus, he chews over the orphanage directors' words.

"Your age may go against you, but since your wife is much younger, we may be able to do something. You certainly have the financial credentials."

As he approaches his front door, Naguib sees Zeina and Yousra waiting outside. When Zeina sees Naguib, she becomes anxious, and Naguib rushes over to her.

"Zeina, what is it? What's happened? Is it Hussein?" Yousra smiles.

"No Hussein is resting, and he's fine. You have some visitors." Naguib asks.

"So why are we waiting outside?" All Zeina can say is.

"It's not bad, but it's amazing." Naguib enters the house, and Zeina and Yousra tiptoe behind him. In the main room, Naguib sees three men, and a boy of six or seven. In that moment, the entire room freezes, and time stops.

"Anwar, is that you!?"

Anwar leaps to his feet and embraces Naguib. They both hold on, and neither of them rushes the moment. For sixteen years, they could only express their love in letters, but now their love has a home. Anwar pulls away, and answers.

"Yes, Abbi it's me, and this is your grandson, Farid. I think you recognise Abdel, this is his son, and his name is Hassam. He's named after his grandfather."

Anwar holds Naguib's hand and leads him to the sofa. Naguib has a thousand questions, but he cannot speak. Anwar sits next to Naguib, and in a flash Naguib lunges at Anwar. He holds him in a strong embrace and bursts into tears. The two men hold each other until both their tears subside.

The emotions run high, and there isn't a dry eye in the room. After a minute, Naguib asks.

"When did you arrive?" Anwar answers.

"About an hour ago, and we came straight from the airport." They carry on talking late into the night. Before Farid goes to bed, Naguib speaks to him.

"Farid, I have something for you. Wait one minute." Naguib goes to the bedroom and pulls out the old suitcase from under his bed. Then he looks into Farid's eyes, and he places a ball in his hand.

"My dear child, you left this behind. And I kept it because I knew, one day, I would return it to you." Farid stares at the ball, and then he stares at Naguib.

"My wonderful Jadd, I've missed you." Once Farid goes to sleep, Naguib, Anwar and Abdel sit on the veranda and talk

245

until the sun rises. Zeina stays awake all night. She makes sure they have food and drink. And Anwar speaks to her.

"Shukraan Zeina Ummi. It's not just for the food and drinks. It's for everything you've done for Abbi. You've made him happy, and I'm eternally grateful for that." Anwar's smile is sincere and warm, and Zeina answers.

"I couldn't have asked for a better man in my life. I see it as an honour to look after Naguib. And I'm honoured to have met you Anwar."

As the sun rises, Abdel asks.

"Uncle Naguib, I want to visit Abbi and Ummi, can you help with this?" Naguib's answer is immediate.

"Yes of course I can. There's nothing to fear, and there's a modern highway out of town. I know that Hassam and Samir will be overjoyed, when they see you and their beautiful grandson."

Abdel still has contacts at the U.S. Embassy, and when he shows them his credentials, they loan him a big estate car. There's enough room for all of them including Sultan, who doesn't want to miss the chance of seeing his old friend Sadiq.

On the journey, Sultan starts to teach Arabic to young Hassam.

"I don't think your grandfather and grandmother speak any English, so you'll have to learn Arabic." To everyone's surprise, young Hassam can speak a lot of Arabic, although it is often with an American accent. Abdel explains.

"Shadia insists that we speak Arabic at home. Hassam has no choice but to speak it." Naguib smiles.

"She's a good girl."

The reunion at the Bedouin camp is joyous, and tearful. Even Sadiq sheds a tear, and when Sultan looks at him, Sadiq speaks.

"Some things are more beautiful than the stars. What do you say my friend?" Sultan agrees.

"Yes, but then there's a little star light in all of us."

However, there is also some tragic news. Ismail died the previous year, and he's not there to celebrate. While sad, Naguib also feels blessed, because he can be a part of this reunion.

They stay for two weeks at the camp, and the night before they leave, the men sit by the campfire. Young Hassam is asleep in his grandfather's arms. Abdel turns to his father and speaks.

"Abbi this has been the most perfect time of my life. For a long time, I'd given up of ever seeing you again, please forgive me for feeling this way. I'll never feel like that again."

Hassam stares at Abdel.

"There's nothing to forgive. I never doubted you. For me this is also the perfect moment. It's a moment that is shaped in heaven, and we are all blessed."

Chapter 47 - Time

A month has passed since Anwar's arrival, and now it's time for him to return.

Naguib spends every minute with his son and grandson. He tries to stay awake, and Zeina complains.

"Naguib, you must sleep. You stay awake and wait for others to wake up. You need to rest." Naguib holds Zeina in his arms.

"Plenty of time to rest once they return to America. And in any case, it's your fault." Zeina sits up and snaps.

"My fault, how is it my fault?" Naguib pulls her back.

"For being so beautiful." Zeina smiles and lies down.

The day of the departure arrives. Naguib has ordered two taxis. Yousra, Zeina, Sultan and young Hassam travel in one, while the remaining group are in the other. Naguib sits between his son and grandson, and he holds their hands for the entire journey.

At the airport, there's sadness, but also a feeling of hope.

"Abbi, I'll come back as often as I can. Next time I'll bring Nawal and the girls. Rafa wants to come, but she's expecting her first child. Soon, you'll be a great grandfather."

Naguib stares at Anwar with wide-eyes, and he exclaims.

"You waited all this time to tell me this news. I have a million questions. Anwar this is big news, and you have to go in five minutes. Anwar, I have not bought a gift for my great grandchild!" Anwar hugs Naguib.

"Abbi, I wanted it this way, because it will give us both something to look forward to." Naguib stare softens, and he breaks into a smile.

"You're right, but you must let me know when the child is born. Straight away. Don't wait until she's three years old." Anwar laughs.

"Abbi, I'll tell you as soon as the baby arrives." Just before they go through to the departure lounge, Naguib shouts.

"Farid, do you have your ball?" Farid reaches into his pocket, pulls out the ball and waves it in the air.

"Yes Jadd, I'll never lose it again."

That night Naguib sits on the roof with Sultan. They drink tea and Sultan asks.

"How are you feeling Naguib?" Naguib puts his cup down.

"A little sad, but I guess it's natural." Sultan agrees.

"Naguib, remember this time. Time passes quickly. It seems like yesterday that I last saw Rania, and the next time I see her, I'll know that my time on this planet is over." Naguib understands.

"Is your Rania still a star?" Sultan points to the sky.

"Yes, there she is, and she's with Rashida. The two stars just next to each other, can you see them? They haven't changed. They're the same as the first time, I pointed them out to you in the desert."

Naguib stares at the sky.

"Yes, I can see them, and I believe some things are eternal. Some things never erode with the passing years. Love is timeless."

The End.

Printed in Great Britain
by Amazon

25897346R00148